Jacob's Plan

A NOVEL

PETER DAVID SHAPIRO

PenLane Press
Lexington, Massachusetts, USA

This book is a work of fiction. References to real establishments, organizations, or locales are intended only to provide an air of authenticity, and are used fictitiously. All characters, and all procedures, processes, incidents and dialogue, are products of the author's imagination and are not construed to be real.

Cover art from "Self Portrait" by Adam Shapiro.

For more information please visit:

www.peterdshapiro.com

ISBN 978-0-9839244-6-3 (pbk)
ISBN 978-0-9839244-7-0 (ebk)

FIRST EDITION 2019

One

Every day starts the same.

Get up, stride vigorously down to the Charles River, huff and puff along the Charles embankment, walk briskly back to Mass Ave., grab a take-out coffee at Starbucks, leaf through the *Boston Globe* at breakfast.

Bad stuff in the news as always, but not to worry, most of the *really* bad stuff is far away.

Meanwhile here in enlightened Cambridge, garbage gets collected regularly, drivers almost always stop for red lights, police officers are poised to serve and protect, and the big brains at our famous universities are on call whenever our Government needs help.

So, not to worry.

After breakfast, I commute upstairs to my home office, global headquarters of my management consulting practice, JM Consulting. There I do what consultants do to bring in work and keep clients happy.

I'm a normal kind of guy. Ordinary looks, long face, strong nose, normal height. Reasonably fit in my mid-forties. No glaring character flaws. Adequate social skills, although people say I can be a tad mouthy. Also stubborn, but then, who isn't?

I know what you're thinking. So, yes, I do get out on occasion, and frequently I'm joined by women friends who are attractive, smart, and single, lately Shannon, who works in a biotech lab at MIT, or Maura, a newly-minted lawyer, and we like each other, though there's nothing serious at the moment.

From time to time I bring a friend to dinner at my parents' house in Winchester, a leafy suburb north of Cambridge, where I lived until college. My mother looks like a kindly little old lady with twinkly eyes but once she gets started on an interrogation, she doesn't let go, like a terrier with a bone. She asks my friend probing questions about family, work, and interests, and shares fond anecdotes about my childhood and adolescence. At the end of the evening, she clutches my companion's arm and declares, "We hope to see you again very soon."

When we're alone, my parents wonder aloud why I'm not yet married unlike their friends' kids who've already started their families.

"You're too picky," observes my mother.

I smile sheepishly and shake my head.

"In case you don't realize," she continues, unamused, "you're not such a terrific catch as you might think."

"I beg to differ. I'm a great catch."

"Don't be cheeky. Maybe if you had someone, you wouldn't be so depressed all the time."

I assure her, and my father who's watching us, that I'm not at all depressed.

Which, by the way, I'm totally not.

I like my life just fine as it is, and wouldn't change a single thing.

Then comes the shocker.

A dangerous buffoon takes over the White House.

Political pundits assured us that this would never happen. It's inexplicable, and unthinkable. How could he win the election? *Any* election? He's a joke, has been for decades, his business scandals, marital cheating, and vulgar narcissism out in the public eye for all to see.

Tens of millions of my fellow citizens actually voted for this moron despite his flagrant incompetence and corruption.

Our country has lost its fucking mind.

Time to rethink not worrying about the bad stuff...

Like the disasters that you need smarts in high places to head off because in every respect, in every possible way, the cretin in the White House is doing the absolutely wrong and stupid thing.

He rejects the science on climate change, exposing us to ever-deadlier floods, heat waves, hurricanes, fires, and droughts. He deregulates banks and provokes trade wars, setting us up for the next Great Depression. He degrades our protections against fanatics who'd detonate nukes in our cities, and against cyber-sabotage of our electric grid. He debases political debate and aligns with neo-Nazis. He undercuts nuclear non-proliferation.

He appoints bozos, lobbyists, sycophants, and grifters as his Cabinet secretaries so that when disaster strikes, their gutted agencies will have nothing to offer. Emergency response? *Fuhgeddaboudit!*

When nothing works and no help is on the way and food and water and shelter are in short supply, public order collapses, and chaos reigns.

Is catastrophe imminent in Cambridge?

Maybe not. Or maybe so. Given the shambolic regime in DC, who knows? Anything is possible.

In the circumstances, denial and complacency won't cut it.

I'm preparing for the worst.

I prefer not to perish from starvation, thirst, exposure, or getting shot, victimhood not being my thing.

If taking action now makes me a *survivalist*, so be it.

I haven't changed. I'm the same normal guy that I was before. I don't wear camo; I don't loath Government; I don't flaunt a deadly weapon; I don't belong to a militia; I'm not counting the minutes until the rapture; I don't subscribe to wacko conspiracy theories; I don't line my hats with tin foil; I'm not a tech billionaire with a walled compound in New Zealand and a private jet at the ready.

What's changed is my reality.

Make that *our* reality, and I, for one, am acting on it.

Two

Neighbors would notice all those boxes going into my house. "Expecting a long siege?" they'd ask, joshing, but curious.

"I'm opening a halfway house," I'd tell them. "Level 3 sex offenders. Great guys! But their appetites, you wouldn't believe!"

They'd chuckle, thinking, Jake has a mouth on him for sure.

"Keep this to yourselves, okay? We don't want folks around here getting riled up."

Now they'd be thinking, he doesn't look like he's joking. Better check with the city, or the state, or whoever the fuck, Jesus H. Christ, first thing!

Harmless neighborly fun.

But later after the disaster they'd remember and come begging, "Please, can you share with us?"

I'd want to help them. Honestly, I would. But real life isn't like a feel-good movie where you open your door to the needy, learn significant life lessons, and everyone is better off by the closing credits. Or like in biblical times when a few loaves of bread and a couple of fish satiated multitudes.

In the real world, parceling out my water and food would put my own survival at risk.

I'd have to tell them, "I'm sorry. There's no way."

Huddled shivering and desperate on my doorstep, they wouldn't leave quietly, not before tearful pleading, and maybe bricks thrown through my windows.

To avoid all that, I wait for cover of darkness to lug in my supplies, staying as quiet as possible.

I stack on racks in my basement sixteen five-gallon plastic jugs of water; military surplus MREs that don't require cooking; sealed bags of nuts, dry cereal, salt-free crackers, peanut butter, canned meats, canned fruits, canned vegetables, canned milk, canned juice, and cans of soup that can be eaten cold; a hatchet, Leatherman multi-tool with fold-out blades, screw driver, pliers, and bottle opener; flashlights, batteries, battery powered radio, hand-cranked charger for cellphones, candles, and matches; toilet paper, paper towels, household bleach and heavy duty garbage bags; burn ointment, antibiotic ointment, bandages, aspirin, anti-diarrhea tablets, and eye wash; pandemic kits of protective clothing, respirator mask, nitrile gloves, and safety goggles. Plus a self-contained breathing apparatus, plastic sheeting, silver foil emergency blanket, fireproof steel safe, fire extinguisher, fold-out cot and sleeping bag wrapped in plastic, and a five-gallon bucket for a toilet.

By my calculations, enough for two months for me and for my parents, assuming they're able to make it to my house from Winchester.

After collapse of public order, armed marauders will roam the streets and anyone unarmed will be at their mercy, not an appealing prospect. Normally I wouldn't want a gun in my house, but I'm not preparing for *normally.*

Firearms Institute is sandwiched between AAA Auto Insurance and Russo's Pizza in a strip mall in Medford, a blue collar town north of Cambridge. To announce myself, I press a button beside the entrance, "My name is Jacob Morais. I'm here for the firearms safety course, for my license to carry."

Loud buzz, a click, and a voice through the grill under the button, "Come in, Mr. Morais."

The receptionist apologizes for the locked door. "We have to be careful. We wouldn't want our firearms getting into the wrong hands, what with terrorists and all."

"Amen to that!" I say.

After charging my credit card for the tuition, she directs me to a room just off the lobby.

"Class starts in ten minutes. Your instructor is Captain Rory Moore. Everyone loves Captain Rory."

It's a plain windowless room with three long tables each with chairs lined behind them, all facing an identical long table at the front. On the side walls are posters depicting guns and admonishments, "Be Safe, Not Sorry," and "Check, and Double Check." Also a certificate from the Commonwealth of Massachusetts affirming that Firearms Institute is authorized to provide officially-sanctioned firearms safety courses.

Already in the room are six others waiting for class to begin. I take a chair at the first table, next to a woman reading a paperback.

Finally, in comes our instructor, round face, short hair, glasses, wearing a blue denim shirt with a Firearms Institute logo on the shirt pocket.

"My name is Captain Rory Moore," he says, in a booming drill sergeant voice. He stands ramrod straight, legs apart, hands clasped behind his back. "This morning I will teach you about gun safety. You will learn how to aim and fire a gun, and you will practice shooting. Then you will get a tip sheet on applying for your license to carry in the Commonwealth of Massachusetts. Any questions?" He cocks his forefinger at each of us in turn and when no one speaks, he says, "Let's get started."

He holds up a handgun that he identifies as a Glock, one of his favorites. He demonstrates how to verify that there's no bullet in the chamber, how to engage and disengage the safety, how to insert a magazine of bullets, how to assume a two-hand shooting stance, how to squeeze the trigger, how to remove the magazine, and how to store the handgun back in its secure case.

Then he hands each of us similar metal cases.

"They're unlocked," he says. "Take a look inside."

Inside my case is a handgun, dull grey black metal, giving off a faint smell of lubricant.

"Check that there's no bullet in the chamber, like I showed you."

Which we do. Then we practice the steps that he demonstrated until we get them right with no mistakes.

"Now for the fun part," Captain Rory says. "Live fire."

We follow him to a shooting range in back where we're sorted into separate shooting booths looking out towards our targets.

On a shelf in my booth are safety glasses, ear protectors, a Glock 19, and a magazine loaded with bullets.

"Suit up," says Captain Rory. "Then insert the magazines into your handguns and assume two-handed firing stances, but don't start shooting until I tell you."

He travels from booth to booth checking and correcting. To me, he says only, "Looking good."

Then, standing behind us, he says, "Commence firing."

At first I totally miss my target, the outlined shape of a man. I adjust my aim and get better at managing the recoil, and my shots punch holes inside the concentric circles drawn on the target's midsection. Amidst the smell of gunpowder and the *crack crack crack* of pistol shots, I hear the townspeople cheer as my bullets tear into the outlaw who murdered their sheriff, commandeered their only hotel and bar, taunted their men-folk, and harassed their women. No one has dared to oppose him, which led him to underestimate me, a fatal error on his part. And now, thanks to my deadly Glock 19, he is thoroughly deceased, a shredded remnant of his former self. The grateful townspeople shout, "You da *man!*"

When we're done Captain Rory says, "Targets don't shoot back. It will be different if you have to use your gun to defend yourself. For one thing, your adrenaline will be pumping like crazy. So make it easy for yourself. Aim for the largest body mass, chest and stomach, and keep firing until you drop the SOB. Okay?"

Back in the classroom, Captain Rory hands us our Firearms Safety Certificates, along with a list of what else we'll need for our LTC applications that we'll submit to our local police departments, plus coupons for Firearms Institute discounts on guns, ammo, and accessories. He promises they'll give us a great deal when we come back with our LTCs.

On my way out, I tell him, "I've never held a gun before."

"How do you like it?"

"Have to admit, it feels good."

"Nothing to be ashamed of."

"I'm not."

Captain Rory nods approvingly. "So, if you don't mind me asking, why do you want a gun?"

"For protection, in case of a major disaster when there's no point calling the police."

"Too true, brother. Better to be armed when all hell's breaking loose."

"Right. Well, thanks for the session."

"You're very welcome."

Thinking we're done, I'm moving on towards the door when Captain Rory adds, "Same time, you've got to think a couple of steps ahead, like in your disaster scenario, about what happens after you shoot an intruder."

"I'd have to dispose of the body."

"Yeah, there's that, but what if your vic has friends and family who come after you to even the score? What do you do?"

I don't have a ready answer and Captain Rory gives me a helpful teacher look. "You'll need a Plan B."

Now he's talking in riddles.

"Plan B?"

"To get the fuck out of Dodge, excuse my French, when you're outnumbered or outgunned or for whatever other reason you have to bug out and disappear to somewhere they can't find you."

"Feels cowardly not to stay and fight," I say, recalling my heroic shootout with the outlaw.

"You'd rather stay and be killed?"

"No."

"So, Plan B."

"Plan B," I repeat, making a mental note. I do need to get on top of this. Turns out that survival will require more than emergency supplies in my basement and a gun.

"Leave no breadcrumbs when you go," says Captain Rory. "No credit cards, no cellphone, and get fake ID."

"Okay."

Leaning towards me, he lowers his voice to a confidential rumble. "You want to disappear for real? Tell no one what you're planning. You understand?"

"Got it. No breadcrumbs."

"Except you've got to tell your wife, assuming you want her to come with you. Are you married?"

"No."

"That's actually better."

I return to Firearms Institute after receiving my license to carry from the Cambridge PD.

Captain Rory is unavailable when I arrive, but there's an affable sales guy in the showroom who helps me decide on my purchases, a Glock 19 handgun like the one I fired there earlier, an over-the-shoulder leather holster, four hundred rounds of Speer Gold Dot bonded core hollow point 9mm bullets, and two ten-round magazines, the maximum legal size in Massachusetts.

Three

I snag a cab outside Penn Station and ask the driver to take me to Roosevelt Avenue in the borough of Queens.

"It's a rough area," says the driver while observing me in his rear view mirror with droopy basset hound eyes that are no longer surprised by anything.

"I'm aware," I reply.

I'm also aware that Roosevelt Avenue is ground zero to obtain fake IDs, according to credible sources on the Internet.

He shrugs. "You're the boss." Meaning, you're a fool, and you're not my problem.

On Roosevelt Avenue, each block under the elevated subway tracks looks much like the others, so I pick one at random. "Let's stop here."

"You sure?"

"Yeah, thanks."

NYPD cops are everywhere patrolling on foot and in slow moving cars. Normally I'd find that reassuring. Now it makes me jumpy. To blend in, I'm wearing scruffy blue jeans and a grey hoodie. But still I feel conspicuous, like a duck in a flock of geese. Time to decide: Retreat back to Boston or do what I came to do.

Two men standing on the sidewalk in front of a 99-cent store eye me as I sidle towards them.

"IDs?" I ask, trying not to move my lips.

They just stare at me, sucking on their cigarettes, blowing out smoke sideways that nonetheless wafts in my direction.

I move on.

A stout woman is sorting fruit in front of a corner grocery.

"How much for an apple?"

"Two dollars."

As I pay for one of her apples I try again, "IDs?"

She looks at me for a moment then jerks her head towards a corner across from us. "Cross there and wait by the light."

I cross the street and wait, as instructed.

About five minutes pass. It makes me uncomfortable just to stand there doing nothing in particular. I'm sure the cops will notice. I pretend to study my phone and resolve to give whomever I'm waiting for another minute or so, and then I'll try somewhere else.

A skinny teenage boy on a skateboard comes rolling towards me.

"You want ID?"

"Yes."

"Shoe store behind me half a block."

The light turns green and he pumps across the street, not hanging around for my thanks.

The display in Glamor Shoes' front window features dusty shoes and boots behind a sign proclaiming BARGAIN SALES/REBAJAS. Inside, a man and a woman seated on a bench are being attended to by a salesman, and an older gent is standing farther back at the cash register. After the older gent catches my eye, he steps into a storage room behind the register. I follow him. He's waiting for me beside a rack piled with shoe boxes.

"ID?" he asks.

"Yes."

"What kind you want?"

"What are my options?"

"We do New York State ID cards."

"Okay, then a New York State ID card."

"Hundred now, fifty more when it's done."

I give him the hundred in cash, and he points a gnarled forefinger towards a space in front of a light grey poster board. "Stand there. Look at the camera. No smiling."

He clicks the camera a couple of times and then turns a screen towards me which has several headshots, none of which is a handsome devil, unfortunately. The photo I select comes as close as I can manage to an image of a model citizen.

He hands me a sheet of paper on a clipboard and a ballpoint pen. "Name, address, date of birth, signature, we'll fill in the rest."

For my name, I wrote John S. Dobby. For my address: 41 Lake Street, in Sprightly Falls, New York, a rural town near the western Massachusetts state line that I once traveled through. For my date of birth: One day, one month, and one year earlier than my actual DOB, to help me recall it, if asked.

Why *John S. Dobby*? Because it's a name that doesn't attract attention. To me, it conjures up nobody special, like a mid-level manager who comes to work on time every day and does his job but invariably gets overlooked when bonuses and promotions are handed out. Maybe others will hear the name differently and become curious to learn more. I hope not.

The older gent says, "Wait in the Queens Café up three blocks on the right. About an hour."

"Then come back here?"

"No, stay there."

I nurse a coffee and read a *New York Times*. Around forty minutes in, two uniformed cops enter the café for coffee and then just loiter outside the door, sipping, chatting, and scanning the street. I'm convinced they'll blow the whole deal until, eventually, they move on.

No sign of anyone after an hour and ten minutes. I toss my empty coffee cup into a trash receptacle and consider returning to Glamor Shoes despite my instructions not to, but a couple of minutes later a guy with a ratty beard and pony tail pushes through the door and gestures with a jerk of his head for me to follow him.

"Where are we going?"

"Not far."

We stop in front of the corner grocery where earlier that morning I bought the apple.

"Examine the fruit," the guy says.

I'm studying bananas when through the corner of my eye I see a man tuck an envelope under the windshield wiper of a car parked nearby. My guide glances around, saunters briskly to the car, and retrieves the envelope.

"Let's go," he says.

He leads me to a side street where there's no one in sight in either direction, and hands me the envelope. "Check it."

It's a laminated card. Inscribed along the top over blue mountains and a yellow rising sun are NEW YORK STATE and the signature of the Commissioner of Motor Vehicles. Below, on the left, are my headshot and my signature. In caps in the middle and lower part of the card are the words IDENTIFICATION CARD and JOHN S. DOBBY, plus a nine-digit ID number, my address in Sprightly Falls, my DOB, my SEX: M, EYES: BR, and HT: 5-10, and dates when the card was issued and will expire, all superimposed over the crest of the State of New York and assorted hieroglyphics.

The card looks official, probably good enough to get undocumented immigrants hired on work crews and underage drinkers into clubs. But would it withstand a bureaucrat's gimlet-eyed scrutiny? Maybe it's missing a holographic code, or something. How would I know, until it was too late?

Still, it's a start, and better than nothing.

"Looks good," I tell the bearded guy as I pass him two twenties and a ten that I've folded in the palm of my hand.

"Pleasure doing business with you," he says.

Four

I receive Grandpa Alain's letter about a week after the phone call to let me know that he died:

Jacob, my good friend Gavin McNair has transcribed this brief letter from my dictation. I'd write it myself except that my arthritis makes it too difficult. I have had a long and rewarding life, and now face the end, as everyone does eventually. I'm being well cared for here in the Residence, as well as can be expected. I have no complaints. Grandma Yvonne and I greatly valued your phone calls and visits after you moved away from Montreal and we welcomed the news of your many accomplishments. I'll look for you in the next world, Grandpa Alain.

At Grandpa Alain's service at Musée McCord in Montreal, Gavin McNair taps on a glass for everyone's attention. "I'll say a few words now about Alain."

McNair is stooped and wispy-haired but his voice is strong and he's fully in command of the room.

"Just a few words," calls out a man with a large forehead and a neat low-cut beard like Sigmund Freud's.

McNair raises his hand to acknowledge knowing chuckles from the crowd. "I promise."

"A force of nature," McNair continues. "You felt his presence. And he was glad to share his opinions."

"Not a shrinking violet," interrupts the bearded man, again.

"No, nothing like you, Barry," says McNair, to more laughter. "But what was special about Alain was that he also listened. You knew that he cared, this man of so many accomplishments. He was a true hero during the war flying over eighty missions and when he came home, he built a successful business that provided good livelihoods to many."

"Hear, hear," someone says.

"He was a generous man, including to the Musée McCord where we are gathered today to remember him. And how he loved his family, his beloved Yvonne with whom he shared a blessed and loving partnership until she passed, and his son Jean Michel, daughter-in-law Marilyn, and grandson, Jacob, all back here with us now to celebrate his life and memory."

McNair gestures towards the three of us. Many in the room give us sympathetic looks.

He concludes, "Alain was my mentor as well as my dearest friend, and I'll always owe him."

Then after a beat when no one says anything, not even Barry, McNair turns towards my father and with an encouraging smile hands him the mic.

My father wears granny-style rimless eyeglasses, has rosy cheeks, and presents a comfortable pudge. If he had a white beard he could pass for Santa, a role that he plays each year for sick kids in Boston Children's Hospital. While growing up I avoided being seen near him in public. When forced to occupy the same sidewalk, I stayed at least ten feet behind or ahead. Not for any good reason; he never mistreated me. But we weren't close, not like I was with Grandpa Alain. I'm trying in these pages to report my story as honestly as I can, so let's be honest: I was a total shit, always comparing my father to Grandpa Alain and finding him wanting, and he was a saint for putting up with it. If I were in his place, I would have chucked my snotty younger self out into the snow.

"Hello, everyone," my father says. "Seventy years ago Alain and Yvonne arrived in Canada as refugees from the war. Then my dad returned to Europe to help defeat the Nazis. After the war, he made good lives for us here. In his own way, he was a loving dad. Although he was not an easy man to please."

My father sighs, swallows, and closes his eyes. McNair edges towards him to take the mic but my father shakes his head and manages to continue, "We didn't always get along. He didn't want us to move to the US. After we left, he and I didn't talk much. I'm sorry about that. I never told him that I loved him. That's not how we talked in our family. I'm sorry about that too."

Silence in the room.

My father hands the mic back to McNair, who catches my eye. I take the mic.

"My name is Jake Morais. When I was a kid and we were visiting Grandpa Alain and Grandma Yvonne, I remember him gazing at me under his eyebrows which were like steel wool..."

Someone murmured, "Got that right..."

"...and he was smiling, or I hoped he was, and I wondered, did he find me amusing? Or was he masking his disappointment that the scrawny boy in front of him showed few signs of growing into a man who would be large in size and in spirit, as he was himself? I resolved to prove my worth in his eyes and somehow, someday, to make him proud. He showed me what it means to be a man. I realize now that I'll never be able to live up to his example but thanks to him, I know what to strive for."

I raise my glass. "To Grandpa Alain, with love and respect!"

"To Alain!" people say, their glasses raised.

Then follow wonderful words from others who knew him, former employees, a longtime neighbor, and a caregiver at his hospice. Several choke up before they're done.

The reality of Grandpa Alain's death hits me after his service, after I arrive back in Massachusetts.

He is gone.

Alain Morais? No one here, nothing to see, move along please!

Silence.

For the first time, I *know* that his absence is absolute and forever and I'm sobbing, for him, and for me, great gulping sobs, until I get a grip.

Gavin McNair emails me that Grandpa Alain's will has been read, and that he left me a property in Montreal, a three-story building within walking distance of McGill University on the corner of Avenue Duluth and Rue St. Dominique.

According to McNair, Grandpa Alain wrote that he hoped his bequest of this building would "renew my grandson Jacob's connection with Montreal and with Canada."

"Probate will take a while," McNair says, when I call him. "But I wanted you to know what's in store."

"Thanks," I say. "I had no idea."

"It's a fine building," McNair continues, perhaps sensing that I need reassurance. "It's in excellent condition, apart from the usual aches and pains that you'd expect in a structure built in the early 1900s."

"Does it have tenants?

"An antiques store on the ground floor and McGill grad students in two apartments on the second floor. The third-floor penthouse is vacant. Alain was planning to get it fixed up."

"Will I have to deal with them?"

"A building manager does that. Alain never had anything to do with his tenants. Nor with maintenance. He hired Lepine Associates, a reputable Montreal firm."

"So Lepine Associates is working for me now."

"When you get title, if that's what you want."

"Yes, please."

I'm contemplating my prospective status as a property owner in Montreal when I realize: If I have to get out of Dodge, I can run to Canada!

I've read that survivalists have cabins in rural areas or in the mountains, out of sight and off the grid, where they can live self-sufficiently for as long as they have to.

Hiding out in Montreal doesn't fit the profile but maybe that's a good thing. I've never had outdoor survival training. In Boy Scouts I didn't get beyond marching in formation and tying knots. Out in the woods I'd probably get eaten by bears. Not to mention the boredom.

Crossing the US-Canada border won't be a problem. Although I'm a naturalized US citizen, I'll still also hold Canadian citizenship until I contact Ottawa to renounce the land of my birth, which basically no expatriate Canadians do.

Neither the US nor Canada interrogates departing travelers at the border. For travelers between Boston and Montreal, those heading north through Vermont drive right past US Customs and stop only for Canadian Customs in Philipsburg, Quebec. Travelers heading south to the US from Canada similarly drive past Canada's Philipsburg building directly to US Customs in Highgate Springs, Vermont. The two facilities are a half mile apart.

Canada will have no reason to inform the US that a run-of-the-mill Canadian citizen has just returned to his home country.

Nor will the US have cause to alert Canada about the return of one of its own US citizens.

To prepare for Plan B, from now on I'll cross the border by bus, train, or air, instead of in my car with its Massachusetts plates.

On entering Canada, I'll show my Canadian passport to the Canadian customs officer, who will ask, "Where do you live?" and I'll reply, "Montreal."

On my re-entry into the US, I'll present my US passport to the US customs officer who will ask, "Where do you live?"

To which I'll reply, "Cambridge, Massachusetts."

Unless I get confused and hand over the wrong passport, never the twain shall meet.

Eight months later...

McNair reports that probate is complete. I receive title to my building in Montreal.

All fine, except that my name is now accessible in a public record associated with the property, not good for Plan B.

I use an online incorporator to set up BLT Properties, LLC, a shell company in the Caribbean nation of St. Kitts and Nevis; BLT *aka* bacon, lettuce and tomato.

BLT Properties' beneficial owner is identified in the founding documents as John S. Dobby of Sprightly Falls, New York, but his ownership is shielded from public view by Nevis' secrecy laws, thereby providing me with two layers of protection.

BLT Properties offers one hundred US dollars for my building on Duluth and St. Dominique, which I, as Jacob Morais, am pleased to accept.

From now on, a Google search will reveal that Jacob Morais sold his property.

Nothing will be known about the new owner except that it's an obscure LLC domiciled on a small island in the Caribbean.

Five

I visit Montreal to examine my building and I like what I see.

Its basic shape could be drawn by a child, a three-story rectangle that's a bit longer on its Avenue Duluth side than on its side facing Rue St. Dominique. It has brick walls painted brown at street level and tan on the higher two levels. English ivy covers much of the lower portion of the building like an unkempt beard. Although open to cars, the block of Avenue Duluth where the building is located also looks welcoming to pedestrians, brick surfaced, with trees in large wooden planters on both sides.

Through an Internet search, I identify a prospective building manager, Réseau Appartements au Québec. Reviewers on Yelp have written mainly positive things about RAQ's owner Sara Shahanagi apart from griping about lack of responsiveness on weekends. Good enough! RAQ is located nearby on Rue St. Denis, a thoroughfare packed with small shops and restaurants.

RAQ's small office has a couple of desks in the back, along with a row of filing cabinets. A middle aged woman at one of the desks glances up as I come in.

"Welcome to RAQ," she says, following up with "Bienvenue," to cover the linguistic bases.

I tell her, "My name is John Dobby. May we speak English? My French is not too good."

"I prefer English," she replies. "My name is Sara Shahanagi. How can I help you?"

"My company has just purchased a building on the corner of Duluth and St. Dominique which has a store on the ground floor and renters in two apartments on the second floor."

"The one with the antiques store?"

"Yeah."

"I know it. Good building."

"Thanks. I'm looking for a manager to collect the rent, pay utility bills, take care of maintenance, things like that."

"That's what we do."

"The former owner had a different building manager. Can you manage the transfer?"

"What's their name?"

"Lepine Associates."

"Sure, okay, they're a big operator. I know them. They'll require confirmation from the former owner."

"No problem."

"And your name, again, is…?"

"John S. Dobby. Call me John."

"And you call me Sara."

"Excellent!" I give Sara my New York ID card. "Take my info off of this."

She photocopies my card and hands it back.

"Where is Sprightly Falls?"

"Near the state line with Massachusetts. My place is on a lake about a mile out of town center."

"What do you do, John, for work I mean?"

"Various things," I reply, with modest vagueness. "Mostly real estate investments. Which is how I ended up with the building here in Montreal."

"Should I forward your mail to Sprightly Falls?"

"Sure," I say, and then make a show of re-considering. "You know what, let's use my PO Box in Boston. It's more reliable than in Sprightly Falls where our general store operates as our post office."

"What if I need to call you?"

"Email me at JDobby1974@gmail.com and I'll get back to you."

She jots that down. It is amazing how readily my fake identity is accepted, no questions asked. This is going to be easier than I thought.

"How about money," asks Sara, "like from rent payments, where do I send that?"

"I'll get you a bank account number after I open an account in Montreal. Meanwhile you can draw on the rent payments for your fees, building upkeep, and other expenses."

"Okay."

"There's a third floor penthouse that's currently unoccupied. The former owner was planning to renovate it prior to taking on another tenant. I'll rent it myself so that I have a place to stay when I'm in Montreal. Have the utilities bill me personally rather than billing BLT Properties, and then pay them on my behalf."

"Also from the rent money?"

"If there's enough…"
"Should be, from a store and the two apartments."
"Then we're good to go."

Six

I knew no one at Winchester High School where I was enrolled after my parents moved us down from Montreal.

To me everyone at WHS was a stranger, in the corridors, in the classrooms, and at cafeteria tables, which was totally fine. I kept my head down, minding my own business.

Towards the end of my first semester, the phys ed teacher called me over.

"We could use you on our track team," he said. "You run fast, faster than most, and you don't get tired."

"Sure," I replied with manly nonchalance as if my being noticed at WHS was an everyday occurrence.

Then one afternoon while I was collecting my stuff after a training run, I heard someone ask, "Want to run with me tomorrow?"

Turning around, I saw Sophie Whalen. Sophie wasn't just anyone. She was an acknowledged WHS superstar famous for excelling at everything she did.

"Me?"

"Yes, Jake, you. We can keep each other company."

Sophie Whalen knew my name!

The next day Sophie and I ran side by side, as we did every following day, after school and on weekends, pounding around the soccer and football fields, the town pond, the town center, and along the town's tree-lined streets. As the fall days grew shorter and colder, we ran through pools of light cast by streetlamps.

I looked forward to our runs. Sophie was my first real friend at WHS, my only real friend there, to be honest.

She wasn't a Barbie-type beauty. She combed her hair for tidiness rather than for style and didn't waste time with make-up. And yet she had a personal magnetism that placed her at the center of any group. Perhaps it was her self-confidence. Given her formidable brain, to Sophie it must have seemed that everyone around her was slogging through mental molasses, including those of us who were her acolytes, and we weren't dummies, although we did tend to be fucked up.

Like Dennis who stayed up night after night slaving over computer code and went to MIT where he suffered a nervous breakdown. Like Cheryl who was accepted at Juilliard but decided instead to join the Air Force and moved to Texas with her husband, also military. And Beth who indulged a wonderfully robust enjoyment of sex with both males and females although not with me, to my regret, and then found religion and became a rabbi in Minneapolis.

Sophie, our lodestar, kept her thoughts to herself except to murmur encouragingly when one of us mused about our aspirations, whether it was Dennis on joining NASA for a mission to Mars, or Beth on becoming a top runway model, or me, on getting posted to London as an international correspondent for the *New York Times*.

"You'll get there," she assured us.

Mostly when we were together she puttered about doing her thing and contentedly shared the weed that was passed around. We felt relaxed in her company. It didn't matter that we were shunned by WHS's cool kids, rich kids, jocks, and nerds, because here, with Sophie, we belonged.

One day Sophie suggested that I should campaign to be elected WHS senior class president.

To which I replied, "You're joking."

"No, really, you should. "

"I'm not into being publicly humiliated."

But she persisted. She predicted that I would surprise people, including myself, because of my special gift: People trusted me. They believed that I harbored no hidden agendas, that with Jake Morais, what you saw was what you got. I found it vaguely insulting that people assumed there was nothing going on behind my long-in-the-chin honest-Abe mug. In fact yours truly had *plenty* going on, fantasies, fears, resentments, piercing insights, and even a scheme or two! I wasn't a guileless innocent. But that's how I came across.

Sophie said, "You'll appeal to classmates who aren't invited to parties or selected for teams."

"Like me."

"Exactly!"

Sophie was right. Although I didn't win, I came in a respectable second. My platform, Voice for the Rest of Us, touched a nerve. I was accosted in hallways by students who wanted to thank me. They knew they could trust me, they said, unlike the guy who won, one of WHS's hulking football heroes.

Even students who voted for the brute let me know that I was their strong second choice.

More than once, I was told, "What counts is that you're authentic."

After WHS, Sophie and I stayed in touch online.

We exchanged email congratulations on our respective achievements, when she graduated from Harvard, when she married Caleb Bronstein, described by many as the most brilliant Harvard law student since Barack Obama, and when she sold her first startup for north of seventy million dollars; and for my part, when I graduated from UMass in Amherst, first with a BA and then with an MBA, and was hired as an analyst by Blair West International in Cambridge, and when I left BWI to launch JM Consulting, and subsequently when I was cited prominently by one of my clients as their key advisor in a high profile merger.

So when the *Globe* reported that Sophie Whalen Bronstein was appointed CEO of Dazzle, a Boston-based online marketplace for fine jewelry, I emailed her, "Great to hear about your new CEO post! All the best, Jake."

I didn't expect a response beyond her usual, "Many thanks, hope all is well."

Instead, my cellphone chirped with a text, "Can we talk?" which I admit that I interpreted as a consulting opportunity. A consultant rooting for gigs doesn't wallow in nostalgia.

I researched Dazzle, Sophie's new company.

Displayed on its website were rings, earrings, necklaces, bracelets, brooches, cufflinks, and *objets d'art*. They ranged from elegant to downright ugly, in my opinion, but I don't own any jewelry apart from my sixty dollar watch, so what do I know? The site's confections of gold, silver, jewels, and gemstones were priced from hundreds of dollars up to tens of thousands. Most sellers on Dazzle's platform were artisans selling items they'd made themselves, but also represented were the august stores that you see in *The New Yorker* ads, fine establishments that cater to the crème de la crème.

Dazzle's partner Island Bank (Antigua) provided an escrow service to receive, hold, and forward buyers' payments subject to confirmation that their purchases were delivered and met every expectation.

The company was growing fast and hiring aggressively.

Its last round of venture capital was raised from a foreign VC called Bracket Group, based in Ukraine. Three Boston-area VCs that were investors in earlier rounds remained committed to the company.

In short, Sophie's company was a tech player with a lot of potential.

I replied to her text, "Love to talk whenever convenient for you. Best, Jake."

Seven

Dazzle's receptionist is seated behind a desk that looks cobbled from recycled wood and other found objects, as you might expect of a tech company that occupies the second floor of formerly derelict shoe factory in the Fort Point section of Boston's sizzling hot Seaport district.

Sporting stubble and horned rim glasses, he greets me with a cheery smile, "Welcome to Dazzle!"

"Thanks. I'm Jake Morais, here to see Sophie Bronstein."

"So glad to meet you, Jake! I'm Brett. Sophie's expecting you."

"Brett," I say, repeating his name to lock it in, and he nods to confirm. I'm terrible with names, good with numbers. I can count a room, no problem. Following Brett past work tables, I count fifty one staff staring at their computer screens and tapping on keyboards, plus seven others wandering about.

Dazzle's open office space gives off a laid-back tech vibe, with its knotted pine wood flooring and exposed steel beams, pipes, and air ducts under a high factory-era tin ceiling. Natural light pours in through a line-up of large windows. Its 'eatery' comprises rustic wooden picnic tables in front of a live wall of cascading plants, and baskets heaped with bags of healthy nut mixes and granola bars, an expresso machine, a keg of craft beer, a tray of canned energy drinks, and a massive glass door refrigerator stocked with chilled bottled water and organic fruit juices, cartons of yoghurt, and assorted cold snacks.

Past the eatery, Brett points out a mural created by Dazzle employees a hodge-podge of cartoon drawings and pithy sayings. "Everyone says it's amazing."

"Amazing," I have to agree.

We walk by a pink papier-mâché Miss Piggy; "rub her head for good luck," says Brett, which I do; and by a mobile of red lobster claws suspended from the ceiling.

In the far corner, there's an enclosed office with a glass front wall and door. Inside the office, Sophie Whalen Bronstein leans forward at her desk, staring at a screen.

Brett taps on her door. "Jake Morais is here."

She looks like the Sophie I recall from decades earlier although her face is thinner and she's added a few lines at her eyes and mouth.

"Jake!" she exclaims, grasping my outstretched hand and holding it for an extra second or two. "You haven't changed at all!"

"Neither have you," I reply. "And now you're CEO of another hot start-up."

"For my sins."

"It's been a long time."

"Too long."

"And Caleb is being talked about as a Supreme Court nominee."

"So we've heard," says Sophie. "His name gets floated to cover the political bases. We don't take it seriously anymore."

"How's Steve doing?" I ask.

The last time I saw Sophie's brother Steve Whalen, his red hair was already thinning although he was only two years older than us. Stocky, disheveled, and impatient with lesser minds, he was nothing like Sophie except that intellectually he may have been her only equal.

"Fine, I think. I assume so. He doesn't talk a lot about his job at Homeland Security. You know Steve."

"Yeah, I know Steve."

Actually I don't know Steve all that well. When our paths crossed back in the day, he made his opinion clear that I was just another oddball hanging around his sister. In a nod to my Canadian heritage, he called me Nanook which I guess meant that he knew who I was. Other than that we didn't interact much. From what I saw, he and Sophie didn't interact much either. She paid no attention to him and he'd ignore her in return. I suspect that when we weren't around he found ways to get under Sophie's skin which he could do, even to her, because he was older. Maybe that's normal. Having never had sibs, I don't know anything about living with a brother or sister.

Sophie asks, "Do you like being a consultant?"

"Usually."

"Still feeling challenged?"

Finally, the opening that I was waiting for. "Why? Do you need a consultant?"

Sophie checks that her glass door is closed.

"I want to hire you," she replies. "Full time."

I like what I'm hearing. One of the most lucrative consulting gigs is to camp at a client's premises and bill full-time hours.

"I'd have an office here?"

"Of course! Right next door! You'll be on my exec team."

"As your consultant?"

"As my VP Strategy. You'll help me set a new direction for the company."

"Hmm," I say, trying to keep up. This is not what I expected. I'm a consultant. I undertake projects and I move on after they're over, like a rolling stone. Working inside a company and having a boss would be new. On the other hand, the title does roll nicely off the tongue: VP Strategy. I've never been a VP before.

Sophie continues, "We're facing big challenges, Jake, so it won't be easy. But that's also why we'll have a lot of fun."

In retrospect, I should have asked what Sophie meant by *big challenges*. In retrospect, a lot of things are clearer.

"I know zip about jewelry," I say.

"Do I look like an expert?"

She is wearing plain gold earring studs and a gold wedding band.

"Well, you're a quick learner."

"So are you, Jake. I saw that back at WHS. Also being a consultant involves thinking strategically, which is what I need here as well. You've built a great consulting practice. Your clients give you very high marks."

So I wasn't the only one doing background research!

Sophie continues, "You're one of my oldest friends. And you don't have ties to anyone else in the company..."

She stops there, waiting.

"I don't."

"So I know that I can trust you. I need you here, Jake, or I wouldn't be asking. You said once that you'd do anything for me."

"Did I?" It's a rhetorical question. I recall perfectly well telling Sophie how she could always count on me. Maybe at the time it was the marijuana talking, but I meant it.

"I'm calling you on it now."

I never could say no to Sophie, and certainly not after she brings up my long-ago pledge. Also, I'm intrigued. Anyway, if my new exec role at Dazzle doesn't work out, I can always return to consulting.

"I'll need time to wrap up a project for one of my clients."

"You can do that while you get installed here."

She hands me a manila folder.

"Here's your employment offer, the usual stuff."

It all looks fine, title, money, stock options vesting over three years, health coverage, life insurance, allowance for personal days. Plus a confidentiality agreement and a non-compete for a year after leaving the company, which nowadays is typical at tech companies.

Sophie's signature as CEO is already on each of the two copies of my offer letter.

"You were prepared," I say, as she looks on.

"I knew you wouldn't let me down, Jake."

I sign the offer letter, both copies, handing one of them back to her.

Sophie extends her hand to clinch the deal.

"Welcome to Dazzle! Now, before you change your mind, I'll introduce you to the others on my team."

She presses a button on her desk phone.

"Brett."

"Yes, Sophie?"

"Please ask Viktor, Maggie, and Toby to join us."

"Will do."

Eight

First in the door is a man who's as pale as a fish's underbelly. He's gaunt, verging on cadaverous. His hair is cut down to his scalp. He has sharp cheekbone ridges, bulging grey eyes, a beaky narrow nose, and a bony chin. He looks wary, like an ex-con.

"You called a meeting?" he asks Sophie. His accent sounds Russian.

"Yes, Viktor," says Sophie. "Please say hello to Jake Morais. I'll tell you more when the others arrive. Jake, this is Viktor Rost, our Chief Financial Officer."

"Glad to meet you," I say.

"Yeah," he mutters.

After a limp eyes-averted handshake, he slumps into a chair.

Perhaps Viktor is just having a bad day and deep down, he's a warm human being.

Next in is a man who's smiling like he's enjoying an internal amusement.

Sophie introduces him as Toby Ericsson, Chief Technology Officer.

"How're ya doin?" he says.

"Great," I reply. "How about yourself?"

"Couldn't be better!"

About a minute later, a woman bustles in. Large purple-rimmed glasses frame her round face. In her hand are loose papers, like she's just grabbed them on her way here.

"Sorry," she says. "I was on a call."

"Not a problem," Sophie replies. "Maggie Chen, meet Jake Morais."

Then to me, Sophie says, "Maggie is our Marketing VP. We've been friends since business school and she reached out to me after Danny Hughes, the former Dazzle CEO, left the company."

"Danny was encouraged by the board to explore other opportunities," says Toby, clarifying.

"They fired his ass," Viktor grumps.

Maggie reaches towards me to shake hands.

"Hi," she says.

Maggie, I like.

Sophie tells them, "Jake is our new VP Strategy, effective immediately."

I give them a friendly smile as Sophie continues, "I'm confident that Jake will be a tremendous asset as I'm sure you'll agree when you get to know him."

"You should have consulted us," Viktor says. "No offense to Jake but this is the first time we're meeting him."

Sophie replies, pleasantly, "It's my decision, Viktor."

Viktor pouts his thin lips, not buying it.

Maggie says, "If Sophie believes in Jake, so do I."

"Me too," echoes Toby.

"Okay," Sophie says. "I want to talk some more with our new team member so thanks to each of you for coming in."

After they leave and Sophie's door is closed, she says, "Viktor's a handful."

"So I noticed."

"He was upset that I was hired as CEO. He thought he'd get the job. Anyway I'm stuck with him for now. He's tight with a leading member of the board."

I take a stab based on Viktor's Russian accent, "The Ukrainian VC?"

"Right, the Bracket Group, which *is* Ukrainian, but Russian speaking, represented on our board by Oleg Krulik. Viktor is Oleg's guy."

"So you're warning me to keep my distance from him."

"On the contrary, I want you to become his friend."

"Why? Is he lonely?"

"I've tried with Viktor. Flattered him. Met for coffee off-site. The whole thing. It turns out that for me and Viktor, nothing works. He sees me as a rival."

"You're not his rival. You're his boss."

"As I said, he's connected."

"I got the impression he didn't take to me either."

"His nose is out of joint. He'll get over it if you approach him the right way. It's amazing how people trust you, Jake. They let down their guard. I saw that back in high school. Not that you don't deserve their trust, of course."

"You're pimping me out."

Sophie laughs and touches my arm, reassuringly. "It's for a good cause. If you and Viktor get along, maybe you'll pick up things that I should know. You'll give me eyes and ears where I need them."

"What about Toby? Do you want me to befriend him as well?"

"If you two hit it off, sure."

"And Maggie?"

"She's terrific. When I'm not around and you need the straight scoop, go to Maggie."

Nine

On my return the following day, my first as an exec at Dazzle, Brett escorts me to my new office. It looks like Sophie's: white walls on three sides, and a glass front wall and door.

"Sophie told me to set you up here," he says. "Call me if you need anything."

Then, seeing my laptop, he says, "I'll give you a company laptop. Meanwhile, Sophie wants you to join a meeting in her office."

Viktor, Toby, Maggie, and a man I don't recognize are seated in visitors' chairs in front of Sophie's desk. I roll in another chair from my office and they make room for me to squeeze in.

The man I don't recognize leans across Viktor to shake hands. "Gary Pollack."

"Jake Morais," I reply, "Glad to meet you."

Sophie says, "Oh, sorry, I forgot you haven't met. Gary is our external counsel from Skiffington, Skiffington and Mohr. Gary, Jake is our new VP Strategy. Gary's enlightening us on what would be involved in a public offering of Dazzle shares."

"Great," I say.

"Which Viktor thinks is a bad idea," adds Sophie.

"We're not ready for an IPO," says Viktor. He's slumped in his chair, evidently his usual posture when visiting Sophie's office.

"Well, for now, we're only exploring it as an option, but we do need to prepare, just in case. It doesn't hurt to get the ball rolling so that we're ready."

Pollack says, "You need to follow certain steps, submit filings to the SEC…"

"The board won't approve," Viktor says. "This is a waste of time."

"Viktor, let's let Gary talk since he's taken the time to come here."

"We're *paying* for his time. Unless he turned off his meter."

"Meter's always on," says Pollack.

Staring hard at Viktor, Sophie's tone is unusually sharp, for her, "I want to hear from Gary."

"Sure. Fine."

Sophie turns again to Pollack, "Go ahead."

"First step is to hire a brand-name outside accountant to provide credible financials."

"What's wrong with Anton Belsky?" demands Viktor.

Pollack replies, "With respect, Viktor, nobody's heard of Mr. Belsky. You'll need an auditor with a reputation."

Ignoring the lawyer, Viktor says to Sophie, "You're heading down the same path that got Danny Hughes fired."

Maggie Chen snaps, "That's enough from you about Danny. At least he was doing his job. Which is more than anyone can say about you."

"Whoa!" says Viktor, raising his hands in mock surrender. "Maggie has claws!"

"That was then and this is now," Sophie says. "What do the rest of you think?"

Maggie says, "I'm for following Gary's advice, obviously."

"Toby?" asks Sophie.

"Yeah, sure."

"Jake?"

Viktor sourly regards his hands clenched on his lap. He knows how I'll vote, being Sophie's new poodle.

"As a management consultant," I say, "I learned that companies benefit when they defer to their CFOs on financial matters. Given that Viktor is our CFO, it seems to me that his opinions on this matter should carry a lot of weight."

Sophie asks, incredulous, "You mean, to keep Belsky as our auditor?"

From the corner of my eye, I catch Maggie glaring daggers at me.

"If that's what Viktor recommends."

"Which I do," says Viktor. Then, to Sophie, "Are we done here?" raising his thin upper lip above his teeth in a tight fuck-you smile.

Fact check: I made up the bit about companies that benefited by deferring to their CFOs. But Viktor is pleased, which is what counts.

"Yes, we're done for now, Viktor," Sophie says.

Maggie and Toby follow him out.

Sophie motions with her hand for me to stay put so I sit back down.

"Time for me to go," Pollack says. He slides his manila folder and writing pad into his leather briefcase.

"You'll send me an IPO roadmap?"

"Yes, within a couple of days."

"And give me contact names at the big accountants?"

"You still want to proceed with that?"

"Of course I do!" says Sophie, sounding surprised at the question. "Send me the contact names directly. I'll follow up and get Viktor on board later, when the time is right."

"Will do," says Pollack, glancing at me.

After he leaves, Sophie turns towards me. She's glowering, rigid with fury: "You're full of surprises!"

"You asked for my opinion."

"And it was certainly appreciated, especially by Viktor."

"You wanted me to be his friend."

"Yes, fine, but what you said, was..," she stops there, jabbing her desk angrily with a forefinger, leaving the rest for me to fill in.

I'm speechless. I've never seen Sophie lose her temper. At worst, I've seen her disappointed, which she showed by going quiet and withdrawing into herself for a while. I feel chagrined to have let her down. At the same time, although I keep my mouth shut, I'm seething at being reprimanded and having to sit here and take it. Evidently my run as a VP is already coming to an end. I'll leave Dazzle as a one-day wonder. I don't need this.

"Keep looking defensive," Sophie says. "I want people who are watching us to think I'm berating you."

"You're not?"

"No, I'm definitely not!" Still scowling, she jabs her desk again. "Jake, what you did was inspired! You're well on your way with Viktor. You'll be his friend, about that I have no doubt."

She strides past me to lower the privacy blinds on her office's glass wall and door. "Now they'll think I'm ripping into you for real."

"Should I cry out?"

"No, show's over. You were great."

"I wasn't acting."

"Well, sorry if I alarmed you, but you delivered your part perfectly."

A few minutes later, I open Sophie's office door, look around, and then slip out closing it quietly behind me.

I'm stony faced. Anyone watching would conclude that I'm more than a little pissed off after my thrashing by my new boss.

I step directly into my office and shut my door.

Ten

Later, Toby Ericsson, Dazzle's technology chief, is pecking on his keyboard when I materialize in his office doorway.

"Good time for a chat?" I ask.

He tears his attention away from his screen. "Whenever." And then, with a sly grin, "You're quite the stud, voting with Viktor against our CEO."

"Was I out of line?"

"With Sophie, that's hard to tell," says Toby, thereby proving that he's smarter than he looks. "She held you back and closed her privacy blinds after the rest of us left. What was that about?"

"Just letting me know she was listening."

"Did it hurt when she spanked you?"

"We had a civilized discussion. Sophie asked for my opinion, which I gave, and she accepts that."

"Uh huh."

"Anyway, I thought I'd say hello outside of her office."

"Yeah, good idea."

"So what are your folks working on?"

"A video chat feature for sellers and buyers. Also how to make our site work better on mobile devices. Stuff like that. Why do you ask?"

"If I'm going to think about strategy, it helps to know what we're already doing."

"Do me a favor," Toby says. "Don't bug my engineers. They're slammed right now and I don't want them distracted. No problem with you talking to them, but come to me first and I'll set up your meetings. Okay?"

"Okay."

"I still don't get why you'd side with Viktor when Sophie was on a different page."

"Why does that seem so strange? He is our CFO after all."

"He's an odd duck and not just because he's Russian. We're all busting our butts to make Dazzle more competitive while Viktor could care less."

I give Toby a few seconds to elaborate. He doesn't.

"Well, let's you and I stay in touch," I say.

"Yeah. Good chat."

Maggie Chen waves me into her office with a flick of her hand. She points to a chair covered in files and magazines. "You can sit there. Just put that stuff on the floor."

I try to keep the pile in order as I lay it down amongst the other piles covering much of Maggie's office floor.

"Hope I'm not disturbing…" I say.

"It's fine. What's on your mind, Jake?"

"Just wanted to get better acquainted…"

She cuts me off.

"What you said in the meeting wasn't helpful. Doesn't bode well."

"Sophie asked for our opinions."

"Your opinion was bullshit."

"Why don't you tell me what you really think?"

Maggie laughs, despite herself, which cools her down somewhat.

"Sophie said I could come to you for the straight scoop about what's going on at Dazzle."

"Did she now?"

"Yep."

She ponders for a moment, then, "What do you want to know?"

"What's the real story about Danny Hughes?"

"They pushed him out because he was trying to do his job."

"They?"

"The board, meaning Oleg Krulik."

"Why did they push him out?"

"Okay, so Danny was scrambling to raise cash. Our investors expected our next round would devalue their holdings. They were excited when Oleg Krulik's group offered a premium. They pressured Danny to take Oleg's money, which he did, and Oleg's Bracket Group became Dazzle's largest investor. Then Bill Harris, our CFO, just stopped coming in. He emailed Danny that it was time for him to move on."

"He gave no other reasons?"

"Just goodbye and good luck. It was a huge surprise to everyone. After Bill left, Oleg pushed Danny to hire Viktor as his replacement. Danny agreed. Once Viktor was in the door, he picked Anton Belsky as our outside auditor. Given that Belsky was and is unqualified, this time Danny objected. And they fired him."

"So Belsky is an ongoing issue."

"You could say that."

"I noticed that you and Viktor don't get along."

"Viktor has it in for Sophie. He slithers around looking for dirt to report to the board. Like he did to Danny."

Maggie looks down towards her desk. I can't tell for sure but it seems to me that she's tearing up.

"I feel so guilty," she says. "It's my fault that Sophie's here."

"And that makes you feel guilty?"

"I put her in this situation, having to fend off Viktor and deal with Oleg. After they fired Danny, Oleg asked around for suggestions to help them find a new CEO, ideally someone well regarded in the Boston area, and I told him about Sophie. When they offered her the job, and she asked what I thought, I sold her on Dazzle. I really wanted her here."

"It's not on you. Sophie makes her own decisions."

"I realize that," replies Maggie, "but still I feel responsible. You're her friend, Jake, so I'll give you this advice free of charge. Keep Viktor at arm's length. He's toxic."

The urge to meet must be contagious: Viktor's standing in my office doorway.

"Got a minute?"

"Sure, what's up?"

He searches for the right words. "You and me... We got off on the wrong foot."

"That can happen. No harm done."

"Still I must apologize for my bad manners."

Again he lifts his upper lip in what passes for a smile, which I reciprocate.

"I accept your apology, Viktor. Not a problem."

Viktor edges the rest of the way into my office, pulls out one of my chairs, and takes a seat.

"Do you mind?" he asks.

"Please."

"You should be aware... What Sophie says is not always right."

I don't reply. Keep my face neutral.

He continues, "You are loyal to her."

"She is an old friend and my boss. But also I try to keep an open mind."

"Like about Anton Belsky?"

"Like I said, our auditor is primarily your responsibility as CFO so we should respect your opinion, all of us, even Sophie."

Viktor nods. "You and me, Jake, we should get to know each other better."

"We should, I agree."

He pushes up from his chair, reassembling his bony Ichabod Crane frame to a standing position. "No one in this company likes me."

"Why do you say that?"

"You were talking with Maggie Chen, so you know what I mean."

"Actually I don't..."

"You'll find out, when you ask around. But in case you're curious, just between us, I don't give a fuck what they think."

"Okay."

"Really, I don't fucking care."

"Yeah, okay."

"But if *we* can be friends…"

"No reason why not," I say, standing behind my desk and returning his grey-eyed stare, sincerely, eye to eye.

Eleven

Sophie allows me a few days to get organized before calling me into her office for my first assignment as her VP Strategy.

"I want you to analyze our business. Let me know what patterns you find that we can build on."

Handing me a thumb drive, she says, "This has our sales data. Good place to start."

Then she adds, "Don't lose it and don't make any copies. Competitors would kill for these data."

My analysis reveals that just two sellers, out of the one hundred and seventy thousand on our platform, account for a high percentage of our sales.

When I report this finding to Sophie, she asks what these two sellers are doing that's different.

"Looks like they sell only the most expensive items, primarily to international buyers located in Russia plus a few other countries. They've got around eighty buyers in total, repeat customers, apparently very loyal."

"So, two sellers and relatively few buyers."

"Yep."

Sophie is scratching her right hand absent mindedly, more caressing than scratching, which I recall she used to do at WHS while she was thinking.

"Who are these sellers?"

"Arthur's of New York and Tamara's Fine Jewelry, both based in New York. They first posted on Dazzle only six months ago and began producing big numbers almost immediately. I tried to contact them to learn more. My phone calls went straight to voicemail and they haven't responded yet to my emails. I visited their New York addresses online via Google Street View: Looks like they don't have storefronts. They must operate out of offices on higher floors."

"Let's discuss this at our Monday morning exec meeting," says Sophie.

First up at our exec meeting the following Monday is Toby, who reports on his video chat project. Five sellers are testing the feature now and loving it, and twenty more will start testing it when we're ready for them.

Maggie reports that she's secured a high profile speaking role for Dazzle at an upcoming conference in Las Vegas. Also she says that a writer at the *Wall Street Journal* wants to interview Sophie for a piece on luxury e-tailing.

"Great work, both of you," says Sophie. She turns to Viktor, "What do you have for us this week?"

He shakes his head. "Nothing new."

"No problem," says Sophie. "So, for my news, I heard back from Gary Pollack on a choice of auditors. I plan to review his recommendations with the board, and with Viktor, of course."

Viktor doesn't respond.

"Also, I asked Jake to analyze our sales data for patterns that suggest how we can update our growth strategy. I'd like your opinions on what he found."

I tell the team about the two New York sellers.

Maggie says, "We should find out how our platform works so well for them."

"I tried to contact them," I say. "They don't answer their phones and haven't responded to my voicemail and email messages."

"So go down to New York," says Sophie. "Pay them a visit in person."

"Will do."

Now Viktor jerks to life. "You want to visit Arthur's of New York and Tamara's Fine Jewelry?"

"That's the plan," I say.

"They won't talk to you. I'm their designated contact here. Only me. They came onto our site because of Oleg Krulik and that was the agreement."

Sophie says, "So let them know that we'd really like to learn more about what they're doing. Introduce Jake. Ask them to meet with him."

"Oleg doesn't want anyone talking with them except for me."

"What a load of crap!" says Maggie.

"That's the way it is," replies Viktor. "So get used to it."

Sophie says, calmingly, "I'll have a chat with Oleg to get this straightened out."

I say to Viktor, adopting an agreeable, cooperative tone, "Meanwhile, you and I can work together on questions that we want to ask them and then you can meet with them to put the questions."

"Okay," says Viktor, with a shrug that I take to mean *not going to happen*. I let it go. No point in antagonizing my new friend.

Late that Monday afternoon, Sophie drops by my office as I'm collecting my stuff to go home.

"I've just spoken with Oleg Krulik about the two New York sellers. He confirmed that Viktor is the only one they'll talk to. He said this was agreed when the sellers were recruited to post on our platform, but he promised to get back to them to work it out. He thinks they'll go along with changing the arrangement but it could take time. He asked for patience."

"And you said?"

"That I'll be patient, within reason. He told me that he appreciates my understanding."

"So we're on hold for now."

"Only until we hear back from Oleg. But keep digging into those data. Let me know what else you find."

"Okay."

"On a different note, Caleb and I are hosting a barbeque at our house in Cambridge on Saturday. Can you come?"

"What time?"

"Starting around six o'clock."

I pull up my calendar on my phone. This is for show. I don't need to check the date or time. Nowadays, my weekends are uncluttered.

"Love to," I say.

"There's something I need to tell you."

Sophie is watching me closely like she expects that I won't like what she's about to say.

I brace myself. "Okay."

"I know Annie Kane."

"Annie? My ex?"

"From way back. Our families used to summer together on Martha's Vineyard. I hadn't seen her in years but a couple of days ago we bumped into each other and got to chatting, and she told me that she'd become single again, and then she mentioned your name."

It takes me a few beats to process that Sophie and Annie know each other. Did Annie tell Sophie about the supplies in my basement, as evidence of my strangeness? How could she not? In return, did Sophie reminisce about the Jake Morais she knew in high school, sharing tidbits that would make Annie laugh? Probably she did.

Fuck.

I ask, "How is Annie?"

"She looks good. She asked about you."

"Great."

"I'm sorry it didn't work out for the both of you."

Even with Sophie, I'm not about to share what Annie and I had together, nor why it ended.

"Annie has her own life to live," I say. "We both do."

"And now you've moved on."

"We have."

"Glad to hear that. Because I invited Annie to our barbeque."

"Okay."

Still looking concerned, Sophie adds, "Hope that's alright with you."

"Absolutely."

Actually it's more than alright. Since she moved out, Annie hasn't replied to any of my emails and texts, and I've sent quite a few along the lines of, "Hi, hope you're doing well, let me know anytime you want to talk," and so on. Maybe Annie will stop ghosting me, if that's what she's doing, after we see each other at Sophie's.

Twelve

Annie.

In a gallery at the Boston Museum of Fine Arts, a docent announced, "I'll be leading a tour shortly. Please gather around."

My heart skipped a beat when I saw her. Slender. Lustrous dark hair. Startling light brown eyes. Sensuous lips. Bright smile. With one arm raised to collect her group, she moved with the grace of a ballet dancer.

I elbowed through her clump of art lovers to get close enough to read her name on her MFA badge, Annie Kane.

She led us from painting to painting, pointing out each work's notable aspects of composition, style, influences and history.

"This one has quite the story," she said, when we arrived at Alfred Tilley's *Mrs. Mabel Morgan*, which depicted a waspish woman perched rigidly on a red velvet loveseat. "Mabel and her husband hated the painting. They ordered Tilley to destroy it but since they didn't pay him, they had no say in what he did with it, and Tilley refused. For the rest of his life Tilley kept this portrait in his studio and insisted on showing it to visitors."

"Seems he didn't like Mabel Morgan very much," remarked a woman in our group.

"Tilley painted what he saw," replied Annie. "If Mabel wanted to appear more pleasant in her portrait, she should have faked it."

She led us to a portrait of a portly red-cheeked man who looked abundantly well satisfied as he studied a book of accounts on the table in front of him.

"This is Desmond Wilkin's *Elijah Price*, who was obviously a much happier subject. Mr. Price was a prosperous Boston merchant in the late 1800s and one of our outstanding philanthropists. He had a personal connection with the subject of another portrait in this gallery. Does anyone know what that connection was?"

No one did.

She pointed towards a portrait on the opposite wall of a fierce looking dandy wearing a purple silk cravat.

"The man in that other Desmond Wilkins portrait is Ignatius Jones, a celebrated psychic. He was notorious for his affairs with many Boston society women. One such affair was with Elijah Price's daughter, Melissa. In 1903, after Melissa was discovered to be pregnant, Ignatius Jones was murdered by one of Melissa's brothers, who happened also to be his best friend."

"*Former* best friend!" I observed, wittily.

"It was a complicated situation," said Annie, perhaps noticing me for the first time. Best of all, I earned a half smile.

"Concerning that portrait of Ignatius Jones," she continued, "it was completed in 1896 and went missing in 1903 on the day of his murder. Recently it turned up in a church rummage sale in Vermont, and it was gifted shortly thereafter to the MFA."

A woman said, "I heard another story, about how Ignatius Jones communicates from the Other Side through his portrait."

"Well, he *was* a psychic," replied Annie, "and that story is definitely out there. People do claim they can hear his voice when they're near his portrait."

She gestured towards the visitors clustering in front of the portrait. "Whether you believe that or not, as you can see Mr. Jones attracts a lot of attention."

I stayed back after our tour ended and the rest of our group had dispersed.

"Annie Kane, you're terrific," I said.

"Why, thank you!"

"My name is Jake Morais. Can I get you a coffee, or lunch?"

Evidently I passed her initial inspection because she replied, "Sure, why not?"

She selected a table in the MFA's New American Café, in the atrium at the entrance to the Americas Wing.

After our waiter left with our orders, hers for a cheese plate, and mine for a hamburger, I said, "You really know your stuff."

"I should. In my day job, I'm a fine arts professor at BU."

"Now I'm impressed for real!"

"You're just trying to flatter me."

"No, I mean it. You're amazing!"

"Please stop. You're making me blush."

There actually *was* more color in her cheeks, which made her even more enchanting.

"I could go on and on," I replied. "But I won't, if you'll tell me more about yourself."

"I'm also a painter. I take commissions for portraits in the Desmond Wilkins style."

"Would you do my portrait?"

Using the thumbs and forefingers of her hands she framed a square which she raised in front of me.

When I asked what she was doing, she replied, "I'm judging how you'd look on canvas."

"And?"

"You have an interesting face."

"That's one way of putting it."

"Could be a while, though. I've got a waiting list."

"No problem," I said, writing my name, email address, and phone number on a scrap of paper that I handed to her. "Please add me to your list. Here's my contact info."

"Nicely done," she said, slipping the paper into her purse. She bit off a portion of a small toasted baguette after dipping it into a cup of maple honey. "So, Jake, what do you do when you're not picking up docents at the MFA?"

I was about to take a chunk out of my hamburger but put it down instead, to avoid having to reply with a mouth full of meat and trimmings.

"I should let you finish that," she said.

"It's okay. I'll chomp it down while you're talking."

She laughed. "A delightful prospect!"

Annie appeared to be interested as I described the life of a management consultant: High stakes! Exotic travel! Then she asked, "What about Jake Morais, the person?"

"Came down from Canada when I was a teen-ager, went to high school in Winchester where my parents still live, no siblings. What about you?"

"My parents are both lawyers and like you I'm an only child."

"Any significant others?"

"None currently," Annie said. "You?"

"Nope. We have that in common as well."

"While we're talking about we have in common," she says, giving me a let's-cut-the-bullshit look, "I have to ask…"

"Sure," I chirp. "Ask away!"

"Did you vote for you-know-who?"

"Are you kidding?"

"So that's a No?"

"A huge flopping No and I'm shocked, *shocked*, that you could ever think…"

"Sorry, I had to know."

"Did *you*?"

"Let's put it this way, you know the old prayer, 'Now I lay me down to sleep…?'"

"I do."

"Well, though I'm not religious I mumble it to myself every night at bedtime."

"So you're covered, just in case."

"Right, then I stick a pin in an old rag doll that a friend gave me after the election, and every morning when I get up I check the news for the results, hoping..."

"It's not working."

"Maybe I need a bigger pin."

After lunch, as we were leaving the café and about to go our separate ways, Annie stuck out her hand, "Thanks for lunch, Jake. I enjoyed it."

I said, "Let's get together again."

"I'd like that," Annie replied.

We did get together again, at first on weekends, then also on weekday evenings.

One Saturday, Annie and I were at an indie theater in Harvard Square watching *Behind Enemy Lines*, a classic 1940s movie about US airmen whose B-24 bomber was shot down over Nazi-occupied Yugoslavia.

The lead character, co-pilot Rob Rifkin from Long Island, everyone called him Rifkin, was played by an actor whose long face resembled Spock's in Star Trek, first gen version, except that the Rifkin actor had curlier hair, thicker eyebrows, and human-shaped ears.

Annie, leaning towards me, whispered, "He looks like Spock."

"Yep."

"Also like you, sort of."

"Maybe on one of my good days."

Someone behind us hissed, "Shhh!"

Annie snorted and straightened in her seat, but allowed herself one more whisper, drawing it out, "Sp-awww-ck!"

The movie opened with carefree bantering among the six crew members before they took off for their bombing run. They hailed from the North and South, cities and farmland, inherited wealth and working class, but they were all Americans united by their common cause.

Their bantering ceased once they were airborne. From then on, each crew member spoke only to update the others as necessary, shouting over the interphone to be heard above the whine of their B-24's engines. Each focused intently on his respective task, well aware that their lives were at stake.

They made it through rough weather and heavy enemy fire to drop their bombs. On their return, they were congratulating each other when they were hit. One of their engines began to spew flames and smoke.

While parachuting from their crippled plane, two of the six crew members were killed by ground fire. The remaining four made it safely to the ground although Rifkin suffered a broken arm when he landed. They hid in the Bosnian woods until nightfall. When they emerged from cover, they were stopped by a partisan, a young woman, who promised she would get them to safety. She carried a rifle, a shoulder-holstered handgun, grenades on her belt, and bandoliers of bullets. She looked about nineteen years old. She told the Americans that her name was Lejla.

As the plot unfolded on screen, I was wondering how airmen like these characters found the courage to embark repeatedly on their terrifying missions in their thin-skinned aircraft, without cabin heating in the bitter cold, hurtling through flak and bullets. How did Grandpa Alain head out time after time in allied bombers over Germany despite dismal odds of returning safely?

Lejla led Rifkin and the others to a barn where she set his broken arm, replacing the rough splint that his buddies had fashioned in the forest, and brought them food and water and blankets.

"Stay here tonight," she told them. "Tomorrow night we'll walk."

Rifkin wasn't much older than Lejla and there was an attraction between them. That night, while the others were sleeping, Lejla crept back into the barn and joined him under the blanket, just to lie closely with him for mutual comfort and warmth.

The following night they began their walk to the coast, following Lejla in single file. Their progress was painfully slow as they hiked in the dark through the deep woods, dodging Nazi patrols and suffering constant torment from mosquitos and black flies. When dawn came, Lejla told Rifkin and his crew to wait in the woods while she checked nearby farms and hamlets for Nazis.

"It's good," she'd tell them, and introduce them to a farmer who would let them stay in his barn.

For six weeks they pushed on.

Each night, Lejla joined Rifkin under his blanket.

Finally, they arrived at a coastal village near a landing area. Partisans there made radio contact with the Americans in Italy, and a small plane was sent to pick them up.

"Join us," Rifkin begged Lejla, "You'll be safe with us. I'll take care of you."

"I cannot," she replied. "I must stay to fight the Nazis and free my people."

Rifkin had tears in his eyes, and Lejla also did, and they hugged farewell. He promised her, "I'll come back for you."

Six months later, after the Nazis were expelled from Yugoslavia, Rifkin wangled permission to return to the Bosnian village where he and Lejla had parted.

He asked a partisan who came out to his plane if there was news of Lejla. The partisan didn't know her name but said he would check. Rifkin was eating dinner with a family in the village in whose home he was staying, when the partisan returned and said to come meet his commanding officer.

The officer saluted Rifkin when they entered his hut. His name was Josip, and he did have news of Lejla.

"She died fighting the Nazis. She killed four of them before she ran out of ammunition, and then they shot her."

Rifkin's face froze in shock and despair as the screen faded to black.

Annie gripped my hand. I looked away briefly from the on-screen drama to glance at her. Her eyes were streaming.

She let my hand go as we filed out of the theater, and took hold of it again once we were on the street.

"Let's go to your house," she said.

When Annie's lease on her Beacon Hill apartment came due for renewal, I asked her to move in with me instead.

She said, "Are you sure?"

"I'm very sure."

We converted one of my upstairs bedrooms into a studio where Annie set up her painting paraphernalia. We hung her work on walls throughout the house. Her favorite sofa took the place of honor in the living room, in front of the fireplace. Her chest of drawers joined mine in our bedroom.

I led Annie down to my basement to show her the racks of supplies.

"What's all this for?" she asked.

"In case of an emergency when nothing's working, to be able to outlast it."

"Like what, a huge blizzard that shuts the city down?"

"Sure, or any kind of catastrophe that's followed by breakdown in public order."

She glanced at me quizzically. "Are you one of those doomsday preppers?"

"If I were, would you think I was a nut case?"

"Not in a bad way," she said, squeezing my arm reassuringly.

One warm evening when we were both feeling frisky, Annie said, "Let's play a game. One of us will play a famous character from the world of fine arts and the other will just act naturally, like improv."

"I'm up for that," I said.

We started that evening with her first scene. She banished me from our living room, and then, after about ten minutes, called me back in.

She'd tossed a white sheet on our sofa, and lay naked on the sheet on her side, her back to me, one of her arms splayed over a pillow.

"Behold Renoir's *Rest After The Bath*," she said.

Annie was less voluptuous than Renoir's model but her lovely backside was no less alluring.

As instructed, I acted naturally. I shucked off my own clothing and lay against her, pressing against her soft skin, exploring the parts of her body that Renoir left to the imagination.

"Why Monsieur Morais," she said demurely, "I do believe you have a stiffie!"

And then we got busy,

There were so many great works of art for us to emulate!

On another memorable evening, Annie lay on her back, her breasts pointing up, her hips slightly raised on one side, in the style, as she said, of Modigliani's *Reclining Nude With Arms Behind Her Head*. Soon I was finding my way around her exquisite form. She held her pose as long as she could.

In her interpretation of the sublime *Frau bei der Selbstbefriedigung* by Gustav Klimt, Annie played the *Frau* reclining in an armchair, her head tilted back and sideways, her eyes closed, her lips slightly parted, wearing a white frilly nighty that was pulled up to her waist, the fingers of her right hand touching herself gently.

I joined in.

At home or out and about, Annie and I came as a pair. We looked out for each other.

We were a couple.

We enjoyed each other's company.

We loved each other.

What we had together was *magic*.

Annie missed her period. We tiptoed on eggshells until she did the test. The results showed false alarm and I could breathe again but Annie didn't seem relieved. If anything, she became more preoccupied and moody.

"What's wrong?" I asked.

"Nothing."

"What? Tell me."

"Alright," she said. "We've been living together for a year."

"Yes."

"Where do we go from here?"

"I like where we are. We're great together."

"Where we are now is not enough for me."

Picking discretion over valor, I didn't say anything.

Annie asked, "Do you see a future in our relationship?"

"Of course I do."

"Because I need to hear you say it."

"I do see a future in our relationship."

"Otherwise I'm wasting my time."

"Why wasting? We're enjoying…"

"…and I won't. I can't. I'm running out of time."

Annie wanted an engagement ring. Lately her hints were downright pointed and she was increasingly impatient with my attempts to deflect.

To prove in a different way that I was thinking about our future, I showed her where I'd added more supplies on the racks in the basement. "Now we'll have enough for both of us to hunker down together, if and when."

She didn't respond as I hoped.

"Oh wow! That's amazing! So glad to hear you weren't just going to evict me, if and when."

"I thought you'd be pleased."

"I'm ecstatic. Can't you tell?"

Plan B was the problem.

I ran the scenarios, over and over.

What if I made the commitment, the ring on Annie's finger and all the rest, and we had a kid or two, and then came disaster and hunkering down wasn't a viable option?

I'd have to tell Annie about Plan B.

Best case, she'd join in the plan. We'd manage somehow, the two of us along with any hypothetical kids.

But what if Annie refused? She'd have good reasons. No appetite for life on the run. Her tenure at BU. Her reputation in Boston as a portrait artist.

Plan B would be compromised.

If I took off anyway, she'd know. And meanwhile she couldn't move on with her life until I was officially dead or divorced.

Except there's no way that I'd leave without her, so no more Plan B.

I was stuck. I couldn't decide what to do.

For a while she and I hardly talked, but whatever she was thinking was making her visibly sad.

I was losing her.

On a Sunday morning, I watched Annie across our dining room table reading the newspaper and she looked beautiful. I broke our silence. "Let's get married."

She lifted her eyes from the paper. "Are you serious?"

"Very."

"What brought this on?"

"I can't imagine living without you."

"That's a start," she said.

Kneeling by her chair and taking one of her hands in mine, I asked, "Annie Kane, will you marry me?"

"I'd love to say yes."

"So say yes."

She shook her head. "But first there can be no secrets between us, and you're keeping something from me."

"May I get up? My knees are killing me."

With a quick smile, her first after weeks of gloom, and with a regal wave of her hand, she said, "You may rise."

After taking my place again at the table, I asked, "What would you like to know?"

"Do you have another family somewhere, a wife and kids and a dog?"

"No, absolutely not!"

"Are you wanted by the police?"

"No."

"Deadly disease?"

"Not to my knowledge."

"I'm not going to play twenty questions, Jake."

I didn't say anything, and she asked, "Who is John Dobby?"

"Who?" Keeping my voice neutral.

"John Dobby."

"I'm not sure I recognize…"

"There's a letter on the desk in your office addressed to John Dobby care of a PO Box in Boston, from a sender in the Caribbean."

"Oh, yeah," I said, "the letter. I saw it on a bench on the Common and brought it back with me. I've been meaning to drop it off at a post office."

"You found it on Boston Common?"

"I was walking across. I had a client meeting in Boston."

"The letter on your desk was opened."

"I opened it to see whether it was junk mail, in which case I'd have tossed it."

"And?"

"It's about a business deal, so I was going to drop it off."

As I weaved this tale, I longed to hear Annie say let's forget about the bloody letter, all that matters is for us to stay together! I wanted to tell her about Plan B, about everything from start to finish with nothing held back. I wanted to lead her hand-in-hand to our bedroom where we'd put a sweaty and satisfying end to all doubts and hesitations.

Annie watched me, silently, waiting.

Fucking, fucking, fucking Plan B! If I revealed it now, all that I'd prepared would be blown, my shell company in Nevis, my alternate ID in Montreal, everything I'd need to get the fuck out of Dodge. If, if, if…

Annie, Annie, my love, we came so close. I was almost the luckiest man alive.

"I don't know what more I can tell you," I said.

Thirteen

"Come see my newest toy," Viktor says.

By 'newest toy,' Viktor may be referring to the sporty red Mercedes convertible that he's parked just outside Dazzle under the *No Stopping Anytime* sign, or possibly to the woman in the Mercedes' passenger seat, high cheekbones, short spikey hair, violet eyes, and a model's glamorous vacuity, which is unfair, I know, I shouldn't judge by superficial appearances, but that's how she looks to me.

"Jake, meet Irina Melnitsky, my very personal companion. Irina, say hello to Jake."

She glances up at me.

"Hello," she says. Her voice is husky, and toneless, and her accent is Eastern European, maybe Russian.

"Pleased to meet you," I reply, but she's already facing forward again, disconnected.

"Climb in," Viktor says. "I'll take you for a spin."

I clamber into the back and am still fumbling for the seat belt when Viktor guns the engine and squeals our wheels through a tight U-turn. We race up Dazzle's narrow building-shaded Farnsworth Street, jerk to a notional stop at the corner, spin left and tear down Congress Street to the penile tip of the

Seaport District, then swerve left and left again onto Seaport Boulevard, dash up Seaport Boulevard and over the bridge that crosses into mainland Boston, swing right on Atlantic Avenue and slalom like a maniac between tour buses, trucks, and cars.

I have to shout from the back seat to be heard over the noise from the car and the wind. "Where are we going?"

"To my condo," Viktor shouts back. "You are my guest."

He lurches the car into the entrance for underground parking at Rowes Wharf.

The living area in Viktor's condo opens through French doors to a deck overlooking Boston's harbor.

Viktor spreads his arms wide, presenting his view, his windows, his light, his costly furnishings, his incredible life.

"Not bad for an accountant from St. Petersburg, don't you agree?"

"I do, no question."

"Me, my three sisters, my mother, my useless drunk fuck of a father, and my old granny all lived together in an apartment smaller than this."

"You've come a long way," I say, admiringly.

"Let's go out to the deck."

I follow Viktor outside. Irina stays behind, draping herself silently in an easy chair.

Across the harbor, planes are descending in a strung out conga line for their landings at Logan Airport and other planes are taking off, rising and receding into the distance until they vanish from view. On the harbor, boats of all descriptions busily crisscross the choppy waters. Closer in, boats are tethered to buoys or nestle at their docks. Directly below us at water's edge, there's a bricked pedestrian walkway along which people are strolling and taking selfies.

"Those *hoi polloi* have no idea that we're looking down at them," Viktor says. "You want a beer?"

"No thanks, I'm good."

He turns towards the open French doors into his condo.

"Irina!"

She looks up from her magazine.

"Bring me a beer. And ice water for Jake."

She unfurls her long body from her chair and glides into Viktor's kitchen, and emerges a minute or so later carrying a tray with two large glasses, a frosty bottle of artisanal beer, a bottle of water, and a bowl filled with ice cubes.

"Thank you, my sweet," Viktor says. He pats her rear as she leaves the deck, and gives me a broad wink.

"Irina's been good for me. And for my friends on special occasions."

Before I have a chance to ask what he means, Viktor continues, "Would you like to know Irina better?"

"I'd be delighted."

"Well, anything is possible, if you play your cards right."

He sips his beer, exhales a satisfied sigh.

"You're wondering, how can Viktor Rost afford all of this?"

"You do have a lot."

"You want to know how?"

"Sure."

He gives me a sly glance, like a canny shopper at a bazaar.

"Can I trust you, Jake?"

"That's up to you. We've just met and you don't know me, not really. I haven't done anything to earn your trust."

"You backed me up on Belsky."

"I might not back you on a different matter. It depends."

"You're speaking honestly," Viktor says. "I like that." Leaning forward, he stage whispers, "I make a lot of money, a *lot* of money, much more than my salary."

I offer a congratulatory smile. "Good for you. That's great!"

"I work with the right people. I mean, like Oleg Krulik. Not Sophie Bronstein. Word of advice, you want to do well for yourself, pick the right side."

"Are they on different sides?"

"You'll find out," confides Viktor. "If you're smart, you also will get to enjoy the good things in life, like a condo on the harbor, and a hot car, and an Irina."

Hearing her name, Irina glances up from her magazine. But Viktor keeps his focus on me. He doesn't need her right now.

"I'm confused," I say. "What are you suggesting?"

He taps the side of his nose. "You'll know when the time comes."

"I'm not following you, about Sophie not being on the right side."

"She doesn't respect boundaries. She's fine as long as she doesn't poke her nose into places that don't concern her. Seems she didn't get that memo."

"Still, I don't..."

"Like with the New York sellers. She was pressuring Oleg to let you talk with them. She doesn't know Oleg like I do. What she doesn't realize is that no one pressures Oleg Krulik. Makes him angry."

"I hope I'm not responsible for getting her in trouble with Mr. Krulik."

"Who cares? You don't need Sophie. If I vouch for you, you'll get a seat at the grown-ups' table."

"That's where I want to be, with the grown-ups."

"She lies about me."

I don't respond to this, and he continues, "If you tell me what she says, I'll give you the facts so you're not misled."

Still I don't say anything, and Viktor asks, casually, "Has Sophie said anything you want to check with me now?"

"She told me she's tried to get along with you but you aren't interested."

"See, that's what I mean! Totally false! Sophie was turned against me from the start by Maggie Cher. She'd fire me in a second if Oleg weren't looking over her shoulder."

"Well, that does put a different light on it, Viktor," I say. "It's good to know the real story."

"You're welcome," says Viktor.

"Should we get back to the office? People will wonder where we are."

"Yeah, let's go. But we'll do this again, right?"

"For sure!"

"Irina can't wait to spend more time with you."

He gives me another suggestive wink.

Irina, who's still curled in her chair inside the condo, provides no sign that she hears Viktor talking about her. About her eagerness to spend more time with me, she gives no sign of that either. Intent on her magazine, she neglects to acknowledge my departure. Nor does she acknowledge Viktor's departure, for that matter.

Fourteen

Sophie's place on Willard Street, just off of tony Brattle Street, is one of those elegant Cambridge houses that you know must be occupied by people of impeccable taste, powerful intellect, and family lineages that go way back.

It's a cream-colored stucco house with a steeply-pitched roof accented by gables. It has true-divided-lite windows set inside dark red frames. Its driveway leads to an open space in the back that's edged by low-rise curved rock walls containing lush plantings of shrubs and flowers.

Sophie ventures out to greet me on the driveway with an awkward hug. Neither of us is a natural hugger.

"Time to meet Caleb," she says, grabbing my arm.

She guides me to the barbeque being tended by a fit-looking man with a sculpted jaw and prematurely white hair, cut short and brushed straight back.

"Jake Morais, meet Justice Caleb Bronstein."

"Very funny," Caleb says, having heard this before. "Call me Caleb."

He gestures towards hot dogs, hamburgers, and chicken drumsticks that are sizzling on his plus-size gas barbeque. "What's your pleasure, Jake?"

No one else is eating yet and I don't want to be the first.

"For now I'll just get a drink, thanks."

A man drifts over to say hello to Caleb.

"Hey, Eric" Caleb says, "Great to see you. Just a sec…"

Then to me, he says, "Let's make sure we talk when we get a moment."

"Sure, I'll look for you."

Behind me, a familiar voice, "Fancy meeting you here!"

"Annie!"

Her light summer dress hangs nicely on her slender frame. In the dappled late afternoon sunlight, she looks more alluring than ever.

We exchange two Euro-style cheek kisses, the second one slipping for old times' sake accidentally-on-purpose into lips-on-lips.

"How are you, Jake?"

"Doing fine, and you?"

"All good. So, you've joined Sophie's company."

"Yep."

"She's an old friend."

"So I heard. Small world."

She pauses like she's unsure how to say what's on her mind, but then just comes out with it, "Sorry about not replying to your emails and texts."

"No problem."

"It's just…."

"I wasn't stalking you. Just trying to stay in touch."

"Sure, I understand."

"Was I creeping you out?"

"A little," says Annie.

"No more, I promise."

"Okay, good."

We share a moment of silence.

Then she asks, "Are you seeing anyone?"

"Nope. You?"

"Nothing serious."

"What about unserious?"

Annie laughs. "That would be telling."

I touch her arm. "I miss you."

She pulls back, just a flinch, but enough for me to notice.

I tell her, "Watching you move out, that was hard."

"Moving out was hard for me too."

We're standing close, and all I see is Annie's face, her eyes, her lips. Everyone else fades into the background. Just the two of us in our bubble and it feels completely right, the way it should be.

Until Annie, glancing past me, says, "Excuse me, I need to..."

"Sure."

Sophie introduces me to various friends whose names I promptly forget. Like us, they're mostly in their late thirties to mid-forties, and they hold well-informed opinions on politics and social trends. They're well educated, well groomed, and well off, and dismayed about the latest outrages in Washington, hardly surprising at a summer party on Willard Street in Cambridge.

After a few hours, the party winds down, guests start to leave, and I notice Annie saying her good-byes to Sophie and Caleb. I hustle to catch up to her as she walks up the driveway.

"Great to see you," I say.

"Great to see you too, Jake."

"We could keep this going."

"You mean, now?"

"Caleb asked me to stay back for a chat but I could visit you afterwards. Or tomorrow. Whenever."

Annie appears to consider the idea.

"Strictly as friends. I promise."

I hold my breath.

"No, I don't think so," she replies.

"Too soon?"

"Yeah, sorry."

Fifteen

Caleb Bronstein's home office is lined with hard-bound books on oak bookshelves. Papers and folders are stacked neatly on his oak wood desk. In front of his desk by a fireplace are two creased leather easy chairs, a matching leather sofa, and a sturdy oak wood coffee table.

I ask Caleb, "Should we wait for Sophie?"

"She'll be awhile, picking up from the party. She said to go ahead."

"Feels like we're deserting her."

"She likes to pick up, says it gives her space to think. She'll join us when she's ready."

"Okay."

"So, tell me, Jake, what do you think of Dazzle?"

"It's a good company. Lots of potential."

"Notice anything strange?"

"Not sure what you mean."

"Unusual. Not quite right."

"Like any company, we have strong personalities. People don't always agree. They take sides."

He's shaking his head. I'm not giving him what he wants.

"What are you getting at, Caleb?"

"Are you aware that your board member Oleg Krulik is a criminal?"

"No."

"I warned Sophie not to take the job but she didn't want to disappoint her friend Maggie. She told me not to worry. She doesn't want me involved. She says she can handle Mr. Krulik."

He leans forward, a lawyer making his case. "I can't help her if I'm kept in the dark. I'm asking you to let me know if you see or hear anything that doesn't pass the sniff test. Obviously I won't reveal that you're my source."

"Sophie would figure that out in a heartbeat."

"Fair enough," Caleb acknowledges. "But will you at least keep in mind that you can call me anytime, day or night, totally up to you?"

"That I can do."

He writes a number on a small white card and passes the card to me. "Call or text me at this number, 24/7."

A soft double knock on Caleb's office door and Sophie pokes her head in. "I was wondering where you boys had gone."

"We're getting better acquainted," Caleb says.

"Are you harassing poor Jake about Dazzle?"

"Why would you think that?"

"What have you told him?"

"Only what I've already discussed with you."

"I'm still here, guys," I say.

Sophie laughs. "Sorry, Jake, indeed you are."

"Caleb tells me that Oleg Krulik is a criminal…"

"True. That's how business is done in Ukraine. He plays by their rules. Oleg doesn't deny it. He even jokes about it."

"I met Mr. Krulik at your welcome party," says Caleb. "He looks and talks like a thug."

"He's also a Harvard MBA and a major donor to the university. He endowed a scholarship for students from Eastern Europe."

Caleb says, "The price of his ticket to respectability."

"I knew about Oleg," says Sophie. "I joined the company anyway. I can manage him. I was intrigued by what I could do as CEO. Dazzle is just getting started, not just as a marketplace for jewelry but also down the road for other luxury items like works of art, antiques, rugs. There's so much we can do once we build the brand."

"Except," I say, "we're blocked from interviewing our most successful sellers."

"What's that about?" asks Caleb.

Sophie replies, "Two New York sellers on our platform are amazingly successful. Their sole contact in the company is Viktor Rost, as they and Oleg agreed when he recruited them to post on Dazzle's site. I'm unclear why they wanted this but that's their deal."

"You're the CEO," Caleb says. "You should have access to anyone involved with your company."

"I discussed this with Oleg and he promised to fix it with them."

"I wouldn't hold your breath," I say. "Viktor told me that Krulik was irked by your call. He doesn't like to be pushed."

Caleb asks, "Viktor confides in you?"

"Sophie told me to become his friend."

"And now you're his friend?"

"Seems so."

"Good for you," says Caleb, with a measuring look.

"What else did you learn from Viktor?" asks Sophie.

"That his waterfront condo at Rowes Wharf is amazing. That he has a girlfriend named Irina who looks like a model. That he wants me to know that he's making a ton of money, well beyond his salary, and that if I want to be successful like he is, I'll stick with him and Krulik, rather than with you. When I asked what he meant, he said you aren't respecting boundaries. He also said you lie about him."

"He *is* a challenge," says Sophie. "Did he tell you how he's making the extra money?"

"No details, except the part about sticking with Krulik. I didn't want to push."

"Okay."

"But I did find more interesting info in the sales data you gave me, in this case about Island Bank."

I glance towards Caleb, and Sophie says, "Tell us, Jake. Caleb can hear what you found."

"Okay. For your benefit, Caleb, we offer buyers a feature that allows them to place their payments in escrow until they receive the items they've purchased. Island Bank manages the escrow payments for purchases on our platform. We get a percentage of the bank's fees."

"It's a good deal for us," says Sophie.

"What's interesting is that our revenue stream from the bank started only six months ago, although Island Bank has partnered with Dazzle for five years, since Dazzle's inception."

"Six months ago would be around the time that Oleg's VC made their investment in Dazzle."

"Interesting coincidence," says Caleb.

"See if you can find out from Viktor what's going on with Island Bank," Sophie tells me.

"Yes, ma'am."

Sixteen

Viktor and I are chatting about his to-die-for waterfront condo and how everyone who's seen Irina is just blown away.

"She really is something," I admit.

"Yeah," replies Viktor. "I'm pleased with her."

After a brief silence between us, I say, casually, "By the way, before I forget, in my analysis of our sales data I noticed a couple of things about Island Bank."

Viktor goes still. "Like what?"

"Our revenues from the bank are reported each month as a single number with no detail, and no supporting backup."

"That's our arrangement with the bank. We trust their reporting."

"So we don't get any more information from them?"

"No, and I don't ask for more either."

"Also, our revenues from them became significant only six months ago even though Island Bank has been handling payments for transactions on our platform for much longer."

"For that, we can thank Oleg. That's the deal he negotiated. Why are you asking?"

"I mentioned these findings to Sophie and she wanted me to follow up with you."

"I thought so," says Viktor, not pleased.

"Is that a problem?"

"Again, she's poking her nose into things that don't concern her, first our top sellers, and now our partner Island Bank. And you're her errand boy."

Time to backpedal vigorously.

"You're right, Viktor," I say, "Let's drop it. I don't want to jeopardize our friendship by passing along questions that Sophie could ask herself."

"Good choice," he says.

"But I'm curious, for myself, not for Sophie, why we need to partner with the bank in the first place. Why don't we just tell our buyers to use credit cards or PayPal as they do on other e-commerce sites and allow them the usual returns and refunds if they're dissatisfied with their purchases?"

"Well, for one thing," replies Viktor, "we have good customers who are not too popular at the moment with the US government. They can't use credit cards or PayPal. Fortunately Island Bank isn't picky about where the money comes from. You understand what I'm saying?"

"Yeah, you don't get rich by refusing to take people's money."

"See, Jake, we do think alike," says Viktor, allowing me back in his good graces with his thin-lipped smile. "That is why we're friends."

I visit the Island Bank website where management team profiles reveal that the general manager and other execs were appointed just a year ago. Among the bank's nine directors, five are Antiguans, while four have Russian-sounding names. Each of these four is associated with an investment group called Island Partners, LLC.

A Google search produces an article published a year ago in the *Antigua Observer*.

Island Bank Purchased by Investment Group.
One of Antiqua's oldest local banks, Island Bank, founded in 1964 and headquartered in St. John's, has announced its purchase by Island Partners, LLC, an international investment group. The purchase for an undisclosed amount ends the bank's ownership by its founders the Reynolds family. Meanwhile, police have not yet determined the cause of death of the bank's general manager Mr. Michael Reynolds, whose body was found four weeks ago in English Harbour. Initial reports that he died from accidental drowning were cast into doubt by information from the family that Mr. Reynolds was a championship swimmer and that his boat was still at anchor when his body was discovered. Police say that their investigation remains open.

Sophie is at her desk in her glass walled office. I don't want Viktor to see us together so I send her a text: "More info on bank. Best to talk unobserved."

Sophie replies, "Come to my house after work."

That evening, in Caleb's home office, I report to Sophie and Caleb what I've learned from Viktor, that Krulik negotiated the deal that during the last six months boosted our revenues from Island Bank, and that the bank manages payments from customers who can't use PayPal or credit cards because they're subject to US sanctions.

"Sanction busting," mutters Caleb. "Another feather in Dazzle's cap."

"Also," I say, "the bank was purchased a year ago by an international investment group called Island Partners, LLC. Directors that the group placed on the board appear to be Russian, based on their names. The purchase occurred shortly after the bank's former general manager was found dead under mysterious circumstances."

Caleb, staring at Sophie, asks, "Would you agree it's time now to connect some dots?"

"I do," Sophie says. "I'll start…"

"Good. Finally!"

"So, a year ago, Island Bank is acquired by an investment group following the death of its general manager. Six months ago, Oleg's VC becomes lead investor in Dazzle. At about the same time, Oleg gets two New York sellers to post on our site and they rapidly become our biggest sellers serving international buyers based mostly in Russia. Also Oleg negotiates a new deal with Island Bank that produces a revenue stream from the bank. Dazzle's CFO quits for reasons unknown and Oleg gets Viktor appointed in his place. And then, about two months ago, when Viktor proposes hiring Anton Belsky as our outside accountant, Dazzle's CEO Danny Hughes objects and is fired by the board."

"The two New York sellers don't even have storefronts," I say. "How were they able to sell so much so quickly? And to buyers who are far away, in Russia? And how do they obtain expensive jewelry in the large quantities that they're selling?"

Sophie replies, "Are you familiar with Ockham's razor?"

Caleb says, "Remind us, for Jake's benefit."

"When you're faced with two explanations, the Ockham's razor principal says to select the one that's simpler."

"Which is?"

"The New York sellers are less amazing than they appear because they are not actually shipping all those expensive jewelry items."

"We'd hear about it," I say. "Their buyers would complain."

"Unless the buyers don't expect to receive their purchases."

"So, no jewelry changing hands. No real sales. Just money sent to Island Bank."

"Right."

The penny drops.

"Money laundering."

"Yes," replies Sophie, as if that were obvious all along.

"Sophie, you've got to bring in the FBI," Caleb says.

"I can't do that."

"That's nuts! Cut this off now. Call the FBI. Otherwise you'll be complicit."

"Maybe there's an innocent explanation."

"Yeah, sure."

"Word would get out that the FBI's investigating Dazzle. It would destroy us. As CEO, I have a responsibility to my company. I just got there, for heaven's sake. I'll deal with it."

"How?"

"I'll tell the board what we've discovered. They'll agree with me that we need to sever our ties with Island Bank and the two sellers."

"Krulik will deny everything," I say.

"Oleg is not the only board member. I know the Boston VCs on our board. They'll outvote him."

"They sided with Krulik when they fired Danny Hughes."

"I'm better placed with the board than Danny was, at the end. They knew what they were getting when they offered me the job. They assured me that I had discretion to do what's best for the company."

"What if they don't support you?"

"Then I'll contact the FBI."

Caleb says, "Take a moment to think about the bank manager who died in Antigua just before his bank was taken over, and the former Dazzle CFO who suddenly quit for no reason, which just happened to provide an opening for Viktor to join the company. These people are dangerous."

"I'll be careful," replies Sophie. "And if I get the FBI involved, we'll be perfectly safe."

"I wish I had your confidence."

I ask Sophie, "So, in retrospect, are you glad you accepted their offer to become Dazzle's CEO?"

Sophie laughs. "Knocking heads with Viktor and Oleg, working with you and Maggie and Toby, seeing our staff putting everything on the line every day, I wouldn't trade that for anything!"

Seventeen

The following Monday morning when I arrive at work, the light is on in Sophie's office but she's not there, nor is she in the eatery or anywhere else that I can see in our open workspace. I call Brett. "Where's Sophie?"

"At a special board meeting down at the Westin."

As a rule, the board meets at the Westin Hotel in the Seaport District since it's only a ten minute walk from our Fort Point office.

"What's going on?"

"No idea," Brett says. "Sophie dashed out. She just said she'd been called to join the meeting, and waved goodbye."

"And Viktor?"

"Maybe he's already at the meeting."

"Any idea when she'll be back?"

"She didn't say."

At eleven fifteen, I receive a message from Viktor that's copied to all Dazzle employees. "All-hands meeting at noon in the eatery. Attendance mandatory."

Once again, I call Brett. "What do you know?"

"I don't think Sophie is coming back."

Viktor stands on one of the eatery tables to address Dazzle employees who've gathered to hear what's happened. His bony face is shiny with sweat and his gangly frame jerks nervously as he grips the mic, not exactly a charismatic presence.

One of the employees calls out, "Where is Sophie?"

"The board has decided to change our leadership to build for the future. I've been appointed as interim CEO during a search for a new CEO."

"You? Interim CEO?"

"Yes."

Gusts of muttered imprecations ripple around the floor, "Unbelievable!" "We're so fucked!"

Another question, "Why did Sophie leave?"

"I'd prefer not to go into the details."

"Why not?"

"It's a sensitive matter."

"Now you have to tell us."

"It wouldn't..."

"Come on, Viktor."

"Okay, okay, if you insist," says Viktor, making a show of surrendering reluctantly to popular demand but only because he feels obliged to share vital information with the company's loyal employees.

"The board was made aware of suspicious attempts to gain access to confidential information held by our partner Island Bank."

"By Sophie?"

"Yes."

"Bullshit!"

Viktor presses on, "There is evidence that Sophie was involved and that she tried to cover her tracks. When she was challenged, she refused to respond directly to questions about these attempts. Naturally our bank partner is very upset. The board had no choice but to dismiss her."

Stunned silence in the room.

"We have alerted the authorities. Sophie Bronstein is not permitted to re-enter these premises. Anyone contacted by her must inform me immediately or face severe consequences. Also the board instructed me to assure all of you that Dazzle will continue on its current growth path. The board recognizes the great work that you are doing to build our company and appreciates your loyalty. We will not allow rogue actions by one person to detract from everyone else's valuable efforts."

I'm staring at my reflection in my office's glass front wall when Viktor steps inside.

"What are you thinking, Jake?"

"What you said about Sophie."

"She threatened us. Naturally we have to defend ourselves. The question is, What are you going to do?"

"I don't know."

"I stood up for you in the board meeting. I told them that you've shown you can recognize your own best interests."

"Thank you for that. But, still..."

"You heard what I told you, in my condo?"

"I did."

"So?"

I wrestle my face into a surrendering smile.

"You did make a strong case."

"And?"

"And what?"

"Are you with us?"

"Yes," I tell him, "I am."

"You sure?"

"I'm sure, Viktor. I'm with you."

"Good! Now the board wants to meet you."

"Now?"

"They're still in session. They told me to bring you over."

A security guard in a tightly fitting uniform recognizes Viktor as we approach the closed door of the meeting room on the mezzanine floor of the Westin Hotel.

"Mr. Rost," he says.

"Hey, Charlie. This is Mr. Morais, here to join the meeting."

Charlie looks me over. "Sir, I need to wand you. Please put your cell, keys, and any other metal objects you're carrying into the basket, and then raise your arms and stand with your legs apart."

He runs a handheld black bar over my back and chest, along my arms, and between my legs. No squeals or beeps.

"Everything okay?" I ask.

"All good. You can collect your stuff from the basket, except your cell, which I'll return to you when you come out.

Viktor explains, "Our board meetings are highly confidential. Charlie is required to check for recording devices."

"Also weapons," Charlie says.

"No worries," I assure him. "Just doing your job."

The five board members are slouched around the table looking grumpy. They've had a difficult morning and I'm yet another issue to be decided. No one rises to greet us. Nor are we invited to take any of the vacant chairs at the table. So we remain standing.

Viktor tells them, "This is Jacob Morais, our VP Strategy."

He recites their names which I quickly forget after I circle the table to shake their hands. As I've already admitted, I'm terrible with names and no-one is wearing a name tag or has a name-plate in front of him. Viktor doesn't identify which VC each of them represents, but it's clear who's here for the Bracket Group, based on the Euro cut of his open-neck shirt and his head being closely shaved like Viktor's, except that his head is larger and thicker necked. His name I do remember, Oleg Krulik.

Krulik bares his big square teeth, Teddy Roosevelt size choppers. "So you're the famous Jacob Morais."

His accent is Russian plus a touch of New York.

"Yes, sir."

"Where are you from?"

"I grew up in Winchester, Massachusetts, and live in Cambridge. My grandparents emigrated from Alsace-Lorraine, in France."

"So you're French."

"American."

"Harvard?"

"No, UMass Amherst."

"Sophie Bronstein went to Harvard."

"Yes."

"I did too."

"I know, sir. Great school."

Baring his large teeth again, he says, "And yet, she hired you."

I assume that Krulik is teasing so I chuckle to show I can take a joke, "Hard to explain," I say, adding, in a nod to today's events, "We've known each other since high school. I still consider Sophie to be my friend."

One of the others at the table, probably in his thirties, power-groomed with slicked back hair, asks, "Why are you making a point of telling us that she's still your friend?"

"Because Viktor announced to the company that the board suspects she has done something shady. Knowing Sophie, I find that hard to believe."

"But you're keeping an open mind, aren't you, Jake?" says Viktor.

I take his hint.

"If the evidence does point to wrongdoing, I'll have to accept that."

Krulik, again: "You are aware of our relationship with Island Bank."

"Yes, sir. At a very high level."

"At a very high level, what do you think about it?"

"I understand that it's quite lucrative for us."

"Do you have a problem with that?"

"No, sir."

"Viktor says you want to join us in making a lot of money."

"I do."

"So you're with us?"

"I am."

Another board member speaks up. He's distractingly obese, and I try to avoid looking at the glistening rolls of fat under his chin. "Sophie is making wild accusations. When the FBI asks questions, you will support our version of the situation."

"I don't know anything. The FBI would figure that out."

Oleg Krulik says, "So you will tell them you have no information that supports Sophie's accusations."

"What accusations?"

"She made statements to us that I won't repeat because maybe she didn't know what she was saying. She's emotionally upset."

"Okay."

"Don't let us down," warns the Ukrainian.

"No, sir."

As we walk back to our office, I ask Viktor, "Did I do okay?"

"In the end, yes, but you had me worried."

"You mean, what I said about Sophie?"

"No one wants the fuck to hear how she's your friend, and how you find it hard to believe she did anything wrong. Oleg especially. He has a very suspicious temperament."

"He knows about me and Sophie. Why try to deny it?"

"You raised a question in his mind. You do not want Oleg to entertain questions about you. It's unhealthy."

"Thanks for the warning."

"I put my neck out for you. Don't make me regret it."

Eighteen

Text from Sophie: "Call me. Use your cell."

She picks up on the first ring, and I ask, "What happened?"

"I made my pitch. Initially they seemed to be listening, but then Oleg denied there were any problems. He said there was no need to sever our relationships with the two New York sellers or with the bank. He said he was working on the sellers to get them to agree to talk with me and I should be patient. He said that once I was talking with them directly, I would be reassured that our relationship was mutually beneficial. He said he would put me in touch as well with Island Bank, with the same result. I replied that my concerns needed to be addressed immediately. Then Viktor jumped up and down complaining that I was out of control. He accused me of threatening the board, and Oleg, and him personally. Oleg said Viktor was making a valid point. He said I should try harder to work with Viktor. He said that maybe I needed time off to regain emotional balance, as he put it. None of the other board members took my side. I collected my papers and left."

"So, not a huge success."

"No."

"The board appointed Viktor interim CEO."

"I heard."

"Viktor claimed at an all-hands meeting in the eatery that you were fired by the board because you tried to break into the database at Island Bank."

"You do know that's a lie, right, Jake?"

"Well, I know it, but that's their story, and I expect the bank will support it, if asked."

"I can't do anything about that."

"Viktor took me to meet the board."

"Did he now? I really did underestimate him."

"Krulik said that you made accusations and that I should expect to be questioned by the FBI, but he wouldn't tell me more, except to warn me not to take your side."

Sophie is silent for a moment, and I ask, "Are you still there?

"I should have been more careful," she says. "I got angry when the board refused to listen. I mentioned that an objective observer who looks at the facts might suspect money laundering. They took great offense that I would say such a thing."

"So now what?"

"I've contacted the FBI."

"And?"

"I reached an agent in their Boston office who covers organized crime, named Patrick Reilly. He said he'll get back to me to schedule an interview. He also revealed that he's aware of the company's complaints against me."

"Already? From the board?"

"They must've worked out that I'd contact the FBI and wanted to get there first. Agent Reilly said he has a lot to sort out."

"Viktor wants me to stay in the company."

"Glad to hear it."

"Eyes and ears."

"Exactly."

"I'll keep you posted."

"Thank you, Jake. Watch your back."

"You too."

Nineteen

Newly ensconced in Sophie's office, Viktor beckons me in and asks how I'm doing.

"Doing well. Why?"

"No second thoughts about staying with us, after Sophie?"

Viktor watches me closely, checking for wobble. In return, I give him full-on commitment, rock-solid, with church-on-Sundays sincerity.

"No, Viktor. None whatsoever. This is where I belong. If you still want me here, I'm staying."

He seems persuaded.

"Then I've got excellent news. I just heard from Oleg, two of the American VCs have pulled out. Between you and me, Oleg pushed for it. He's very pleased."

"I would have thought..."

He interrupts, as interim CEOs can do. "You would have thought wrong. They pull out, it's a good thing. There's more for us. Oleg is buying out their interest, no big deal."

"Good to know."

"About your role here, going forward, Oleg agrees with me that you should remain our VP Strategy, and also now I'm appointing you VP Marketing, taking over from Maggie. She's gone, left yesterday with no notice. It's just as well. She won't be missed. You can do her job, no problem."

"Glad to try," I say. "But shouldn't we look for a marketing person to replace her?"

"No rush," says Viktor. "The board wants us to cut spending. We have a new strategy to focus much better than we did before. We'll improve how we serve our biggest buyers and our top sellers. The rest, the small fry, don't make us the same kind of money. I got sick of hearing Sophie blab about investing in our platform to attract more buyers and more sellers. So we're done with that."

"Okay."

"From now on, we care only about where we make the most money. For a change, also, we'll treat Island Bank like the valuable partner that it is. No more mistrust. You okay with that as well, Jake?"

It's nice of Viktor to ask.

"Of course."

"We're going to right-size for our new strategy. I've decided to make cuts, starting with those collecting the highest salaries, top down."

"How many?"

"Twenty for now."

"That's a third of our staff."

"Yeah, and maybe we'll cut more, depending on how things go. I'm putting you in charge. No need to check with me on names. Just do it. Make the announcement, send out the notices, hustle them out the door. Can you handle that?"

Viktor's bulging grey eyes all but dare me to raise an objection. Now I know what's meant by making a pact with the devil.

""I'll do it," I say.

"Also put Brett on your cut list. He was too close to Sophie for my taste. I think he still talks to her."

"Okay."

"We should spend more time together, Jake. Irina keeps asking about you."

Tech workers are in high demand in the Boston-Cambridge-Somerville corridor. No doubt after hearing about Sophie many at Dazzle have started returning recruiters' messages. Still, there are no happy faces looking up at me in the eatery. I'm standing on the same table on which Viktor announced that although Sophie was gone no one should worry because the board appreciated the great work that everyone was doing.

"Bottom line," I tell them, "the company has to right-size, which is doubly painful because we'll lose valuable people who have worked very hard for our success, a really bitter pill."

"More bitter for us than for you," says a man whom I recognize as one of our web designers. "When will we hear who gets whacked?"

"By end of day, today," I reply. "The details are still being worked out."

Actually, I've already compiled the list of Dazzle's soon-to-be-departed. It didn't take me long, starting with the highest paid within each category, engineers, product managers, designers, and marketers, until I reached twenty.

Then, getting us to twenty one, I added Brett. He's standing towards the back of the group not far from his receptionist desk, looking distinctly less cheery than usual.

Dazzle's HR person is even now assembling the lay-off notices and supporting documentation for unemployment insurance and health coverage.

"Why isn't Viktor making this announcement?" demands one of our lead engineers whose name, though she doesn't know it yet, is on the list. "Is he scared?"

"Not at all. Viktor believes in delegating and I agreed to do it."

"Well, can *you* tell us how this supports the board's growth strategy that Viktor told us about?"

"Even the most famous growth companies have to right-size from time to time," I reply. "Google, Apple, Amazon, Microsoft, they all do it. We're no different. The board and Viktor are totally committed to Dazzle's growth. They see this right-sizing, however painful, as essential to build a strong financial foundation to support our growth."

Proving yet again that I can sling bullshit with the best of them! And, anyway, if neither our board nor our interim CEO cares how Dazzle will perform after losing a third of our staff, it's not up to me to save their company.

Toby bursts into my office, shoving the glass door so hard that it bangs against a chair.

"You're firing four of my best engineers! Do you know how hard it is to recruit good engineers? Why didn't you consult me?"

"I'm just doing what our interim CEO told me to," I reply. "Following orders."

"Fuck your orders!"

He slams back out of my office and into Viktor's.

There is yelling, Viktor responding in a quieter voice, more yelling, Viktor pushing his chair back to stand behind his desk, and then Toby knocking over his own chair and storming out of Viktor's office.

Raising the number on the layoff list to twenty two.

Viktor calls me a few seconds later.

"Now that Toby's gone, I'll promote one of our engineers to take over as interim Lead Engineer."

"Other engineers will follow Toby out the door."

"We'll survive," says Viktor. "We don't need a big staff."

Twenty

Everyone at Dazzle knows that interim CEO Viktor Rost and I are best buddies.

Each morning our new receptionist Brittany greets me with a bright smile, as bright as Brett's was, maybe even brighter.

"Good morning, Jake!" she says.

"Morning, Brittany."

A celebrity shock wave ripples through Dazzle's open work space as I trek to my office. Staff glance up from their screens, smiling.

"Hi Jake!"

"Hi, how're you doing?"

There are too many of them for me to remember their names, even if I were good with names, but they know mine. I try not to let it go to my head.

My cell buzzes with a text from Sophie. I take a seat in the eatery with my back to the live plant wall where no one will be able to read my phone over my shoulder.

In her text, Sophie says, "Appointment with FBI agent Reilly set for tomorrow morning. Please update me if news on your end."

I reply, "No news since layoffs. Very quiet here "

"Anything from V. about Island Bank or the two sellers?"

"Not a peep."

"Much to discuss with FBI tomorrow. Will let you know what happens."

"Please do."

I think we're done but after a moment or so, Sophie follows up with another text: "This weekend Caleb & I are heading down to our cottage in Martha's Vineyard Can you join us to get caught up? Lots of room. Beautiful view. Fresh ocean air. You'll be very welcome."

"What about risk of being seen together?"

"Very low risk on MV unlike in Cambridge/Boston. Cottage has great privacy."

"Then yes, thanks, I accept."

"Wonderful! We'll email you directions."

After work, I'm at home boiling water to make spaghetti for dinner when my doorbell rings.

As I make my way to my front door, the *birg bong* of the doorbell is replaced by insistent knocking.

The man and woman on my porch both wear dark suits, white shirts, and somber expressions. The man is white, middle-aged, and fleshy, the woman younger, slightly darker complexion, maybe Hispanic, with a butch haircut.

They aren't as young and eager looking as typical pleaders for the environment or social justice, so I guess they might be selling a more traditional product, maybe religious salvation.

No matter, I'm not buying.

I call out through the door, "Not interested!"

"Mr. Morais?" asks the man.

"Yes."

"We're from the FBI. We'd like to talk with you, sir."

"Show me your IDs through the side window."

They do so: FBI agent Patrick Reilly and FBI agent Charlene Rivera.

We sit at a table in my kitchen. The agents decline coffee or tea. They promise they won't take much of my time.

"We received reports about your company," says agent Reilly. "I assume you know about that."

"I do."

"What can you tell us?"

"Not too much. I'm new in the company."

"Well, just fill us in as best you can."

"Alright. Our CFO, Viktor Rost, is now also our interim CEO. He told us that the board fired our former CEO Sophie Bronstein for an action she took involving a partner company called Island Bank. I find it hard to believe she would do anything improper, knowing Sophie, but I really don't know."

"We were told she broke into the bank's database and then tried to cover it up."

"That's what Viktor told us as well."

"Ms. Bronstein also contacted me," Reilly says. "She made allegations about the board and about Mr. Rost, about criminal activities that may be going on."

"Really?"

"Do you know anything about those allegations?"

"No.

"She never discussed them with you?"

"As I told you, I'm new at the company. I've focused on learning my job."

"So you can't tell us anything to back up her allegations?"

"No, I'm sorry."

Agent Charlene Rivera says, "Ms. Bronstein hired you, right?"

"Yes."

"And you're old friends."

"Yes."

"Even though she was booted out of the company you're still there."

"It's been quite a confusing time."

"In fact," says Reilly, "you didn't just stay put, did you? You took the lead in firing a whole bunch of employees."

"I did what I was told by our interim CEO. Is that a problem?"

"Not necessarily."

"What does that mean?"

"If we find that Ms. Bronstein's allegations are well founded, we may wonder why you stayed with the bad guys."

"I'd have to be pretty dumb to sign on with bad guys just when the FBI is investigating."

Reilly says, "Perps do dumb things, you'd be amazed."

"I just go into work each day and do my job."

"What do you do there, again?"

"VP Strategy, and now also interim VP Marketing."

Agent Rivera says, "You're a big exec."

"It's a small company."

"You make good money there?"

"Enough."

"And yet you don't know anything."

I don't respond, and Reilly says, "If there's anything you *can* tell us, now's a good time."

"Don't think so."

"Do you have any docs from the company that will help us learn the facts?"

"No."

"That Ms. Bronstein gave you, for example."

"I told you, no."

Reilly leans forward, "If you hold back, we'll have you doing a perp walk as a co-conspirator."

Agent Rivera smirks. "Love those perp walks."

"I'm not holding anything back. Let's just finish this so I can get back to my dinner. I suggest that you talk to Sophie. Basically I'm a bystander in all of this."

"Ms. Bronstein is unavailable."

"Why?"

"You haven't heard?

"Heard *what*?"

"She's unconscious."

"*What*?"

"She was mugged earlier this evening when she was out jogging near her house."

I must have gone pale because agent Rivera asks, "You need a minute?"

I shake my head. "You don't find that suspicious?"

"That she was mugged?" asks Reilly.

"You just told me she's making accusations and now she's been attacked. Why are you here? You're wasting time."

114

"We don't do street muggings. Cambridge PD are looking into it."

"Where is she now?"

"You'll have to get that information from her family."

"I will, soon as we're done here."

"Talk to us about Viktor Rost and Oleg Krulik."

"I need to call Sophie's husband."

"Just answer our question, Jake, and we'll leave you to it."

"As I said before, Viktor Rost is my interim boss. I don't know much about him. Nor about Mr. Krulik. Check with Maggie Chen. She's been in the company much longer than me."

"We haven't been able to reach Ms. Chen. We left lots of messages. It's real annoying when people don't get back to us."

Reilly slaps a business card on the table and clambers to his feet, followed by agent Rivera. "Give me a call if you think of anything, okay."

"Sure."

"Don't be a stranger."

Lately the *Boston Globe* has run stories about a notorious mobster who operated out of a nondescript Toyota dealership in Somerville. 'Shiny Mikey' Wallace extorted payments from local merchants and drug dealers, tortured brave souls who resisted, and ordered the murders of adversary hoodlums and suspected snitches. The FBI created a task force to bring Shiny Mikey to justice. With the help of courageous civilian informants and undercover agents, they collected enough evidence for his arrest and probable conviction. However, hours before his arrest, Shiny Mikey escaped along with his girlfriend.

An investigation determined that he was forewarned by a Boston-based FBI agent. At the now-former agent's trial, his lawyers implied that he, the former agent, was not alone. The *Globe* reporters surmised that the lawyers might be negotiating for a favorable settlement by enhancing the value of the former agent's cooperation. Whatever their purpose, the lawyers had turned over a rock, perhaps exposing corruption in the FBI's Boston office involving additional mafia moles.

And now Sophie is attacked shortly after making her appointment with agent Reilly of the same Boston office, the day before she's scheduled to go in for her interview. I don't buy the random mugging theory. The timing is way too convenient for Oleg Krulik and Viktor Rost.

My bottom line: It's not safe to trust the FBI, in particular its Boston office, and specifically FBI agents Reilly and Rivera.

Twenty One

As soon as the FBI agents leave my house, I text Caleb: "Just heard about Sophie. Hope she's OK. Don't want to bother you but can you update me when you get a moment."

My cell rings a moment later. Caller ID is blocked but I take the call anyway. "Jake Morais."

"Jake, this is Caleb. Got your text. We're at Mt. Auburn. Sophie's in intensive care. She's unconscious in an induced coma."

"What happened, Caleb?"

"It may have been an attempted mugging. Sophie was out running as she always does to clear her mind. She was found unconscious near bushes on Foster Street on the other side of Sparks, about a block from our house. Neighborhood kids on bikes found her and called 911. She lost a lot of blood. Cambridge police say she has stab wounds in her side and back."

"Did anyone see anything?"

"Police are interviewing nearby residents. No word yet on that."

"She had an interview set with the FBI tomorrow morning."

"I'm well aware. For now I'm just focusing on Sophie."

"What do the docs say?"

Caleb pauses, and then replies, "They tell me they're doing what they can to stabilize her but she was very badly hurt."

"I'm truly sorry Caleb."

"Yeah."

"I'm pulling for her."

"Thank you."

"Let me know when I can visit."

"Okay."

My phone buzzes and Annie's name comes up on caller ID.

She asks, "You heard about Sophie?"

Her voice is ragged like she's been crying, and harsh, like she's beyond rage.

"I just talked with Caleb, at Mt. Auburn."

"Why are you still in that company?"

"Sophie wanted me to stay as her eyes and ears working from the inside."

"Don't give me that."

"It's complicated, Annie."

"No, it's not. We both know they're lying about Sophie. Now they tried to murder her!"

"Current theory seems to be an attempted mugging."

"And you're going along with it! You're with them. One of my friends knows someone at Dazzle. She heard you were in charge of letting people go."

"I'm trying to do the right thing."

"I can't stand to hear your voice."

She disconnects.

Twenty Two

Through the glass wall of Viktor's office I see him leaning back in his chair, his arms behind his head, engaged in an animated phone conversation. He's on the speakerphone so talking more loudly than usual and I can hear well enough to conclude that he's speaking Russian. He barks out a throaty laugh, having not a care in the world.

He sees me, ends the call, and waves me in.

His cheerful expression is gone. Forehead creased, eyebrows knitted, lips pursed, hands clenched on his desk, he looks deeply sympathetic, fully engaged in thoughts and prayers on Sophie's behalf. "I heard the terrible news. A terrible thing! Terrible!"

"Yeah," I say. "Terrible."

"How is she?"

"In a coma."

"You never know," says Viktor mournfully. "Wrong place, wrong time. A drug addict with a knife. Suddenly you're another statistic."

"So it seems."

"Well, what's past is in the past, and now of course we wish her only the best, Oleg and me, all of us here. Please pass that along, if you get a chance."

"I will."

After a pause, Viktor allows a tentative smile to tug at his thin lips. "You've been helpful to me, Jake. We make a good team."

"I agree."

"You stepped up to manage our right sizing which must have been hard for you."

"It's what you asked me to do and it was necessary, so I did it."

"You made the right choice. You proved to me that you are one of us."

"I'm glad you see it that way."

"That choice that you made..." Viktor places his hand over his heart, "...it's important to me personally. And you should know, if you don't already, I take care of my friends."

I wait to hear what he's getting at, and he continues, "What I'm about to tell you, you can't repeat, not to anyone. Just between us. Okay?"

"Yes, just between us."

"I'm a partner in a group that owns Island Bank. I share in the profits which, by the way, are very big. It's like I told you, work with right people, you get what you want. Now that you proved you're on our team, I argued to Oleg that you should get an equity share and he agreed."

Viktor pauses, my cue to thank him.

I'm thinking, are they setting me up? Should I accept Viktor's offer and keep the charade going, or walk away and end it now? Then I think of Sophie and there's no question what I'll do.

I say, "Thank you, Viktor. I appreciate it."

He extends his hand across his desk. "Welcome to the gravy train!"

His hand feels clammy. I try not to shudder or pull away too abruptly.

"We need your signature to make this official."

He slides towards me a sheet of paper already carrying his signature and an 'X' on the line where I'm to add mine. In lawyerly language, the document states that I, Jacob Morais, am hereby granted a quarter of one percent interest in Island Partners, LLC, the group that in turn owns one hundred percent of Island Bank Ltd., based in Antigua. The document stipulates that I will receive proceeds amounting therefore to a quarter of one percent of Island Partners' total income, with the first payment to be received twelve months from date of signature, to be deposited directly into an account that's been opened in my name in Island Bank, unless said payment is forfeited due to actions by me or to other circumstances preventing Island Partners from distributing its earnings to its partners. Under a paragraph titled Confidentiality, I agree to keep confidential all information concerning Island Partners and Island Bank, subject to forfeiture of my interest and exposure to lawsuit for breach of contract.

"Looks good," I say, scribbling my signature.

Viktor inserts the signed form into a manila folder and deposits the folder in a side desk drawer.

"Don't worry," he says. "No one will see this except for me and others in Island Partners who need to know. I'll lock it away as soon as we're done here."

Glancing around Viktor's sparsely furnished office, I don't see anything that looks like a safe.

"Not here," he says.

He slides over another sheet of paper.

"Login info to access your account. You just need to create your ID and your password, and you're all set."

"What will I get for my quarter of one percent?"

"That depends," Viktor says. "The equity partners don't get dividends because the bank is managed not to produce net profits which would be taxable."

"Okay."

"Our deal is to take money off the top, twenty percent of the money that our clients process through the bank…"

"Our clients?"

"Certain high wealth individuals. Better not to get into that."

"Fine, no problem. Just curious."

"Anyway," Viktor continues, "our cut, our twenty percent, is divided up based on our equity shares."

He taps numbers into a calculator on his desk. "Currently on an annual basis your quarter of one percent share will be good for thirty five thousand dollars."

"Sounds good to me." Then, keeping my voice casual, I ask, "How much do you own?"

"Eight and a half percent," Viktor replies, with an air of satisfaction. "Only Oleg has a bigger share. I'm one of the founding partners."

"So, you and Mr. Krulik..."

"Yeah, we have history. Anyway, when you sign onto your account, you'll find ten thousand dollars in there already. I made the deposit this morning out of the partners' general fund. Consider it as an advance against your payout a year from now."

"You can do that? Just take money from the general fund and move it to a different account?"

Viktor nods. "I'm the designated admin guy for the partners. I move the money where it's supposed to go, for payouts, expenses, whatever."

"As approved by Mr. Krulik."

"Oleg lets me do what is right for the group. But also he pays close attention, or he wouldn't be Oleg."

"You're taking a big chance on me. What if I don't work out?"

"You will."

Viktor looks at me expectantly like he's waiting for another expression of appreciation, perhaps.

"I thought the advance would be a nice gesture," he says.

"It is, Viktor, it is. Very nice! Thank you."

My cellphone buzzes from an incoming text.

"Sorry," I say. "Let me just check this."

Which I regret doing as soon as I see the source. The text is from FBI agent Reilly. "Need to meet again."

"Any problem?" asks Viktor. "More news about Sophie?"

"No, just a friend. We've been looking for a time to get together."

Once back in my office, I reply to Reilly's text, "I've got nothing to add."

Twenty Three

On my way home, I stop at the Bank of America branch on Mass Ave near my house. At a teller window, I withdraw two thousand dollars, all in fifties.

I try to use a different teller each time I make these withdrawals. They're curious, I can tell. Probably they assume I'm involved in illicit cash transactions of which many possible examples come readily to mind. But they don't ask, and I just say thanks and stuff the cash into my pocket.

At home, I add the cash to my growing Plan B reserve in my basement safe.

In case Plan B turns real, I expect that I'll also need access to email to find out what's happening back home and whether anyone is getting close. But scratching that email itch could reveal where I am when I log in.

So that I'll be able to check email safely, I create multiple email accounts and set up mirroring of incoming messages from one account to the next.

Everyone knows my Yahoo email address, which is the only address that I've used to send emails.

However, no one will know that my incoming emails are mirrored from Yahoo to a second tier address that I open on

Gmail, and from Gmail, mirrored again to a third email address on Earthlink, and from Earthlink, yet again to a fourth email address, on AOL.

My incoming emails will be read only at my AOL address, after they've have been mirrored three times over.

I'll be able to lurk on the email grid without being detected. No one monitoring my Yahoo tier one address will see any activity. Anyway, that's the plan.

Twenty Four

Viktor hosts a party in his condo to celebrate all the great things happening at Dazzle.

Oleg Krulik is there, as is the remaining American VC whom I'd met at the board meeting, the obese one whose name escapes me, and accountant Anton Belsky, also a hefty guy, who's taking full advantage of Viktor's liquor selection, and a clutch of bodyguards, black leather jackets, bald heads, broad backs, bulging arms, and Irina standing by the bar being hospitable, joined by two other slender women with spectacular cheekbones and bored expressions.

Krulik is already well lubricated and in an expansive mood as he surveys the harbor from Viktor's deck.

"Hello, Mr. Krulik," I say. "I'm Jacob Morais. We met earlier at the board meeting."

"Yeah, hello."

"Beautiful evening."

"Yeah."

"Great view."

"Yeah."

Krulik seems more interested in the view than in me and I'm about to return inside when he growls, "Sophie fucking Bronstein wouldn't back off. Got what she deserved."

"You mean the attack that left her in a coma?"

He casts a heavy-lidded glare down at me. "Yeah, so?"

I don't trust myself to reply. Then Krulik observes, "But now you're Viktor's friend."

"I hope so. Because of him, I'm going to make a lot of money."

Krulik coughs up a laugh. "Show me the money! Right?"

"Right!"

I'm struggling to sustain joviality in Krulik's thuggish presence. What's the etiquette for socializing with inebriated hoodlums? I have no idea, except that you want to avoid causing offense.

Looking inside, I see that the American VC has enthroned himself on a sofa with one of the women. She's grimacing appreciatively while His Hugeness chortles at a joke he must have made.

Viktor joins us.

"Can I steal Jake away?" he asks Krulik.

"Yeah," says Krulik. "He's all yours."

"Irina's waiting for you in the bedroom," says Viktor.

"Gosh!" I say. "That's terrific."

Then I hesitate and Viktor asks, "What?"

"I'd feel awkward, since Irina is your..."

He goggle-eyes me like I'm impugning the value of his gift. "You don't want her?"

"I'm not saying that. Of course I do. She is very beautiful."

"So go to Irina."

She's curled in a chair gazing out the window, shoes off, wearing a cotton summer dress that partially covers her long legs.

I check to lock the bedroom door but it doesn't have a lock, which is a downer given the party just outside.

"Hi Irina," I say. "Viktor told me that you were waiting for me."

She shrugs, says nothing, and doesn't fake a smile.

I sit on the bed, facing her. She does have striking features, violet eyes, cheekbones, fleshy lips, and a model's perfect body, thin but still feminine. If we'd met under different circumstances, like in a crowded café in London where we were forced to share a small table and then got to talking, who knows what might have happened? But here, in Viktor's bedroom, it doesn't feel right. Nor does it help that Irina looks as bored as sand as she slips off her clothes.

I don't stop her.

Irina sits her naked body beside me close enough that I can feel her heat and the pressure of her thigh against mine, and I can smell her skin. She reaches to unbutton my shirt.

There's no denying that this is pleasurable, at least to me, but letting it proceed further will carry too high a cost. Reluctantly, but firmly, I tell her, "Hold on."

"You don't like me?"

For the first time, a spark of interest.

"Sure, I do. You are very beautiful. But here…"

"He told me to be nice to you."

"Not like this."

She shifts a few inches so that she can look directly at me.

"You don't want?"

"Not now. I'm sorry."

"Viktor said…"

"I'll tell him that we had a good time. If he asks you, you say the same thing. Be vague. Can you manage that?"

"Yes."

She remains on the bed, uncertain, and I say, "Please get dressed, Irina. It's okay."

She pulls her clothes over her firm slender body, her panties, her bra, her dress, and returns to her chair by the window. I stay where I am on the bed.

I need to consume more time before I emerge from the bedroom with a satisfied smirk and fulsome thanks to Viktor for his generous gift, so to get a conversation going with Irina, I ask her, "How long have you known Viktor?"

"I don't know, maybe six months."

"Did you meet here? Or in Russia?"

"I am Ukrainian, not Russian. We met in New York."

"And you hit it off."

"I don't understand, hit it off."

"Liked each other."

"He told me he would take care of me if I stayed with him and did as he said."

"Has he offered you to others like he offered you to me this evening?"

"Yes."

"Are you okay with that?"

"I do what I have to."

"You are very beautiful, Irina, and you speak English well. You could be a model. Or, whatever…"

"In Ukraine I was a school teacher," she says. "Here, I don't know what I can do. They told me they would help me get papers to work but…"

"Why not return to Ukraine?"

"Viktor has my passport. I can't go anywhere."

"Would you leave, if you could?"

"Yes."

Suddenly her eyes fill. "They gave me drugs. They raped me. Krulik, and others, while people watched. They told me that they would kill me and nobody would know. Or I could go with Viktor, like they wanted."

"Irina," I say. "I don't have any plan right now but if I can, I'll try to help you."

"Thank you," she says, being polite, and not pretending to place any stock in my promise.

She turns to stare out the window again. Beside her chair, there's an old pinewood chest of drawers standing on four legs. On the floor underneath it is a small black safe with a combo lock.

"What's in the safe?"

"I don't know."

"Your passport?"

Irina glances down at the safe like that possibility hadn't occurred to her.

"Do you know the combination, Irina?"

"No," she replies, more engaged now given the direction that our conversation has taken. "When Viktor is showing off, he lets me see him spinning the dial to open the lock, but I'm not close enough to see the numbers."

"Too bad."

"I'll watch more closely," she promises.

I check the time on my cell. Only a few more minutes before I can rejoin the party.

Krulik is hunched over a table, snorting white powder through a tightly-rolled hundred dollar bill. He straightens, wipes his nose with the back of his hand, passes the tube to Viktor who also sniffs heartily, straightens, and wipes.

Viktor sees me and says, "Hey!"

He waves me over. "Take a hit."

"Not my thing. But thanks."

He stares at me for a second, or maybe just past me, his focus dissipated by the powder. Then he recalls where I've been.

"How was Irina?"

"Fantastic. Thank you!"

He gestures towards the fat VC whose face is muffled between the breasts of the woman whom he's been fascinating with his lively wit.

"They need the room. Can you let Irina know?"

"Will do."

Krulik leans over and rests his large arm on Viktor's narrow shoulders.

"People say Viktor is an asshole and he is, but he's my asshole, isn't that right, Viktor?"

Staying completely still, ignoring the weight on his shoulders, Viktor grins and replies, "Always, Oleg."

Looking at me through red-rimmed eyes, Krulik asks, "Will you be my asshole too, Jacob Morais?"

"It would be my honor," I say.

Twenty Five

Brittany buzzes me from her receptionist's desk.

"Jake, two visitors here for you. They're from the FBI."

"Did they say what this is about?"

"They want to talk with you. Shall I bring them to your office?"

"No. Tell them to wait there. I'll be right out."

Agents Patrick Reilly and Charlene Rivera are the only people in the building and possibly in all of trendy Fort Point who are wearing dark suits and white shirts, in Reilly's case accented daringly by a thin dark tie.

"We need a few minutes of your precious time," Reilly tells me.

"Let's go outside."

Too late, I realize that Brittany, her mouth still agape from seeing actual FBI agents, will conclude that I want to talk with them where we won't be overheard, which is true but looks bad. I should have led them to my office in full view of everyone to demonstrate that I have nothing to hide. Seeing the agents in my office, Viktor would have intervened. I'd have made introductions. Everything would have been in the open, giving Viktor no cause to worry. I made a mistake. It happens.

"I'll be back soon," I assure Brittany. "This is probably about Sophie, following up."

Reilly doesn't say anything, either confirming or denying.

"Okay, Jake," replies Brittany, her eyes flicking from me to the FBI agents, and back again.

We walk up the street. Once we're out of view from Dazzle's windows. Reilly and Rivera stop by a parked BMW and slide their butts onto its hood, making themselves comfortable and leaving me standing on the sidewalk facing them.

"What's this about?" I ask.

"Your reply to my text," says Reilly, while agent Rivera looks on impassively behind her dark sunglasses. "When I ask for a meeting, *no* is not the correct answer."

"I've got nothing more to tell you."

"We think you do," says Reilly. "Now that you've gotten so close to Viktor Rost."

"Also to Oleg Krulik," adds agent Rivera.

"I'm not close to Mr. Krulik. I've only seen him a couple of times."

"Like at your good friend Viktor's condo," Reilly says. "Along with party girls and recreational substances."

I could have bleated that just because I went to Viktor's party doesn't mean anything, but what's the use, so I hold my tongue.

"We have our sources," Reilly says.

"What else have your sources told you?"

"That you're Viktor's bum boy."

"I'm just trying to make a living."

"Stop fucking with us. You're one of them."

"One of *them*? Does this mean you believe Sophie? You weren't sure the last time we talked."

"Don't pretend you're stupid, Jake. You know they're dirty."

"Mr. Krulik is one of our investors and he's on our board. He went to Harvard. That's all I know."

"Yeah, well, just to fill you in," says Reilly. "Krulik is a gangster. He was an oligarch in Ukraine until the government fell and he had to leave to save his ass. But his apparatus is still in place and he runs it from here."

"If you know all this, why was he allowed back into the US?"

"That's above my pay grade. But you're going to help us bring him down."

"How would I do that, exactly?"

"Wear a wire."

"Technology is amazing nowadays," agent Rivera says. "Almost invisible."

"No way."

"*Yes* way," Reilly says. "Otherwise you'll go down with them. Think about it, hands in cuffs, perp fame on TV, quality time with horny cell-mates. Time to choose: Are you one of the good guys?"

"I could ask you the same thing. I mean, what happened with Shiny Mikey Wallace?"

"Excuse me?"

"According to the *Globe*, he was tipped off by an FBI agent in your office just before he was supposed to be arrested. If I agree to help you, how long before Krulik hears about it?"

Reilly shifts himself off the BMW and stands up close, getting in my face. "No one would find out. Don't believe everything you read in the *Globe*."

"Okay, thanks for clarifying."

My sarcasm goes over their heads. They just watch me, Reilly up close, Rivera still on the car.

"Wear the fucking wire, Jake," says Reilly, sounding almost friendly, like he's urging me along as a friend.

I shake my head. "No."

Agent Rivera says, "Let's take him in."

"On what charge?" I ask. "Refusing to commit suicide?"

"Lying to the FBI, for starters."

"Okay, take me in," I say. "We'll find out how this plays before a judge."

Reilly says to agent Rivera, "Why don't we give Jake a day to consider his options?"

"Fine," she replies, and then to me, "You've got a day."

Reilly says, "Here, tomorrow, same time."

Viktor is waiting for me in my office, his normal pallor sickened to grey-green. "What do they want?"

I don't try to hide what he probably already knows. "They want my help against you and Mr. Krulik. They claim he is a gangster."

As I suspected, Viktor isn't surprised. "There's no proof," he says. "What they told you, it's just propaganda. Oleg lives openly in Brooklyn. He does business as an investor. He donates to charities."

"They gave me until tomorrow to let them know my decision."

"And, what will you tell them, tomorrow?" asks Viktor, like he's just curious.

"I'll tell them 'no.' They're bluffing. If they have anything, they would have moved on us by now."

"Good answer."

Then, Viktor adds, "We're worried about documents. We're still checking what Maggie took."

"Has she turned up yet?"

"Oleg's guys are looking for her. They'll find her. They have their ways."

"Right."

"The problem is, Oleg is still suspicious about you, no matter how many times I reassure him. He's convinced that Sophie gave you files and you've got them hidden away."

"But that's not true."

"I know that, but Oleg..."

"How can we persuade him?"

"We can't. Better not to try. He can smell fear. It makes him crazy."

"So..."

"Look, Jake, just to make everyone more comfortable, leave your PC here in the office when you go home, okay?"

"Sure. It will give me an excuse not to work nights and weekends."

"And don't take any documents off company premises."

"Okay."

"One more thing, Oleg has arranged for his guys to search people on their way out. Not every day and not everyone but enough to keep people honest."

"People, or me specifically?"

"People, including you."

The large fellow slouching against a car parked outside our office was one of the bodyguards at Viktor's party. He doesn't pretend not to stare at me as I leave our building.

I acknowledge his interest with a genial nod.

"Nice day."

No answer. Maybe he doesn't understand English.

"Would you like to search me?"

No answer.

"Okay, see you later then."

I force myself not to glance back during my fifteen minute walk to South Station. Once I'm on the platform for Red Line trains heading into Cambridge, my quick scan in both directions reveals no sign of him or of other Krulik bodyguards.

Nor on the train.

Nor in Central Square station in Cambridge.

I climb the steps out of the station to Mass Ave.

There I see another heavy set bald guy, one of the others from Viktor's party. He's watching the station, and watching me, as I cross Mass Ave.

They don't need to follow me. They know my routine and where I live. Are they checking whether I meet anyone? Or just trying to spook me?

I walk to my house as fast as I can without breaking into an undignified sprint.

Twenty Six

A question is roiling my mind while I struggle to get to sleep and to resist checking the clock on my side table: How do I know that Reilly and Rivera really are FBI agents?

In the morning I call the general number for the FBI office in Boston.

My call is picked up by a man who drones, "Agent Nick Ahearn FBI Boston Division this call is being recorded."

"Agent Patrick Reilly, please."

"Just a minute."

The line goes silent.

Then Ahearn comes back on. "Who's calling?"

"Isn't my name on your caller ID?"

"Humor me."

"Jacob Morais."

"Just a minute."

After another moment of silence, I hear, "Reilly here."

The voice sounds like Reilly's.

I ask, "Can you tell me a fact that confirms you're the agent Reilly I've met a couple of times?"

"Yesterday we met at your company and earlier at your house in Cambridge, both times with agent Rivera. What's this about?"

"Making sure you're who you say you are."

"Are you convinced?"

"Yeah."

"Okay, see you again this afternoon."

"I won't be there."

"Why not?"

"Because you made a big show of asking for me at my company."

"So?"

"You're trying to get me in trouble."

"Guess what, Jake, you're being watched all the time. Krulik hasn't lasted this long by being a trusting soul. It makes no difference if we meet in plain sight."

"Yesterday Viktor was waiting for me in my office as soon as I got back. The discussion we had wasn't pleasant."

"Let me guess. He asked what we wanted."

"Yes."

"And you told him."

"Yes."

"That's what we expected."

"Did you also expect I'd tell him I had no intention of helping the FBI?"

"Of course. What else would you say?"

"Well, that's why I won't be there. I'm not about to put my life at risk, not after what happened to Sophie."

"It's a free country, Jake. You make decisions and you accept the consequences of those decisions."

"That's what I'm doing."

"So be it."

That afternoon, around four, Viktor beckons to me to join him in his office, and once I'm there with the door closed, gets right to the point.

"What did you tell the FBI today?"

"What I told you, that I couldn't help them."

"Are you wearing a wire?"

"No, I told you…"

He gives me one of his long stares, scanning for tells. Then he looks away. "Okay. I believe you."

"Okay."

"They'll keep after you."

"Not a problem," I say. "I'm not going to work for them against you or anyone else."

"Good."

"Can you tell Mr. Krulik that I said no to the FBI?"

Viktor shifts uneasily in his chair. He looks even paler than usual, and sweaty. He looks scared. "I'm not telling Oleg anything. He's already talking about getting rid of loose ends…"

"Shit."

"…not good for you, or for me either since I vouched for you."

"Maybe I should quit. I'll give back my equity in Island Bank, return your deposit in my account."

"That would make him even more suspicious."

"What do you suggest?"

"We're still friends, right?' asks Viktor.

"Yes, of course."

"So you've got nothing to worry about."

"Okay."

"We'll get through this, believe me."

He starts tidying his desk, aligning papers and folders, putting the cheap ballpoint pens that he uses into a jar. It seems odd, the way he's avoiding my eyes. Maybe I'm getting paranoid.

Krulik's heavies are nowhere in sight when I leave the office. Nor on the T, nor on Mass Ave near the Central Square station.

I've prepared myself for another visit from Reilly and Rivera. At any moment, I expect to hear my doorbell ring, soon followed by impatient banging.

Which doesn't happen. Apparently they have other things to do that evening.

The milk in my fridge has gone sour. If I hurry I can get to Gennaro's Market before it closes at nine.

On my quick walk to Gennaro's, there are no Krulik heavies around, that I see.

On my way back, when I'm still on Mass Ave, I sense that I'm being followed. I stop to re-tie one of my shoes and look behind me, casually. I see no one there except for a homeless guy sprawled on one of the street benches, and a woman heading into a CVS.

My imagination is in overdrive. I need to calm down.

I resume my fast walking pace up Mass Ave, and then turn left onto my street. Two men standing on the sidewalk in front of my house watch me approach. Each has scruffy goatees and mullets and loose untucked short-sleeved shirts.

I cut across a neighbor's patch of grass to avoid them.

One of them asks, "You Jacob Morais?"

"No. I'm just visiting. Jake is away."

"Give me your wallet," the other one says, while the first one pulls up his shirt to reveal a gun holstered on his belt.

I hand over my wallet.

"Smart-ass," the first one says, after opening my wallet and reading my Mass driver's license. "So, *Jake*, why do you think we're here?

"No idea."

"To give you a message: We know where you live."

My legs feel rubbery, and my bladder is screaming. I would run, if I could, but I can't outrun a bullet.

"Why should that concern me?" I ask, in a voice that sounds remarkably normal to my own ears.

"You got documents that were stolen from your employer."

"Not true."

"Just shoot the fucker," the second one says.

"First we need to get the documents," the first one says. "Then we'll snuff him."

"I don't have any documents."

The second scuzzie says, "We'll do it quick if you don't give us trouble. Merciful."

"I'm not giving you trouble. If I had documents, I'd pass them over to you. But I don't."

"Fuck it," the first one says. He looks around. Still no one coming on the sidewalk. Cars passing but not slowing, showing no curiosity about the three of us. "We're wasting time."

He closes the gap between us. I can barely suppress gagging from his reek of tobacco, mossy teeth, and rancid body odor, not to mention the sight of his grey metal gun jammed against my stomach.

"So I'll count to five," he says. "You decide how you want this to end."

"I'm telling you…"

He starts, "One."

"I don't have anything."

"Two."

"You can stop counting."

"Three."

"Do you want to search my house? I'll prove it to you."

My mind racing wildly I think maybe I can get to my basement and get my Glock out of my safe, but even as I imagine this scenario, I realize that there's no chance, not in this universe.

"Nah," the other one says. "We're not going to play hide-and-seek in your house."

"Four," says the first one, the one with the gun.

I give up. I can't reason with these morons.

"Five."

"Don't," I say.

He widens his eyes like he's about to pull the trigger.

"Last chance."

I prepare to die. Clench my jaw. Close my eyes. I don't want my last sight on earth to be the man's repulsive face. Hold my breath. Think of Annie.

Nothing happens and I open my eyes.

The gun holder furrows his grimy brow as if he's thinking, then he says, "He's fucking pissed himself."

Which, looking down and feeling the wet on my leg, I realize that I have.

A Cambridge police car turns from Mass Ave onto my street.

The two sewer creatures slope off, trailing a warning, "We'll be back."

I don't feel like talking to anyone in my present condition, so I let the cops drive by without hailing them down.

You don't get to pick your catastrophe.

The occupant in the White House continues to lurch from one gross stupidity to the next, but right now, at this moment, the threats that I face are different than I anticipated when I stocked my basement.

They're personal.

I'm caught between a homicidal Russian-Ukrainian gangster and FBI agents who might be on his payroll, whether they are or not I have no way of knowing.

I'm menaced by lowlifes who jammed a gun into my stomach and promised to return to finish what they started.

How much good am I doing for Sophie anyway? She's in a coma. None of this matters to her anymore.

There's no one I trust who's waiting for whatever evidence I can collect on Krulik and Viktor and their schemes.

Their money laundering is not my problem Certainly I'm not about to sacrifice my life to stop it.

Annie wants nothing to do with me.

I'm outnumbered and outgunned and hunkering down is not the solution.

It's time for Jacob Morais to go.

Twenty Seven

I pack two bags, an overnighter and a soft-sided briefcase, each equipped with shoulder straps and therefore both portable and inconspicuous. I don't want to be seen on the street with a rolling suitcase.

Question to witness: "Did you see Jacob Morais at any time after the last day he was at work?"

Witness: "When was his last day at work?"

Police officer supplies date.

"Yes, I remember now, I did see him, it was on Mass Ave. What caught my eye was that he was pulling a suitcase, one of those rollers."

In the overnighter, I pack items that no one searching my house will notice as missing, underwear, socks, shirts, an extra pair of jeans, shoes. They'll check for toiletries and my razer, so I leave those behind.

I also leave my laptop, which I hate to do because it's almost new, but it's another possession that, if missing, will provide a clue about the circumstances of my disappearance. I've deleted all files on the hard drive that refer to Canada, my search for a fake ID, or my communications with Sophie. Docs

147

that I want to keep I've copied onto a thumb drive that I take with me.

I stuff cash into my money belt, in pockets in my overnighter and briefcase, and inside my packed shoes, socks and folds of clothing.

In the morning, just after seven, I peek through the shades on my front windows to check the street: No one in view, in particular no bald leather-jacketed heavies or lowlife assassins.

I slip out by my back door and walk up the alley towards Mass Ave.

So far, so good. The street is crowded with rush hour commuters. I join a line boarding a Mass Ave bus, ride the bus across the Charles River into Boston, and get off at the Newbury Street stop.

I hail a taxi and ten minutes later I'm at the Peter Pan ticket counter in the South Station bus terminal.

"Yes?" asks the woman at the counter.

"One ticket to New York City, please, on your next bus out."

She taps at her keyboard and checks her monitor. "Ticket costs seventeen fifty. Bus leaves in twenty minutes, gate eleven."

Before she makes change on a twenty, she says, "I need your name and photo ID."

I tell her, "John Dobby," and hand her my New York State ID card. She gives it a cursory glance and passes it back to me, along with my ticket.

Four hours and twenty minutes later, a little after two o'clock, my bus arrives on schedule at the New York Port Authority terminal.

To get from New York to Toronto, I now have to decide, bus or plane?

Flying would be faster and more comfortable. I could take commuter rail to Newark Airport and Porter Airlines from Newark to the downtown Toronto airport.

But, airlines' res systems match passenger names against a No Fly List maintained by the FBI. I choose not to press my luck.

There's a Greyhound bus to Toronto that's scheduled to depart in about five hours. It's an overnight ride, another ten hours. Again I pay cash at the ticket counter. When the agent asks for my passport, I show my Canadian passport for Jacob Morais.

Now I have five hours to kill.

There's nothing that I particularly want to see outside the bus terminal, not while lugging two bags and carrying wads of cash. I pick up a paperback at a Hudson News store and make myself comfortable in McCann's Pub on the terminal's second level; McCann's is noisy, and dark, which suits me fine.

I'm in an aisle seat on the bus to Toronto. The woman in the window seat beside me says hello, and I say hello back, which is the extent of our conversation. She inserts ear-buds and watches a movie playing on her laptop. I read my paperback. After a few hours, only a couple of reading lights remain on and the bus is mostly dark and quiet, no one talking, just the hum of the engine and rumble of our tires on the road. I'm thinking about the life I'm giving up, leaving behind the person I was, all that I've achieved, the credentials that I've earned over the years, in education, employment, and personal credit, all that comprise my shield and sword for a middle class life. I'm depriving my parents of their only son, and myself of my parents, who are getting older and won't be around forever. No more weekly dinners to receive their counseling on my relationships, appearance, and work choices. They won't know what happened to me. I'll be unable to reassure them, or to help them when they need me. No one I care about will know where I am. I'll never see Annie again. I'm abandoning my home in Cambridge that's given me so many comforts and conveniences. I'm unsure that I have what it takes to pull this off. I'm more alone than I've ever been and feeling sorry for myself. I recline my seat and close my eyes.

Around three in the morning, the lights come on and the driver announces, "We have arrived at the Canadian border. Please stay in your seats. Prepare to collect your bags to pass through customs as instructed by customs officers."

A female Canadian customs officer boards the bus. She announces that we'll disembark five rows at a time to speak with officers inside the building, and that we should bring with us all of our possessions, without exception.

Being towards the back, I'm in the last set of rows to climb off the bus. We're directed inside where I join a short line marked for Canadian citizens.

"Where do you live?" asks the customs officer, this one a middle aged man, as he examines my Canadian passport and then runs it under a scanner.

"Montreal."

"What were you doing in the States?"

"Visiting friends in New York."

"How long have you been outside Canada?"

"One week."

"Why are you going to Toronto instead of directly back to Montreal?"

"Visiting friends in Toronto, as well."

"In your bags, any weapons, drugs, mace, or fresh fruit?"

"No."

"Value of items purchased in the US?"

"Just a paperback, maybe fifteen dollars."

He hands back my passport.

"Welcome home."

Oh Canada, true north strong and free!

Two hours later, at six o'clock in the morning, we pull into the bus terminal in Toronto.

A short taxi ride brings me to Toronto's Union Station.

My ticket for the ViaRail train to Montreal costs one hundred nineteen dollars (Canadian), paid in cash. When asked for a photo ID, I show the ticket agent my New York State ID for John Dobby. He glances at it briefly before completing my ticket. Again, good enough!

My train departs Union Station at nine twenty. It isn't full and I have a two-seater to myself.

My train ride to Montreal's Central Station takes five hours. I doze most of the way.

Twenty Eight

Before long the others in my building on Duluth and St. Dominique work out that the new tenant who has just moved into the top floor apartment is connected somehow with the building's owner.

Mahmoud and Nina Maqbool, the owners of Les Mouches Heureuse on the ground floor, are friendly, but insistent.

Mahmoud catches me one morning on my way out of the building.

"Mr. Dobby."

"Good morning, Mahmoud," I say.

"Yes, good morning. Look, I'm sorry to bother you, but do you have a moment to check our air conditioner? It's not working properly. Only blows warm air."

"I'm very sorry to hear that."

"It's bad for business."

"I understand. You should tell Sara Shahanagi, our building manager."

"I did already. Nothing's been done."

"When you call her again, tell her I asked that this be taken care of as soon as possible."

Mahmoud frowns, disappointed, but too polite to press further.

"I will do that, Mr. Dobby. Thank you."

"No problem."

I'd assumed that I'd be in Montreal for months, maybe a year or so, but now I realize that I hadn't thought things through. What if my exile has no end date?

I'll retain title to my house in Cambridge as long as property taxes and utility bills continue to be deducted automatically from my account at Bank of America, which could go on for several years, and then the utilities will be shut off and the City of Cambridge will take possession of my house in lieu of taxes. My Volvo parked behind my house will deteriorate from lack of use. After a while it will be noticed that my license plate sticker is out of date, and tickets will accumulate on the windshield, and eventually the car will be designated as abandoned and confiscated, again by the City.

People who call my Cambridge landline phone and U.S. cellphone will get redirected to voicemail until the voicemail boxes are full and unable to accept more messages. Texts and emails will go unanswered. No one will come to my front door in response to repeated presses on the doorbell.

My parents will wonder why they haven't heard from me. Maybe Annie will have second thoughts about consigning me to purgatory. Or Sophie will emerge from her coma. Or Viktor will report my unexplained absence from work.

Passersby in the neighborhood will notice the weeds overgrowing my sidewalk. Mail carriers will observe that magazines and packages that are too large to be shoved through the mail slot in my front door are accumulating on my front steps.

A concerned citizen will call the police.

Cambridge police officers will break in, having reasonable cause for concern about my well-being.

They'll see mail piled inside my front door, unopened.

They won't find my dead body.

But they *will* be accosted by rancid smells in my kitchen from soured milk, rotted fruit, vegetables reduced to slimy mush, bread shot through with mold, and other edibles long past their use-by dates.

They'll find my PC which after my password is circumvented will offer no clues about what has happened.

In my basement, they'll discover racks of non-perishable canned and dry food, water, and other supplies, from which they'll deduce that I must be a survivalist, unless I had other more nefarious plans, like holding a kidnapping victim. They'll find my safe and seek Court approval to break it open, which will be granted after due consideration, and then they'll find my Glock, which will make them wonder why I needed it, and whether it had anything to do with my disappearance, and why it's still in my safe.

Also in the basement, they'll wonder about the high-octane vinegar smell from my urine drenched blue jeans and underwear in my washing machine still waiting to be cleaned. Not the best way to be remembered. On the other hand, these pungent items might confuse potential trackers so, on balance, an acceptable embarrassment.

I figure that the police will conclude that I left in a hurry. They'll be unable to determine whether I left willingly.

Speculating goes only so far. I feel an urge to check how things stand for Jacob Morais.

I can't access texts and voicemails on my US cellphone. If I turn it on, even for an instant, it will announce itself to nearby cell towers and thereby let the world know that it's alive and well in Montreal and therefore, most likely, so am I.

I could access the Internet with my new laptop via WiFi in a Second Cup or Starbucks café, but won't my laptop and the café WiFi leave tracks? I've heard that WiFi in a café can attract eavesdroppers. Not being a geek, I have no idea, but it seems plausible.

I call Sara Shahanagi for advice.

I tell her that I'm working on a business matter that's at a very sensitive stage, that I'm looking for secure access to the Internet which rules out WiFi in public areas, and I'd prefer to stay anonymous which means not using my own laptop, nor any device in my apartment.

She says, "You're welcome to use a PC my office. It's no bother. I won't snoop."

"Thanks, but I don't want to be in your hair."

"Try the Atwater Library."

The Atwater Library occupies an early twentieth century brick building on Atwater Street on the western edge of downtown Montreal. It's a community library, officially a charity, and unlike Montreal's municipal libraries it does not require its visitors to register or show an ID. In its spacious, brightly lit, high-ceilinged reading room are twelve desktop PCs that deliver wired Internet access for four dollars an hour, payable in cash.

Bingo!

The Tor browser on the thumb drive that I insert into the library's computer provides access to the Internet via a global network that hop-scotches through a daisy chain of servers, which keeps hidden your location as well as the location of the website you are visiting.

I check my AOL email address to read incoming emails that have been mirrored via Yahoo, Gmail, and Earthlink.

After three weeks away, there are seventy eight messages, mostly spam, but not all.

On Day Three of my disappearance:

From Viktor: "Hi Jacob, No show at work for couple of days. No response to texts or phone or voicemail. You must check in now."

From agent Patrick Reilly: "Call me. No more games."

On Day Seven:

From Viktor: "Certain people are having bad thoughts. Check in now. Your friend, Viktor."

From Annie: "I heard from my friend that you are not coming into work at Dazzle and no one there knows why. You didn't pick up your cell just now when I called and your VM box is full. What's going on? A."

From my father: "Son, we tried to call you when you didn't visit us last weekend and we expected you. No answer. Your mother hopes to see you soon. She sends her love! Jean Michel, your Father."

On Day Eleven:

From Caleb: "Just to let you know that Sophie's condition has not changed. We're transporting her down to our cottage on Martha's Vineyard where I can stay close by while she has 24/7 care."

On Day Fourteen:

From Annie: "I'm freaking out! No-one's heard from you! This is so unlike you, I just can't believe... Call me, A."

On Day Nineteen:

From Annie: "Found out your parents also haven't heard from you. We called the police. We should have done it sooner. Guess we were in denial. Hope you're reading this and are OK. But if you are OK and reading this, don't be such a f***g jerk... call us, A."

On Day Twenty:

An article in the *Cambridge Chronicle* reports that I've been declared missing. The Cambridge PD entered my house by breaking in through the back door. Concerning my disappearance, Sergeant James Murphy said, "We don't know the circumstances. We don't know whether there is any connection between Mr. Morais' disappearance and an assault that badly injured the former CEO of the company where Mr. Morais worked. Currently we have no reason to believe that Mr. Morais is the victim of foul play."

The headshot accompanying the story is captioned, 'Jacob Morais, missing.'

So, my headshot is out there. Anyone I've met here in Montreal who happens to see it will be struck by John Dobby's remarkable resemblance to Jacob Morais. Then it will be recalled how I moved into an apartment on Avenue Duluth at the same time that Jacob Morais disappeared in Massachusetts.

Dots will be connected.

Not good.

Twenty Nine

I'm walking across the McGill campus on my way back to my apartment when I hear close behind me a male voice, "Hey, Jake!"

The shock of hearing my former name is like ice water splashing down my spine.

I force myself not to stop, look around, or alter my pace. I keep walking, not looking back.

"Jacob Morais?" Now a female voice. Again not one that I recognize. I can't turn around to look.

I keep walking, now a little faster.

Again the female voice, "Jacob, is that you?"

The male voice, "Jake? Jesus, wait up!"

The female voice, "Maybe it's not him."

"I could have sworn..."

"So catch up to him. Get a better look."

I keep walking, purposefully, places to go, people to see, no time to dawdle, no one here named 'Jacob Morais.'

The voices stop. I don't hear any footsteps approaching. I don't dare glance back to check.

Now, I realize, I should never have come to Montreal. It's too close to Boston, only six hours away by car. Visitors from

Boston are everywhere. I should've picked a more obscure, distant location, like the interior of British Columbia.

Shoulda coulda woulda.

Too late now.

One thing is crystal clear: I need a new look.

I stop shaving and in a few days I'm growing stubble.

Adding to my new, hip image are tinted horned rim glasses from a costume shop on St. Catherine Street, tightly fitting jeans, and a soft leather jacket.

I'll let my hair grow, aiming for the swirly mane style favored by tenured college professors, revered poets, flamboyant trial lawyers, and man-of-the-people politicians.

Still, people who know Jacob Morais well will not be fooled. My parents could turn up in Montreal at any time. Annie's told me how much she likes the city and she might visit here again.

I'll have to stay vigilant.

Montreal in the summer is one festival after another, jazz, comedy, Shakespeare. I join the throngs at these events, and hang out in cafés nursing cappuccinos and reading newspapers and paperbacks, and browse bookstores, and explore art museums. In the evenings, I sample the city's restaurants, Greek, Chinese, French bistro, Indian, Thai.

The carefree visitor thing begins to wear thin.

I'm not ready for endless relaxing. There has to be a more productive way to spend my time. For example, I could use an additional proof of identity for John Dobby, like a birth certificate.

I search the Internet for hospitals that were operating when John Dobby was born but that have since closed, and find St. Vincent de Paul Hospital in Rushmore County, in upstate New York, which closed in 1993.

According to the birth certificate that I create on my PC, John Steven Dobby, male, was born at 7:20 a.m. on March 5th, 1974, to Joyce Dobby, twenty eight years old, and Martyn Francis Dobby, thirty three. I was born at home with the assistance of Dr. Robert L. Malis, who had admitting privileges at St. Vincent's.

The document bears the signatures of Dr. Malis and of a witness, Mrs. Bethany Fink, midwife. It's embossed with the official circular seal of the Registrar at St. Vincent de Paul Hospital in Rushmore County, New York. The seal appears to be authentic, as it should, since my customized hand-held embosser from eBay cost me twenty dollars. Across the seal is scrawled the signature of Jared L. Adelman, Registrar, which looks nothing like my own signature.

The handwritten number in the top right corner would help to locate the original in the file room at St. Vincent's, except that the hospital and its file room are long gone.

I dab the document with a used tea bag, then with a paper towel to remove excess wetness, and leave it overnight under several sheets of paper towel, a cloth towel, and a couple of heavy books.

By morning, it looks decades old, a work of art, even if I do say so myself.

Thirty

Cash that I carried with me into Canada is dwindling.

Rent from the tenants in my building goes primarily to cover ongoing building maintenance. Some money has to be set aside as a reserve for major expenses. Any day now the gas furnace will need to be serviced, the roof is old, and outside paint is peeling. Which means there isn't enough left over to provide me with a livable income.

I can't access my US bank account.

To get a paying job in Montreal as John Dobby, I'll need a Permanent Resident Card and a Social Insurance Number, and even polite Canadians don't just hand these out. The government official on the other side of the desk will examine my New York State ID card and my birth certificate, and she may even accept them as valid, but then she'll request to see my US passport. No matter how vigorously I wave my arms, unless I produce one, she'll ask, reasonably, "How did you enter Canada without it?"

Fugitives in movies and in novels readily acquire fake passports but I'm here in real life where it's not so easy. No doubt there are passport forgers in Montreal who cater to well-connected criminals. The catch is that to find these forgers, you have to know a guy who knows a guy, which I don't, and in any case honor among thieves, hardly ever a sure thing, won't extend to an outsider like me. In seedy bars in the seedier parts of the city where I might meet the right sort of criminals, I won't exactly blend in, even if I could speak fluent French Canadian. Not to mention that asking strangers where I can buy a fake US passport will probably attract attention.

Another possible source is the dark web, a parallel universe of websites that are invisible to Google. While some sites on the dark web are employed by heroic political dissidents and journalists, most are operated by less savory types, like jihadists, neo-Nazis, and other flavors of terrorists; by sellers of synthetic opioids, firearms, computer hacking software, stolen credit card numbers, and counterfeit cash; by murder-for-hire contractors, child pornographers, cannibals, and sex traffickers; and, for my purposes, by hawkers of fake IDs.

Using a PC in the Atwater Library, I access the dark web via the Tor browser on my thumb drive.

Among the vendors of fake IDs, Forge Central seems as good a choice as any. It promises a 'perfect' US passport that will be totally real because it will be produced by an associate who works in the Passport Agency inside the US Department of State. It asks for my height, eye color, hair color, a shipping address, and an email address. Once these are submitted, I'm told to email a recent headshot and, within fifteen minutes, to provide the equivalent of a thousand dollars in bitcoin.

That gives me pause: What if Forge Central swallows my bitcoin while providing nothing in return? What could I do? Post an angry review on Yelp? Complain to the authorities that I was cheated?

Worse, what if Forge Central is operated as a honeypot by the State Department's Bureau of Diplomatic Security? The feds would ship my new passport to the address that I stipulate, providing along the way helpful shipment updates just like Amazon does, except when I go to pick it up I'd encounter Special Agents in windbreakers, with badges on their belts.

So, forget the dark web.

And, come to think of it, nowadays US passports are linked to a US State Department database. No matter how expert the forgery, the passport will fail as soon as the database is interrogated.

I'm stymied. A US passport for John Dobby is beyond my reach.

So I can't be hired legally in Montreal.

I could work for contractors who aren't fussy about IDs, like on a landscaping crew, or as a housepainter, or washing dishes in a restaurant, but call me spoiled, I'm not ready for that, not yet.

I'll have to work for myself.

Mahmood and Nina Maqbool open Les Mouches Heureuse at ten o'clock each morning and they serve customers until seven in the evening except on Sunday when they close at five.

Nina, dark eyed, head covered with a scarf, operates the cash register. Mahmood roams the store, dusting, tidying, and chatting up customers.

Every inch of their shelves and tables overflows with vintage collectibles, old books, bottles, kitchenware, china plates and bowls and mugs, silverware, dolls, jewelry, pennants, sports memorabilia, oil paintings, prints, posters, lace, handmade marbles, lamps, toys, trays. tools, whatever.

"How's business?" I ask Mahmood.

"Good, and not so good, it depends." He's cautious; an upbeat report might prompt a demand for higher rent. "Could be better."

"You have lots of stuff."

"Is there anything you're looking for, Mr. Dobby?"

"Call me John."

"Thank you, I will," says Mahmood, glancing at Nina, who's watching us. "John."

"So, Mahmood, where do you find these items for your store?"

"From everywhere. Flea markets, estate sales, people bring things to us. Why?"

"I visited your website. It's very nice, has good photos. You show the store to good advantage."

"Thank you."

"But you don't offer a way for customers to buy your items online."

"We have this store," he says. "They can come here to find what they want."

"What if that's too much trouble? Maybe they're far away. And there's never anywhere to park around here."

"Then they won't be our customers," says Mahmood, sounding perplexed. "Our customers enjoy coming to visit our store. They see what we have, talk to Nina and me. And they don't pay shipping charges."

Nina, who's listening from her post at the cash register, jumps in, "Do you have a reason for asking, John?"

She's the sharper Maqbool.

"I have a proposal for you and Mahmood. I'll sell your items online."

"What would we have to do?" asks Nina.

"Nothing, except to keep track of the items that I offer for sale. Let me know if any of these items is sold in the store so that I can take it off my Internet listing. Whatever I sell online, I'll buy from you off your shelf at your full retail price including the VAT, and ship it to my customer."

"You'll do this for us?" asks Mahmood.

"For me too. I'll price the items high enough to make a profit."

They exchange looks. More sales, at zero risk. Nina nods. Mahmood says, "Yes please, John. We'll try your plan."

My first thirty items from the Maqbools are variations on French Canadian rustic, each small enough to ship easily, such as painted plates, teapots, bowls, bottles, small lamps, artifacts that you might find in a habitant farmhouse.

I post photos and descriptions of each item in QuebecHabitant, my new online store in the vintage treasures section of Etsy, a big online e-commerce platform, and on eBay. I write the descriptions in consultation with Nina. Actually, she dictates, and I transcribe, so the Maqbools' contribution to our venture is more than 'nothing,' but Nina doesn't complain.

I price the items thirty percent higher than the Maqbools' prices including VAT.

As I suspect, there's a market in the vast beyond for French Canadiana. Orders drift in, are paid through PayPal, and I pluck the items off the shelves of Les Mouches Heureuse to be shipped.

Soon I'm listing fifty items and selling one or two per day.

Until now, I've walked past the jewelry store up a few blocks on Avenue Duluth without seeing it, perhaps because its window is small and its entrance is below sidewalk level, six steps down.

I press a button by the door and a woman inside checks a screen on her counter. Then a buzzer sounds, and the door clicks unlocked.

"How can I help you?" asks the woman. I guess that she's in her early forties. She has large dark eyes and honey blonde highlights in her swept-back light brown hair, and is stylishly elegant, with a beige scarf that drapes her shoulders.

"My name is John Dobby. I live just up the street above the antiques store on Duluth and St. Dominique."

"Les Mouches Heureuse?"

"Yes."

"Nina and Mahmoud. Nice couple."

"Are you the Paola whose name is above the door?"

"Paola Scaffidi." She smiles and extends her hand across her counter. "Glad to meet you."

"Likewise," I say, as we shake hands.

I scan the rings, earrings, bracelets, and brooches arrayed under her glass counter.

"They're all handmade," Paola says. "Are you looking for a gift?"

"Not exactly."

Paola's lips tighten.

"You're wondering why I'm here," I say.

"Well, yes."

"I operate an online marketplace. Currently I sell vintage items from the Maqbools' store. I could sell your jewelry as well."

"I've only recently opened the store," replies Paola. "Right now I'm not planning to sell online. Maybe later."

I tell Paola what I told the Maqbools, how I'll pay her full price for items that I sell. "As far as you're concerned, I'll be just another customer of your store, a very good repeat customer, if things go well."

"What would I have to do?"

"Just let me know if you sell any of the pieces that I'm posting online so that I can remove the posting."

"That's it?"

"That's it. We don't need a formal contract. Just a mutually beneficial understanding."

"I'll think about it," she says. "Can you come back tomorrow?"

My Jewels by Paola store opens on the Etsy platform with an initial posting of sixteen of Paola's handmade pieces. Like Nina Maqbool does for QuebecHabitant, Paola dictates to me descriptions to accompany the photos, what the items are, and what they're made of.

My pricing rule is simple: Add two hundred dollars to Paola's retail price. A pair of amethyst earrings that Paola sells for six hundred dollars, I post for eight hundred. "Fine with me," she says. "My customers here won't pay what you're asking."

In addition to selling on Etsy, I register Jewels by Paola as a seller on Dazzle. Why not? No-one at Dazzle will connect a small Montreal-based online store headed by John S. Dobby with former exec Jacob Morais.

Jewels by Paola accepts payment via PayPal or, if buyers on Dazzle prefer, via Island Bank.

Within my store's first week on Dazzle, a buyer does select Island Bank to make his payment. Once he confirms that he's received his purchase, the bank transfers the money into the store's account, as it's supposed to.

At a rate of several jewelry items sold per week, I become Paola's best customer. I text her about each sale and by the time I arrive at her store, she has the item boxed and ready to go.

My online stores are generating cash, still not enough to live on, but it's definitely nice to have money coming in. And it's all legal except for not paying taxes, which I'd pay happily but can't while I lack a government-approved identity.

Paola and the Maqbools are selling items that would otherwise gather dust.

All things considered, win win.

Thirty One

Paola is divorced. Her daughter Elise, fourteen years old, attends a French language school.

About me, Paola knows that my real estate investment firm, BLT Properties, LLC, owns my building on Avenue Duluth. I tell her about the small town in upstate New York where I grew up, a great town for a kid on a bike but now unfortunately in decline due to lack of jobs, and about my house on a lake in Sprightly Falls which I'm renting to a couple of men, both artists. I confide that I moved to Montreal for personal reasons but in case she's curious, I'm not married, nor do I have any personal attachments back in Sprightly Falls.

"Not anymore," I add, my voice thickened with emotion.

Being polite, Paola changes the subject. "How did you get started in real estate investing?"

"My grandfather, on my mother's side, was a real estate developer in California. When he died, he left his properties to me and I set up BLT Properties to manage them."

"So if you don't need the money, why are you going to the trouble of selling my jewelry and the Maqbools' vintage pieces online?"

"I'm bored with real estate. My online stores keep me entertained while I think about what I want to do when I grow up."

"Any ideas?"

"Still working on it," I say. "Meanwhile I'm having fun."

The lies tumble out one after another, like bombs dropping from a B-24. It's too easy. I don't enjoy deceiving Paola but what else can I do? By all indications, she accepts my story. Why wouldn't she? I give her no reason for doubt, and nothing that I tell her can be readily checked.

During one of my visits to her store, about a month after I posted Jewels by Paola online, Paola says, "Elise wants to meet you. She told me that we should have you over for dinner."

"What's *your* opinion on that?" I ask.

"My opinion is that we should."

To get to Paola's house, I take the 24 bus which runs along Sherbrooke Street through Montreal and Westmount to points farther west in Notre-Dame-de-Grâce. When I was growing up, I rode this same bus many times between downtown Montreal and our home in NDG.

In case anyone who sees me on the bus might remember me from long ago, I sit in the back so that I can watch who's getting on. If necessary I'll duck my head, or get off, whatever I have to do.

I arrive at my stop without incident. I recognize none of my fellow passengers, women, men, old, middle aged, white, black, Asian, and no one pays me any attention whatsoever.

I'm invisible, a remnant of the vanished past.

Paola's house is in Westmount, on the flat part of Roslyn Avenue below Sherbrooke Street. In general, houses below Sherbrooke are less imposing than the lordly manors on Westmount's upper hillside where Grandpa Alain and Grandma Yvonne used to live, but Paola's house looks eminently solid and comfortable. It's semi-detached, made of brick, and has a generously proportioned white-columned front porch.

A teenage girl opens the front door.

"You must be John Dobby."

"I am. You must be Elise."

She has dark brown eyes like her mother's and appears very grown up for a fourteen year old, apart from her teenager smirk.

"Mom says to come right in."

I follow her into a living room.

"You can sit there," she tells me, pointing towards the sofa,

"Thanks."

"Help yourself to cheese and crackers and hummus dip."

"Thanks," I say again, reaching for one of the crackers in a basket on the coffee table, and for a knife to cut a piece from a round of soft cheese.

"Mom will be down soon."

"Okay."

Elise disappears into another room and I sit back to wait for Paola. Her compact living room space is nicely laid out. The room has style, not interior designer fussy, but confident and tasteful, furnished with two small sofas and a couple of chairs around a square wooden coffee table, an upright piano against one of the walls, and cushions on a window seat under bay windows facing the street.

Paola arrives, wearing form-fitted blue jeans and a stylish red silk jacket.

"Did Elise offer anything to drink?" she asks.

"No, but that's okay. I would have waited for you in any case."

"She's a work in progress," says Paola.

In the dining room, I'm ordered to stay seated while Elise and Paola bring out platters and bowls of food from the kitchen and place them in the center of the dining room table where we can serve ourselves.

We're digging in when Elise says, "I can't find anything about you on the Internet."

"Elise, be polite," her mother warns.

"Just saying." Again the smirk.

"Where did you look?" I ask.

"Facebook, Twitter, on Google. Unless you're the John Dobby from Australia who just had his ninety third birthday."

"Seems I'm not very famous."

"I guess." Skeptical, biding her time.

Paola asks about the tenants in my building, and we talk about that for a while, and I ask what they think about the return of a Trudeau as prime minister of Canada, and Elise says everyone in her school thinks he's a total hottie, and we talk about how she wants to travel when she's older. Paola asks what I think about what's happening in DC, and I say it's beyond disgusting, and she agrees. Companionable chit-chat; the first time in months, since my dash to Canada, that I am not eating dinner alone.

Over dessert, apple pie and ice cream, Elise resumes her inquisition, "Mom said you don't have a car."

"Nope."

"Not even a driver's license."

I don't remember mentioning that to Paola although maybe I did when she was giving me directions to her house and I said I'd take the bus.

"It's on my list to get it."

Paola says, "You don't really need a car in Montreal."

"That's right," I say. "So there's no rush."

Elise asks, "Can't you use your US license to drive here?"

Her expression is pure innocence, Paola's evil spawn.

If I reveal that I have a US driver's license, she may ask to see it and I'll have to explain why I don't carry it with me, which I don't, since a driver's license for Jacob Morais serves no purpose for me in Montreal where I'm known as John Dobby. If I reply that I don't have even a US license, then Elise will ask how I got around a rural area like Sprightly Falls that surely lacks public transportation.

"Only for a short while," I say. "Eventually you have to get a Quebec license."

Elise glances at her mom to confirm that she is paying attention, and then mercifully excuses herself. "Got homework."

"Nice to meet you, Elise," I say.

"Thank you so much for coming," she replies, in the mechanical monotone of a Costco greeter.

Back in the living room, after pouring me a glass of port, Paola says, "Elise wants to protect me."

"That's a good thing."

"We've had a rough time. When my ex-husband took off, I was left on my own with a baby girl. It's hard for either of us to put our trust in anyone."

She brushes her eyes with a sleeve. "Sorry."

"I should go. Thanks for a wonderful dinner, and for introducing me to Elise."

"I'm scaring you off."

"No. That's not true."

She's standing close to me, inside my personal space. It's unsettling, in a good way. It feels like time is slowing down and maybe it is, compared to my heart's beating faster. Softly, Paola asks, "Should we go out, you and I?"

"I'd like to…"

"I think about you a lot, John Dobby. Ever since you walked into my store and became my best customer just like you promised, I look forward to seeing you."

"You mean, when I come bearing cash for more of your beautiful pieces?"

"You know what I mean."

"We hardly know each other."

Her eyes lock on mine, and she says quietly, "I know you well enough."

She places her hands on my hips and pulls me in towards her, and asks, "Will you stay the night?"

I don't want to hurt her. After all, she's just confided that she's not yet healed from the treachery of her ex-husband. But she's lonely, and I am too, and I like her, and I'm attracted to her, and she wants me, and I've almost forgotten what it's like to be so close to a beautiful woman. I'm riding a rush of feeling. I'm off balance, and liking it.

I tell Paola, yes.

Thirty Two

Paola is still asleep when I slip out of bed to shower but by the time I'm getting dressed, she's awake and watching.

"See you later?" she asks.

"Hope so."

I lean down to give her a kiss goodbye.

She stretches and murmurs, "Me too."

Downstairs I meet Elise on her way out the front door with her backpack on.

"Morning," I say cheerily, and receive a stony look in return as she leaves the house.

Elise can't dampen my mood. I won't let her. She'll come around eventually. For the first time, during my bus ride back to downtown Montreal, I'm allowing myself to feel optimistic about John Dobby's prospects. This could work! I won't be alone anymore. I can make a life here.

As I approach my building, Mahmoud scurries out, looks up and down the street, and gestures to me frantically with his hand.

"Come in, John! Hurry! Quickly!"

"Good morning, Mahmoud," I say, determined to share my sense of well-being and keep the glow from fading. "Beautiful day!"

"Yes, good morning," he replies. "Let's go to the back, away from the window."

He leads me to a small windowless office behind the store's cash register. His nervousness is contagious.

"What happened?" I ask.

"A man came into our store asking questions. He wouldn't tell me his name and I told him that I didn't know anything."

"Asking questions? About what?"

"He said that he was looking for the owner of this building, a person named Jacob. I told him I don't know a Jacob and anyway I only deal with the building manager, not the owner."

"Did you give him my name?"

"No, no, I was very careful."

"How about Sara's name?"

"He already had it. When he read it off a piece of paper, I just confirmed it. I didn't know what else to do."

"Don't worry, Mahmoud. You did fine."

"I'm sorry," he says, clasping his hands like he's praying.

"Not a problem. I'm sure it's only a misunderstanding."

Once back in my apartment, I text Sara, "Mahmoud says a man was looking for the owner of my building and may come to see you."

She texts back, "Here and gone. We need to talk."

Sara sits on the sofa at the back of her office, me on a chair, our knees almost touching.

"I don't know what's going on," she says.

"Did he say who he was?"

"I asked him. He evaded my question. All he would tell me was that he's looking for the Jacob Morais who owns the building that I manage, and who he says is a friend."

"What does he look like?

"Stocky, forties, reddish hair."

I try to control my panic. Have Viktor or Krulik tracked me to Montreal? Who is this man asking questions?

"Does he have an accent?"

"Why do you ask that, John?"

"Trying to place him in case we've met."

"No special accent. Basic American, to the extent that I could tell."

"Did you clarify for him that Jacob Morais is not the owner of my building?"

"I did. I told him I've never met Mr. Morais, just the new owner."

"So, then, that's settled."

"Not really." Sara gives me a cut-the-crap look. "The man in the photo he showed me looks just like you used to when we first met, before you grew a beard and let your hair grow longer, so now I don't know what the hell. One thing I do know is that you spun a merry tale for me. And that's okay, people have their reasons. Except that I will not associate with a criminal. So is that what you are, John? Or Jacob? A criminal on the run?"

"No, nothing like that."

"But you're not John Dobby from Sprightly Falls."

"No."

Forcing down a fiery acid surge from my stomach, I can taste the failure.

"Well, okay then," Sara goes on, "Not a surprise."

"It's not?"

"I've known from the first day we met. I called the general store in Sprightly Falls and they told me they never heard of you. They assured me that they know everyone who lives on the lake and you aren't one of them."

"But you went along with it anyway."

"As I said, people have their reasons. As long as John Dobby paid my fees and didn't cause me trouble, I was willing to play pretend."

"Well, I'm sorry. And thank you."

"To be clear, your real name *is* Jacob Morais?"

"Yes. You can google Jacob Morais. You'll find that I'm a missing person from Massachusetts, not a criminal."

"I already did. That's why we're here talking. Otherwise you'd be in a police cell by now. I don't care about the details, and I'm still fine with our business arrangement unless more turns up that you're not telling me. But you need to get this sorted."

"I'm on it," I say.

Why has a stocky man with reddish hair turned up here in Montreal asking about Jacob Morais? And who is he?

Maybe there are developments back in Massachusetts that I need to know about.

I return to the Atwater Library to check my emails.

From Caleb, dated two weeks earlier: "Sophie died early this morning. Annie Kane tells me that you are still missing so I don't know whether you will receive this but I thought you should know."

I stare at Caleb's message on the screen. It's not possible. How could Sophie die? I'd assumed that she would recover. She was always so calm, and confident, and decent. She was an essential part of my world. Sophie dead! I can't believe it! I push the keyboard back and put my arm on the table and lay my head down on my arm and close my eyes. I can hear her asking, "Want to run with me?"

Someone jostles my elbow. "Are you all right?"

It's a teenager who's using one of the other PCs.

"Yeah, sure," I mumble. "I'm just taking a break."

He looks uncertain. "You want me to call anyone?"

"No, thanks, I'm fine."

"Okay."

"Appreciate your concern."

"Okay," he says again, and returns to his PC.

There are more emails. I force myself to read them.

From Annie: "I'm so depressed about Sophie, I don't know what to do. Police still won't say whether she was attacked randomly or intentionally targeted. Also about you they claim to have no leads although they seem to believe you're still alive. Totally fucking depressing. If you're reading this, you're a fucking fucker for not letting us know you're OK. Unless you can't. Then I'm sorry. A."

From my father: "Son, no reports from the police on your whereabouts. Your mother and I hope for good news. She sends her love, your father, Jean Michel."

From Maggie Chen: "Assume you heard about Sophie. Hope you are reading this in a safe place. For myself, I'm staying in a place unknown to Viktor. I'm fine physically but a total wreck emotionally. I knew Viktor was bad but I had no *idea*. Despite appearances I'm aware you were on Sophie's side. Take care, Maggie."

And an article in the *Boston Globe*:

Business Leader Sophie Whalen Bronstein Succumbs
Three months after she was assaulted near her home in Cambridge, noted entrepreneur Sophie Whalen Bronstein has died. According to family members, she never regained consciousness. Ms. Bronstein was most recently CEO of Dazzle, an online marketplace. She left Dazzle due to disagreements with the company's board. Cambridge police are investigating the incident and pursuing certain leads. Coincidentally two other executives of Dazzle who were colleagues of Ms. Bronstein have gone missing, Ms. Maggie Chen, VP Marketing, and Mr. Jacob Morais, VP Strategy. Police are investigating these matters as well. A memorial service for Ms. Bronstein is planned for a place and time to be announced later.

Thirty Three

Walking from the Atwater Library to my building on Avenue Duluth usually takes twenty minutes, plus or minus, depending on my route which I vary in order to throw off possible followers.

Today I take St. Catherine Street, planning to turn left on Avenue McGill College towards the McGill campus, which I'll cut through to get to Avenue Duluth.

I don't see him coming. One moment there's no one around. Then suddenly standing beside me is a paunchy guy with thinning reddish hair, and glasses, and a toothy grin.

"Well, well, well, Nanook!" he says. He's a bit out of breath. Maybe he jogged to catch up to me to make his surprise appearance. "Haven't you been a clever fellow!"

Less hair than the last time I saw him but, without question, Sophie's older brother, Steve Whalen.

"Not clever enough, it seems," I reply.

Neither of us makes a move to shake hands. I don't pretend to be glad to see him although, to be fair, I'm relieved that it's Steve Whalen and not one of Krulik's hoodlums.

I ask, "How did you find me?"

"You mean in the nanosecond that I looked, after Sophie died?"

"I'm really sorry about Sophie. I found out only this morning when I checked my emails."

"Yeah, well, that's why I'm here."

"Tell me how you tracked me down."

"Lots of clues. No sign of struggle at your house, no word from abductors, no corpse. I knew you were Canadian so I checked with our counterparts in Ottawa and they confirmed that you crossed the border three months ago. Then, given your background in Montreal, and your grandfather's bequest, it wasn't hard."

"Okay."

It "wasn't hard?" So much for my numerous efforts to cover my tracks.

"If it makes you feel any better, my being in Homeland Security helped."

"Right."

"And I admit, it took me longer than a nanosecond to work out that you and John Dobby are one and the same, so maybe two nanoseconds."

"Well, Steve, it's been great catching up. What are your plans while you're in Montreal?"

"Let's find a place to talk."

Steve buys a sticky bun to go with his coffee at the Second Cup on Sherbrooke Street across from the McGill campus.

"Feeling a bit peckish," he tells me. "Want anything?"

"No."

He cuts his sticky bun into small pieces and eats them quickly with his plastic fork, chased down with coffee and satisfied grunts. "Hits the spot! You sure? My treat."

"No, thanks." Then, "Tell me about Sophie."

"Not a random mugging. Her wallet was still in her fanny pack along with her phone."

"So, what…?"

"A video from an outdoor video cam at a house on the street shows a man struck her when she tried to run around him. He struck her again when she was down on the ground. We assume he had a knife although you can't see this in the video. He didn't try to take anything from her, and he didn't seem to be in a hurry either, just walked away."

"Has he been identified?"

"Not yet. It's a grainy image from a distance and in afternoon shadows, so we can't make out his face. All we can tell is that he's scruffy and wears a mullet."

I don't say what I'm thinking: I've met him.

"We think he was working for Viktor Rost."

"Not for Krulik?"

"The video image we have doesn't match any of Krulik's thugs. We think he is local talent. Maybe Krulik told Viktor he preferred not to worry about Sophie anymore and Viktor made his worry go away."

"So it's Viktor…"

"We believe so."

"That piece of shit!"

"Yeah."

"What are you doing about it?"

"That's up to you, because we need your help."

"We?"

"The United States of America."

I roll my eyes. "Uh huh."

"I'm not joking," Steve says. "Just do as we ask, and we'll be fine."

"As you ask? Like what, exactly?"

"Return to Massachusetts. Cozy up to Viktor. Rekindle your friendship."

"Viktor would never take me back."

"He will if you play it right. He still wants to believe in you. He didn't have any friends until you came along and he just can't accept that you'd betray him. It's very touching. He'll entertain almost any reasonable explanation for your vanishing act."

"How do you know all that?"

He waggles his eyebrows, like Groucho. "We in Homeland Security have our ways."

"What about Krulik?"

"Viktor will sell Krulik on letting you back in."

"So you say."

"I do."

"Strange."

"What?"

"Originally it was Sophie's idea for me to become Viktor's friend."

"Think of it as completing the mission that she gave you."

"Yeah, except now there's no way I can make nice with Viktor, not when I look at him and see Sophie's murderer."

"You can do it," Steve says. "It's for a good cause, for us to get justice for Sophie. Also because Viktor knows where the bodies are buried. He can help us get at Krulik. That's our holy grail, to have enough on Krulik to convince *him* to implicate his clients, some of them being oligarchs around Putin. The more we can squeeze Putin's cronies, the more leverage we'll have against Putin himself."

"So, it's a big deal."

"Very big."

"And you need me to topple the first domino."

"You got it."

"Okay, Steve, I've heard your pitch. I'm really impressed. Come see me again in a couple of months. I'm starting to make a life here and I'm not ready to go back."

"Nope, now is the time. Tell everyone that you need to go away for a while. It doesn't have to be forever, only until we get the job done."

"Or until I'm dead."

"Could happen. I don't deny that there's a risk. But just because I'm asking nicely doesn't mean you have a choice. If you step up, then afterwards you can keep your game going here as John Dobby if that's what you want to do. But, if you don't step up…"

No question, he can mess with my life in Montreal, although I might be able to deal with that. But what I can't ignore is that my Plan B has failed: Steve tracked me down despite all of my precautions. If *he* could, so could others.

"I have conditions."

"Such as?"

"Arrange my return to Boston in a way that doesn't reveal I was here."

"Already worked that out. You'll fly in from California, tell people you were holed up in a cabin near Mendocino, no Internet, no communications, re-connecting with nature, finding yourself, blah, blah, blah, and you're shocked to learn that you were declared missing."

"Will anyone buy that?"

"People believe what you tell them, Nanook. It's your gift."

"How about calling me Jake?"

"Jake."

"Also, I need a US passport, social security number, and New York driver's license in the name of John S. Dobby."

"Now I'm confused. Which is it then, Jake or John?"

"Here in Canada, I'm John Dobby. I need these docs for when I return. That's the least you can do."

"Fair enough," says Steve. "It's a deal."

"The FBI can't know anything about this. Only you."

"Why not? Agents Reilly and Rivera mean well. They're doing their best."

"Did you tell them you found me?"

"No, it was my personal project."

"I don't trust the FBI. Not after Shiny Mikey Wallace. They've got leaks in their Boston office."

"Could be just one bad apple."

"Except that Sophie was attacked just after she made her appointment for an interview with agent Reilly. How do you explain that?"

Steve shrugs. "Okay, if that's what you want. No FBI. Anything else?"

"No entries in any databases at Homeland Security or anywhere else that connect Jacob Morais and John Dobby.

Nothing written down anywhere about John Dobby except to validate my new IDs. You will be the only one who knows."

"Is that it?"

"Yes."

"Okay, you have my word."

I tell Sara Shahanagi that I have unfinished business in the US so I'll be away, but she should keep everything going as before.

"With you still as John Dobby?"

"Yes, just like before."

"You met the man who was looking for you."

"We met. Everything's all set."

On hearing that I will go away, Nina and Mahmoud both look horrified, convinced that I'm protecting them from the dangerous knowledge that I will be taken into custody and tortured to death, as happened to their friends in Egypt.

I assure them, "I'll be fine."

"Oh John, our dear friend, we'll pray for you," says Mahmoud.

I tell them that I have to stop posting their vintage items on Etsy since I won't be able to handle any transactions while I'm away.

"That's not a problem," Nina assures me. "Thank you for telling us."

"You can post again when you get back," Mahmoud says. His sad watery eyes express better than words that he doesn't expect that to happen soon, or ever.

It's already late in the afternoon when I get to Paola's store and she buzzes me in.

She shimmies around her display case to meet me.

"Hey stranger," she says, with a lewd grin. "I was wondering when you'd turn up."

"It's been a busy day."

She presses herself against me. "Always here for you," she whispers. "Even after business hours."

"Paola…"

"What?"

"I have to leave Montreal for a while."

"So why the long face? Call me when you get back."

"I'm not sure when that will be."

She pulls away, and her smile fades.

"You don't know how long you'll be gone?"

"No."

"So are you saying, maybe permanently?"

"Not if I can help it."

"Where are you going?"

"To the US. Business matter I have to attend to."

"I see."

"I just found out today."

"You didn't know about any of this last night."

"No."

She shakes her head. "Damn."

"I'm sorry."

"I don't believe it."

"You don't believe…"

"We had a one night's stand! For real! I can't believe I allowed myself…"

"We had more than that."

"Was last night too soon? We can ratchet back."

"This has nothing to do with last night. And if it's okay with you, I'd prefer not to ratchet back."

"Who are you, John Dobby? Tell me."

"I'm the same person I was yesterday."

"Really? Then why all the mystery? We were managing when you came into our lives. Not wonderfully, but well enough. You made me want more."

"Same for me," I say.

"I should've listened to Elise."

"I'm not like your ex-husband. I will come back, I promise."

"Sure you will," says Paola.

Thirty Four

Steve meets me in front of the corporate jet terminal at Montreal's Pierre Elliott Trudeau International airport.

"Our plane is waiting in the hanger," he says. "I've taken care of US Customs."

The jet is sleek and white, with engines mounted behind the wings on either side of its tail.

We're greeted by a flight attendant standing at the foot of stairs leading up to the jet's open door. "Welcome, gentlemen. Make yourselves comfortable and we'll get on our way."

There are two leather upholstered seats in the front of the cabin. Towards the back, where the cabin is wider, there are six more seats, four at a small table and two facing each other on the other side of the aisle.

We have the plane to ourselves and take the seats in the front.

"Lots of space to stretch out," Steve says.

"Nice ride for a government employee."

"Thanks," says Steve, as if I'm complimenting *him*. "It's a Dassault Falcon 2000. A gift from a drug trafficker."

"Very generous."

"He lets us play with his toys in return for free room and board."

We take off at a steep angle. Once we level off, our flight attendant appears from the galley. "Snacks to get you started," she says.

She places trays on the small tables in front of each of our seats. On each tray are plates of cold cuts of ham and beef, with small pickles, and wedges of cheese, and crackers, and glasses of ice water.

"I'll bring out lunch shortly," she says. "Meanwhile what would you gentlemen like to drink?"

We land at the airport in San Jose, California, and taxi into a hanger. Our luggage is loaded into an SUV that's waiting for us there. The driver, a middle aged Hispanic man, greets Steve warmly, "Hey, Mr. Whalen, good to see you!"

"You too, buddy!"

Buddy asks me, "Enjoy the flight?"

"No complaints."

"Not a bad way to travel."

"Only the best for my friends," Steve says.

Then, looking at me, he adds, "We'll overnight at the airport Marriott Courtyard. You can catch up on your emails and voicemails."

"I've already been tracking my emails."

"Yeah, but this time you'll do it openly and respond to your messages. Update people on where you were, why you were out of touch, and how shocked you are that anyone thought you were missing."

To Annie and to my parents: "I'm in San Jose California in an airport hotel and will fly back to Boston tomorrow. I've been in a cabin up near Mendocino where I had no Internet or cell coverage or phone line, so I haven't seen any of your messages until just now. I'm fine. I just wanted to get away from everything for a while. I'm sorry that I caused you such worry. Will call and see you soon."

To Caleb: "I've been out of touch, without Internet. Terrible news about Sophie. I had no idea. I wish I'd been there with you. I'm so sorry."

To Maggie: "Just now rejoining the Internet after months off the grid. FYI, before I left, Viktor told me that Krulix's men were looking for you. Be careful."

To Viktor: "I've been off the grid for the last three months. I should've let you know but I wanted a clean break, given all the pressures. After much reflection, I realize now that I acted too hastily and I'm very sorry for not letting you know. I'll reconnect with you on my return. Your good friend, Jacob."

Jacob! I'll have to get used to that name again.

Now, finally, I can listen to my voicemails, twenty eight in all. After deleting the fourteen messages from robo-callers ("This is Rachel, from credit card services..." and "Don't hang up! You have won..."), I hear Annie, and my parents, tell me how worried they are, and implore me to call as soon as possible.

Their most recent messages, before the VM box filled up, tend to be brief: "This is ___ again. Call me."

I decide to call each of them once I'm back in Cambridge. Except for one call that can't wait, which I make to Sergeant Murphy of the Cambridge Police.

He picks up, "Sergeant James Murphy."

"Sergeant, this is Jacob Morais. I've just now discovered that you were looking for me."

"You could say that. Where are you?"

"In San Jose, California. Coming back tomorrow. I was off the grid and had no idea…"

"People here were concerned."

"So I've learned. I'm very sorry about that."

"We had to break into your house. Seems you left in a hurry without telling anyone."

"It was a last minute decision. I wasn't thinking clearly."

"Alright, Mr. Morais, Come see me when you get back so that I can close the file. Bring ID."

An email from Annie pops into my box just before I sign off: "Don't bother calling. Relieved you're alive but totally pissed at you right now. Gone for three months, no word to anyone. You didn't think people would worry? Fuck you."

Thirty Five

My house is a mess, mail and papers heaped inside the front door, muddy boot marks everywhere. Apparently the Cambridge police searched the house when it was wet outside and they didn't think to wipe their boots before tromping through. Three months of dust. Books pulled from the shelves and dumped on the floor. A fetid smell in the kitchen from rotted food, like being downwind from a garbage dump.

My back door frame is cracked where the Cambridge PD forced the door open. I can shut and lock the door but it's not secure. I'll need to get it repaired.

Upstairs, clothes from my closet and chest of drawers are jumbled on the floor along with sheets and pillow cases tossed off the bed.

Medicine cabinets are emptied, their contents on the bathroom countertops.

In my home office, the floor is covered with files from my filing cabinets. My laptop PC, normally on my desk, is gone.

Emergency supplies in my basement are still in place on their shelves. My safe has been opened. No Glock handgun.

My Volvo parked out back in the alley has all its tires and its windows are intact, but the battery is dead.

I'm lugging out bags of garbage when a neighbor ambles over for a chat.

"You've been away a long time," he says.

"Yeah, off the grid, taking a break."

"You know that the police were here, right?"

"So I've heard."

"Saw the piece about you in the *Chronicle*."

"I did too, after I got back."

"Well, is everything okay?"

"Yeah. Thanks for asking."

Thirty Six

I resist the urge to open the water bottle on the table in front of me in the Cambridge Police HQ meeting room. Sergeant Murphy, a veteran cop in his 50s, doesn't offer it for my use. He's barely polite, no small talk. Taking a sip would look suspicious. My dry throat is temporary, I tell myself. I'll be fine once I get into my story.

"I've got a couple of questions," Murphy says.

"Am I in trouble?"

"I want to flesh out the details to close the file on your case."

"Okay, go ahead."

"You were in a cabin for what, twelve weeks?"

"Yes, near Mendocino."

"No communications of any kind."

"No, none. I went off the grid to collect my thoughts."

"How did you get there?"

"Flew to San Francisco, took a bus to Mendocino, hitched a lift from the town to the cabin."

"When we checked your credit card records, back when we thought you'd gone missing, nothing turned up about a plane ticket."

"As I said, it was a last minute thing. I paid cash for a ticket."

"What airline?"

"JetBlue."

I will myself not to glance away, nor to fidget with the water bottle. Hands still. Face blank. Cooperative tone of voice. No hesitations.

"So if I check with JetBlue, I'll find your name as one of the passengers?"

"I assume so."

"What did you do in Mendocino?"

"Listened to the ocean, the waves crashing on rocks, the seagulls, and so on, and breathed the fresh air."

"Food?"

"There was a small market about a half mile up the road."

"Any photos you can show me?"

"Just memories, Sergeant."

"Not even on your cellphone?"

"Never turned it on."

"So then you had enough solitude and decided to fly home from San Jose, where you finally checked your email and found out people were looking for you."

"Yes."

"Were you surprised?"

"I realize now I should left word about where I was going. Just taking off like I did was thoughtless. I wasn't thinking straight."

"Why San Jose?"

"Excuse me?"

"Why not fly back out of the San Francisco airport? You drove right by SFO while you were heading south to San Jose."

"I don't know. No good reason. Maybe because San Jose airport is less crowded. Easier to find an airport hotel room."

"How did you get there?"

"Bus to San Francisco, commuter rail to San Jose."

"All paid in cash."

"Yes."

"Why didn't you use credit cards?"

"I was still trying to stay off the grid until the end. I can't explain it. It was what I wanted to do."

"You were questioned by the FBI before you took off."

"Yes."

"What about?"

"The company where I worked made allegations against our former CEO. The FBI agents were following up."

"Your former CEO who was assaulted and later died from her injuries."

"Yes. Sophie was a good friend. Are you involved in investigating the assault?"

"I'll ask the questions here."

"Okay."

"Did the FBI agents tell you that you also were under suspicion?"

"No."

Despite having a pad and ballpoint pen on the table in front of him, Sergeant Murphy has yet to jot down any notes. Seems nothing I tell him merits recording.

He lays his dead-eyed policeman's stare on me and I look back at him, waiting.

"Here's the scoop, Mr. Morais," he says, finally. "You think I'm just a stupid cop…"

I'm about to claim that I think no such thing but he shakes his head to cut me off.

"Fact is, I'm not stupid enough to believe your line of bullshit. First thing we did when we were told you were missing was put out a standard query to Canadian and Mexican customs and we heard back right away about a Jacob Morais entering Canada around the time you supposedly disappeared. So what you just fed me is a total lie. We clear?"

"Yes."

"On the other hand, so far as I know, no laws were broken. You wanted to get away from your girlfriend, job, whatever, that's your business. You were stressed about what happened to your former boss, okay, that's tough. But you wasted our time trying to find out what happened to you. I don't give a flying fuck where you really went or what you were really doing. But don't pull this stunt again. If you do, I'll find a way to make you sorry. You got that?"

"Yes, Sergeant."

He shoves his chair back, takes his pad and pen, and starts for the door.

"Show yourself out," he says.

"I will," I reply. "Thank you. But…"

"What?"

"Cambridge police took a few things when they were searching my house, including my laptop PC and my Glock."

"Your house was abandoned. The Glock could have fallen into the wrong hands."

"It was locked in a safe."

"Easily opened with the right tools."

"I want it back. I have a license to carry."

"Your basement, with all those supplies, are you one of those weird preppers? Expecting the world to end tomorrow?"

"I believe in being prepared."

He shrugs.

"See the officer at the front desk to get your Glock. You'll have to sign for it."

"And my laptop?"

"That too."

"Did you find anything on my PC that's of interest to you?"

"About where you'd gone? No."

"About anything else?"

"Seems you're as pure as the driven snow."

My parents' ranch-style house in Winchester is the one we moved into when we arrived from Montreal and that they've lived in since.

My father opens the door, unsmiling. "So you're back."

"Yes. I'm sorry…"

"Tell that to your mother."

I follow him to their backyard deck where my mother is waiting. We hug. I hand her my peace offering, a bottle of California wine and a box of Godiva chocolates, which she accepts, and then she pulls back.

"How could you? What were you thinking?"

"I'm sorry. I should have let you know."

They ask the same questions as Sergeant Murphy did, are told the same lies, and respond with similar disbelief.

"It's not like you to drop off the grid," says my father.

"I know. It's hard to explain."

My mother asks, "You remember the Grauls?"

"Of course."

"Bonnie told us they saw you in Montreal."

"Don't see how, since I was in California."

"Bonnie said you were on the McGill campus, and they were as close to you as we are now. She said both she and Mal called your name multiple times but you ignored them."

"They must be mistaken."

"Bonnie is one of my oldest friends. She and Mal have known you since you were born. She said they were very certain."

"Facts are facts," I say. "I was in California. So either I have a double in Montreal or they were hallucinating. Bonnie and Mal *are* getting along in years, after all. Could be early dementia."

"Same age as us," observes my mother. "Your point?"

"Dinner on Sunday?" asks my father, quickly changing the subject.

"Wouldn't miss it."

"Will you bring anyone?" asks my mother.

A leading question. They were disappointed, to say the least, when Annie and I split. They had high hopes.

"No, just me."

"Well, if you do want to bring someone, they're always welcome," she says.

Caleb looks wrecked, dark purple saucers under his eyes, ragged stubble, dead tired.

"My condolences for Sophie," I say. "I still can't believe it."

"Me neither," he says.

He ushers me into his study where Steve Whalen, occupying one of the easy chairs, nods hello.

"I came to see Caleb," I say to Steve. "Not you."

"Not a problem," Steve says. "I told him how I tracked you to Mendocino and persuaded you to rejoin the world."

About my time away and the circumstances of my return, Caleb shows scant interest. Instead, he says, "Steve told me he also tried to get Sophie to refuse the CEO job at Dazzle, like I did."

"I told her it could be dangerous," Steve says. "She disagreed. She told me she could work with her fellow Harvard MBA, Oleg Krulik. And obviously, Jake, she would never have recruited you if she thought it would put you in danger."

I'm not so sure about that but there's no point in arguing. What Sophie was thinking, we'll never know.

"You have to understand," Steve continues. "Sophie was bored. Her whole life, everything she did, she found too easy. She wanted to try something hard for a change. So she wasn't put off by the risks that we were worried about."

"Well, I should have done more to protect her," says Caleb. His voice cracks. "I pushed her to talk to the FBI. I should have known that these criminals would try to stop her. I should have hired body guards for her. Stopped her from going out by herself."

"Don't beat yourself up," Steve says. "What happened was not your fault."

Caleb's misery, the horror of Sophie's death, the futility of my Plan B run to Montreal, suddenly it's all too much. I feel my face turning red, and I'm shouting at Steve, "Cut the shit! You don't get off that easily. You're Homeland Security. You could have persuaded Sophie if you tried hard enough. You *wanted* her in Dazzle to help you get at Krulik. Now she's dead. And you're pushing me to put my head on the block to go after these same fucking hoodlums who murdered her. How about using your billions of tax dollars to put the bad guys away without exposing civilians like Sophie or myself?"

"Like I said," Steve replies, evenly, "Sophie went in with her eyes open. And we'll get justice for her, I promise you."

"*We'll* get justice?"

"Settle down, Jake."

"I *am* settled!"

"So, are you going to bail?"

He doesn't say *again*. Doesn't have to.

"I'm not bailing. But only because of Sophie. The only reason. Nothing to do with you."

"Okay, understood. Now give me your phone."

"Why?"

"So I can teach you a lesson in phone hygiene that may save your life."

He clicks the icon on my screen for text messages.

"You have text threads here you need to get rid of," Steve says. "With me, Sophie, agent Reilly, Maggie Chen. Think how Viktor would react if he saw these messages."

"So go ahead, delete them."

After fiddling with the phone for a couple of minutes, he says, "Gone. Along with emails to and from, and your history of recent phone calls. From now on, immediately delete any text or email message involving me or anyone else that you wouldn't want Viktor to see, likewise your phone call history after every call. If you need to keep track of a number or an address, write it down on a piece of notepaper which you dispose of safely and as soon as possible."

"By chewing and swallowing?"

"Anywhere it can't be retrieved, so not in a wastebasket."

What if Viktor *had* demanded to see my phone? How would I have explained texts to and from Sophie after she was forced out of Dazzle, including on the afternoon just before she was attacked?

I need to up my game.

Thirty Seven

When we met the first time, it wasn't hard to insinuate myself into Viktor's good graces. All I had to do was show respect. For folks who don't get much, that means a lot.

Then after Viktor became Dazzle's interim CEO and plied me with favors, not least offering up his girlfriend, I reciprocated by listening admiringly to his boasts and doing his bidding.

Back then, it didn't occur to me that he was capable of murder.

Now I know. Viktor is a stone-cold killer. When we meet again this morning at Dazzle, I'll be face to face with Sophie's murderer.

I'll do what it takes to regain his trust but I'll have to watch myself, to mask what I'm thinking.

Viktor is still fish-belly pale, bony, and goggle-eyed.

"You fucked me," he says, swallowing hard, his Adam's apple bobbing. "Oleg was convinced you'd gone into witness protection to testify against us."

He seems bereft. If I didn't know better, I'd almost feel sorry for him.

"Believe me, I would never do that," I say.

"I had no fucking clue where you were. Oleg blamed *me* for defending you."

"You're right. I shouldn't have put you in that position with Mr. Krulik. I apologize, Viktor. I'm truly sorry."

"I thought you were my friend."

"I *am* your friend. That hasn't changed."

He seems to think about this for a bit, then asks, "So why are you here?"

"I want to make it up to you if there's still room for me in the company."

Viktor doesn't reply. To fill the silence, I ask, "Who's the guy in my office?"

"Your former office. He's our new VP Marketing."

"He was napping when I came in. He had his head on his desk."

"So what? Maybe he's sleepy."

"I guess."

Viktor must sense an unasked question because he adds, "I hired him as a favor, not for his brilliance, and we're not paying him much. The main thing is, he does what he's told."

"Like I did."

"Yeah, sure," says Viktor.

"Well I'm back now, and I hope you'll give me another chance."

Viktor clasps his hands behind his head and leans back in his chair. "I'll let you know."

He returns his attention to the monitor on his desk.

I'm in a Starbucks nursing a cappuccino and staring at other people who also have nothing better to do when my cell buzzes. A text from Viktor: "My condo tonight at 8. Talk to Oleg."

Irina opens the door.

"Hi, Irina," I say.

No reply. Not even a flicker of recognition. I don't take it personally. After all, three months ago I pledged to help her and then I disappeared. She stands aside for me to enter.

One of Krulik's no-neck heavies stops me.

"Raise your arms."

He runs a wand up and down my torso, along my arms and legs, and around my groin.

No beeps or hisses or whatever.

"Go ahead," he says.

Viktor and Oleg Krulik are sitting on the sofa by a harbor-facing window.

Krulik points to a chair across from them. "Sit!"

"The hot seat," I say. No chuckles from either of them. So much for ingratiating humor to lighten the mood.

"Viktor texted me that you wanted to talk," I say to Krulik.

"You talk, I'll listen."

"Shall I tell you why I went off the grid for three months?"

"Go."

"Because of you, Mr. Krulik."

"Me?"

"You sent two goons who shoved a gun into my gut on my front doorstep. They demanded company documents that I didn't have, and I told them I didn't, but they wouldn't listen. They said they were going to shoot me, and they would have if a police car hadn't come down my street. They said they'd be back, and I believed them."

"I don't know anything about that," says Krulik.

"They made it clear they were sent by my employer, which had to mean you."

"Not by me."

"Then who were they working for?"

"Me," says Viktor. He doesn't sound at all apologetic.

"Why?" asks Krulik, turning towards him.

"Jake was talking to the FBI, he admitted it. He could have taken documents. Naturally we had to remind him not to be stupid."

"I told you that I refused to work for the FBI."

"We needed to check. You passed the test. You proved you didn't have any documents. Or if you did, you were willing to die to keep them. Which I doubt. So we were surprised that you never returned to work."

Time for wounded outrage! "Viktor, you talk all the time about our friendship. And you sent two lowlifes to kill me?

"They wouldn't have killed you. They were just getting your attention."

I raise my voice a notch, getting into it: "They got my attention, Viktor, so don't pretend to be surprised that I took off. But now I'm back. I'm here. If you don't trust me, just say so, and I'll leave and we can stop wasting each other's time."

"Calm the fuck down," says Krulik. "We'll give you another chance."

"Good, okay, I appreciate that."

"Viktor will explain."

He stands and flexes his shoulders and lumbers towards the door, followed by his bodyguard. Not big on good-byes.

"Explain what?" I ask, after Krulik and his heavy are gone.

"First, let's celebrate Oleg's decision," Viktor says. "Irina! Two beers!"

As she's placing them on the coffee table in front of us, Viktor asks her, "You remember Jake, don't you?"

Irina nods, her violet eyes meeting mine for a moment before turning away.

"Good girl," he says. "Now leave us alone."

She goes into the bedroom and shuts the door behind her.

"You're still my VP Strategy," says Viktor. "You'll take a space at a work table."

"No office?"

"I want you in the open work space where you can hear what others are saying and report back to me."

"Okay."

"Also you'll do favors when I ask, with no questions."

"What kinds of favors?"

"Small things, like friends do. For example, three of Irina's cousins are arriving tomorrow at Logan. You will pick them up for us."

"I'm not a limo driver, Viktor."

"See? What did I say?"

"Okay. Sure. I'll do it."

"Anyway, a limo driver is not what I need. This is a special personal favor, as a friend. You will meet them and take care of them for a little while until their employers are ready for them."

"Will Irina want to visit with them first, maybe show them around Boston?"

"Why would she?"

"Because they're her cousins."

"Very distant cousins."

"Viktor, I'm not... I'll do it, but I'm not following what you are asking for."

"It's not important that they are Irina's cousins. Forget about that. What you need to know is that they are escaping from the civil war in eastern Ukraine, here to work for good Boston families as nannies. They need a place to stay for a few days, like your house in Cambridge."

"Why my house, Viktor? Don't you have space for them here?"

I'm once again trying Viktor's patience. He responds heavily, putting an end to our dialog, "My condo is too small. Also it's being watched. Your house is better."

"Sure," I say. "I understand. Glad to do it, as a personal favor."

"Soon as you meet them at Logan, examine their passports to ensure they're who we expect. Their names are Caterina, Gisele, and Nika. Hold onto their passports for safekeeping." He hands me an envelope. "Here's cash for expenses, a thousand dollars. Let me know if you need more."

I pocket the envelope.

"If you want one of the cousins for yourself, we could work that out," Viktor says.

For a moment I think he means as a nanny but then he adds, in a lowered voice, "Or I'll take one of them and you can have Irina. She's very beautiful but I'm getting tired of her and we both know how fond she is of you. Maybe she can help you get it up, unlike last time."

He sees the question on my face.

"Irina told me about your little problem when you were in there with her," pointing at the bedroom. "Next time she'll make you happy, guaranteed."

Thirty Eight

Passengers stream through the swinging doors into the international arrivals hall in Logan's Terminal E, back finally on *terra firma* having survived (once again!) the improbability of traveling in an aluminum tube thirty five thousand feet above the ground. And not just on any *terra firma* but in the United States of America with permission of US Customs. Tired, relieved, and purposeful, they peel off to greet family, friends, and sign-holding limo drivers who stand with me behind the rope, or stride past us to wherever they're going.

Irina's three cousins and their travel escort were supposed to arrive on a Lufthansa flight from Frankfurt which according to a Logan arrivals screen has already landed.

After about a fifteen minute wait in the crowd behind the barrier, I see a squat ill-tempered-looking woman push through the doors followed closely by three girls pulling oversize suitcases.

I hold up a placard on which my name is lettered, JACOB.

The woman escorting the girls sees my sign when I thrust it right in front of her.

"Jacob Morais?" she asks.

"Yep."

She mutters in Russian and the three girls cluster behind her like obedient ducklings. They don't look much alike, apart from being young, physically attractive, and apprehensive.

"Show me ID," the woman says.

I extract my wallet from my pocket and open it to show my Massachusetts driver's license.

Apparently it satisfies her because she says. "Let's find a place to sit down."

A café in the lobby has a spare table where she and I take seats. The girls stand behind their escort.

She hands me three passports. "Check them."

The shorter girl with a round face, watchful dark eyes, and short dark hair is Nika Markov, twenty years old. One of the taller girls, very blond, very blue eyed, and pink cheeked, who could pass for a fairytale milkmaid, is Caterina Zhuchuk, nineteen. The other taller girl, brunette, with long eyelashes and soft Bambi eyes, is Gisele Dryomov, nineteen. Their passport photos match their anxious faces. Each present and accounted for.

"Okay?" asks the woman.

"Yes."

She slaps a sheet of paper on the table listing the girls names, stating that they were "Received at Boston Logan Airport," dated that day and with a signature line over my name, Jacob Morais.

"Sign on the line."

I do as she says.

"Put their passports away," she said.

I comply, shoving them in one of my front pants pockets.

She speaks Russian to the girls. The only words that I recognize are 'Jacob' and 'Morais.'

"I told them to go with you. Nika, the short one, speaks a little English and maybe she's smarter than the others, so talk to her and she'll translate. Good luck."

"Wait," I say. "What's *your* name?"

"Doesn't matter," says the woman, before she marches off and disappears in the crowded terminal.

Nika says, "We need to go to bathroom."

I lead them to a Ladies where I wait for them just outside the door, guarding their suitcases.

After about five minutes, they come out, looking less bedraggled, and I tell Nika, "You and your cousins follow me now to my car."

"They're not my cousins," she says. But she translates what I said for the other two, or at least I think she does, because they keep close behind me as we exit the terminal.

I park my Volvo in the alley behind my house and let the girls in through the kitchen door.

"Your room is upstairs," I tell Nika. "For all three of you. You'll share the room, one on the bed, and two on inflatable AeroBeds on the floor. You can decide who sleeps where."

Nika looks confused. "AeroBeds?"

"I'll show you."

They follow me upstairs, lugging their suitcases, voicing the Russian version of 'ooof' as their heavy cases bump against the steps. Sure, I could help with their suitcases but I'm not running a B&B and it's not like they're my personal guests.

I show them their bedroom and the guest bathroom, and also my bedroom, bathroom, and home office, which I tell Nika are private, not to be entered, and point to locks on the doors.

I've also locked the door to the basement. They don't need to know what I have down there.

Nika asks, "Where are your children?"

"No children."

Not the answer that she expects. Suddenly agitated, she backs away from me, causing the girls behind her to stumble. She'd assumed that she and Gisele and Caterina were in good hands, first under the supervision of their squat escort to safely enter the United States of America, and now guided and hosted and employed by a gentlemanly Jacob Morais, who has a big enough house and looks trustworthy, albeit a bit cold, which is normal for an employer. But now, she's unsure.

"Why no children? We are nannies."

"Ah," I say. "I am not your employer. You will be working for Russian-speaking families. You are only staying here for a short time until your employers come to pick you up."

"Employers?"

"Families with children. Each of you will go to a different home, to take care of different families."

Nika translates for the others. They exchange worried glances.

"We want to go outside," she says.

"Not right now," I reply, as suggested by Viktor, who had anticipated a version of this request. "Police will stop you and demand your work papers which are still being prepared so that you can stay in America. With no papers, you will be arrested and deported back to Ukraine. Maybe you can go out later when you have papers. Do you understand?"

"Okay."

Reading her glum expression, I figure it won't be long before she takes her chances on leaving my house.

"I need to go to my office upstairs," I say. "Take what you want from the refrigerator if you are hungry or thirsty."

"Thank you," says Nika.

"If you have any other questions, you can ask me."

"Thank you," she says again. She seems grateful. I feel almost nauseous from the role that I'm playing to deceive these three innocents.

Caterina opens the refrigerator door and she and Gisele examine what's inside, milk, apple juice, orange juice, a large plastic bottle of Coca Cola, which I wouldn't touch but perhaps Ukrainians are less picky, sliced ham, cheddar cheese, tomatoes, eggs, apples, yoghurts, and so on. Caterina gives me a look, just to be sure, and when I don't object, she starts taking things out of the refrigerator. Gisele reaches in and does the same. Apparently, they're hungry. For now, they're focused on what they'll eat and drink and are no longer paying much attention to me.

Back upstairs in my home office, I call Viktor to report that I've picked up the three girls and we're back at my house.

"Don't let them leave," he says. "Oleg will be angry if they get away. He paid a lot of money to bring them here."

"What am I supposed to do, chain them to the radiators?"

"Good idea. I'll have chains delivered to you."

"Seriously, I don't know what they'll do once they're alone in the house."

"They will be collected by a van tomorrow night. Until then, stay with them, keep an eye on them."

"Sorry, Viktor, I'm not going to stay home all day and I do plan to sleep tonight."

He's silent for a moment, then: "One of Oleg's men will stay in your house until the van comes. They won't get past him."

"Okay."

"Tell me about the girls. Are they beautiful like Irina?"

"No one could be as beautiful as Irina."

"True," says Viktor. "But I want to meet them."

My second call is to Steve Whalen.

"They're giving me another chance. I'm rejoining Dazzle."

"Told you," says Steve. "You're back in the fold."

"Not all the way back in, not yet. I'm being tested."

I describe how, as a 'personal favor' for Viktor, I received the three girls at Logan. "They're in my house now, downstairs. A van is coming tomorrow night to pick them up."

"So Viktor does trust you," says Steve.

"And now I'm a sex trafficker."

"Nanny trafficker."

"It's not funny, Steve. Not for them."

"You still have the girls' passports?"

"Yes."

"Scan the ID pages from each of the passports and email the scans to me."

"What will you do with their IDs?"

"We'll keep an eye out for the girls."

"You'll keep an eye out. That's it?"

"If we extract them now, Krulik will know there's a leak in his organization. He'll conclude that it's you given your history and because you're the one who has them. In any case, since it appears that the girls entered the US voluntarily and legally, we couldn't support a charge of sex trafficking even if we *could* connect their entry to Krulik or Viktor."

"So?"

"Let it go, Jake. When the time is right, we'll pull them out."

"Meanwhile they'll be drugged, raped, prostituted."

"I'm very sorry about that, but we have to focus on our larger objective."

Twenty minutes later, my doorbell rings. On my doorstep is a bald, beefy heavy in a black leather jacket, the same one who searched me at Viktor's condo.

I let him in.

"Where are they?" he asks.

"In the kitchen, getting a bite to eat."

"Introduce me to them."

"It would help to know your name."

"Pavel."

I lead him to the kitchen. The girls are sitting around my kitchen table having sandwiches and apple juice.

They look up at the big guy standing behind me.

I say to Nika, "This is Pavel. He's here to help with your arrangements."

Nika looks him over. Then, with solemn formality, she says, "I am Nika."

Followed by the other two. "Caterina." "Gisele."

Maybe I'm imagining it, but I could swear there's a blush spreading over Pavel's cheeks and bald pate.

Nika asks, "You want sandwich?"

When Pavel doesn't reply, Nika says, "You sit with us."

He does as she says, placing his large body on the fourth seat at the table, and mumbling in Russian. The girls laugh.

"What did he say?" I ask Nika.

"He said Nika is bossy."

Thirty Nine

The girls are still asleep in their room when I creep downstairs.

Pavel is sitting in the living room, watching me come down.

"Everything okay?" I ask.

"Yes."

"I'm going out for a walk. Back soon."

He shrugs and I head out the door.

I'm not looking to go anywhere in particular, just to get outside. I walk down to the Charles, then along the river's edge for a couple of blocks towards MIT, then end up at a Starbucks where I get a cappuccino and read the *Boston Globe*, my old routine, savoring my time alone.

When I arrive back at my house, I discover that I have another visitor, Viktor Rost, in the living room with Pavel.

"Good morning, Jake," he says.

"Why are you here?" I ask, keeping my voice low.

"I won't stay long. I just had to see them for myself."

There's activity upstairs, voices, footsteps, the bedroom door opening and shutting, the guest bathroom door shutting, the shower running and toilet flushing.

Nika is the first to come downstairs. She nods hello to me and to Pavel, and looks curiously at Viktor.

"This is Viktor Rost," I tell her. "He is manager of the nanny agency. He came by to meet you before going to his office."

"My name is Nika Markov," she tells him. "I am pleased to meet you."

"Pleased to meet you too, Nika," says Viktor, staring at her like a *very* fond uncle.

"I make breakfast?" she asks.

"Go ahead," I say.

Caterina and Gisele come down the stairs together.

I put my hand up to stop them before they join Nika in the kitchen, then point to Viktor and say, "Viktor." Then I point towards each of them and they say their names in turn, "Caterina." "Gisele."

Viktor gazes avidly at the two girls like a glutton perusing a restaurant menu.

First he takes Caterina's hand in both of his and holds it as he repeats her name, savoring each syllable, "Cat-er-ina."

Then Gisele's hand, and her name rolls slowly off his tongue, like he can't bear to let it escape entirely, "Gis-ele."

Shyly, embarrassed, they avoid his gaze.

I ask Viktor, "Do you have anything to tell them?"

He stares at them for a moment then speaks to them in Russian. Caterina and Gisele keep their eyes down like serf girls being addressed by their master.

"What did you just say to them?" I ask.

"That I'm sure they will do very well in America."

At my front door, Viktor says, "The blond one, Caterina, she is perfect."

"Yeah, she's very attractive."

"I'll take the girls' passports."

I hand them to him and he looks at each of them in turn. He stares at Caterina's, repeating her name, "Caterina Zhuchuk."

Then, under his breath: "Nineteen! Perfect! Just perfect!"

He puts the passports in his pocket.

"Stay home today," he tells me. "Tonight, when the van arrives, make sure the girls are packed and ready to go. No fuss. No noise. No delays."

After breakfast, I go upstairs to my home office, leaving Pavel with the girls.

Not long after, I hear shouting and wailing, and the door to the girls' room slamming, and then hard knocking on my office door.

Nika stands in my doorway, hands on her hips, glaring.

"Come in," I say.

"No, I'll stay here."

"What's happening?"

"Pavel told us. We are not here to become nannies. We have to go to New York City."

I don't have a good answer to that, or any answer, so I don't say anything.

There's more crying in the girls' room while Nika holds her ground in my doorway. "I worked in store. Caterina was in school. Gisele lived on farm. We are good girls. They lied to us. You lied to us."

"Pavel shouldn't have upset you," I say.

"He answered my questions."
She turns to re-join Caterina and Gisele in their room.

Pavel is back at his post on the living room sofa. For a big man, he looks diminished, like he's been caught in a shameful act.
"You made the girls cry," I tell him.
He shrugs. "Nika asked me, when will we meet our employers to start being nannies? I told her, you are not here as nannies. I don't lie to women."

That night, Pavel places the girls' suitcases by the kitchen door.
Every now and again, Nika meets my eyes, hers questioning, imploring, and then, it seems to me, burning with hatred. Each time I look away. Nothing I can do.
At five minutes after eleven, the van rolls slowly down the alley to my house. There's enough ambient light, apparently, for the driver to navigate the alley without headlights, and the van is moving very quietly and slowly.
It's a plain white van, no lettering on the side or back, and no windows except in the front for the driver and passenger.
The van stops beside my parked car. The driver gets out, goes to the back of the van, and opens its rear door.
Pavel carries the girls' suitcases out and loads them into the van.
Nika stares at me for a long moment. Last chance, eye to eye, will I allow this to happen?
Again, I look away.
She leaves my kitchen, saying nothing. Caterina and Gisele follow.

At the foot of the steps to the alley, Nika spins back towards my house and spits.

I have been cursed, and I deserve it.

Through my kitchen window, I watch them climb into the back of the van.

The driver shuts and latches the door that locks them in.

Pavel climbs into the van on the passenger side, and pulls his door closed.

The van moves on down the alley, headlights off, almost soundless except for a soft rumble from its engine and crunching of its tires on the road.

Forty

Viktor reports that the girls were delivered in New York and Oleg Krulik is pleased.

"Glad I could help," I say.

"Also, the blond girl..."

"Caterina."

"Oleg is giving her to me. Not as a gift. She wasn't cheap. But worth it, don't you think?"

"It depends."

"Well, it's only money."

"What about Irina?"

"I don't have space in my condo for both her and Caterina. You can have her, at no cost."

"That's very generous of you, Viktor, but shouldn't I talk with her first?"

Viktor looks genuinely puzzled. "What about?"

"About what she wants to do."

"I tell her to go with you, she goes."

"I'd prefer that she's willing."

"Oleg's guys will keep her in line. There's nothing to worry about. She's yours."

"Still."

"Fine," says Viktor, vexed by my persistence. "I'll arrange for you to talk."

"Good."

I stand to leave his office.

"Wait a minute," he says.

I sit back down.

Viktor gives me his thin lipped smile. "You took care of the girls like I asked. You showed that I can rely on you, like before."

"I'm glad that you see it that way."

"So I re-activated your account at Island Bank and I deposited a little extra, another five thousand."

"You didn't have to do that."

"You don't want the money?"

"Of course, thank you, really, both for the money and for Irina."

Again I stand up to leave, and again he says, "Hold on."

"Okay."

"How'd you like a weekend in the Caribbean? Get a break from the cold?"

It's not all that cold outside, not yet, but definitely getting cooler. Mid-October in Massachusetts is bringing shorter days, falling leaves, temps at night dropping into the low forties. Winter is coming.

"I wouldn't mind it," I say.

"Antigua. It's beautiful this time of year. I need you to go down there, meet a new friend of ours who works for the government, Melford Smith. He's just been appointed as chairman of the national banking commission that oversees Island Bank. We need to establish our relationship with him, which can only be done in person, face-to-face. I'd do it, but I can't go. I've got personal business in New York, Caterina's coming out party. After Oleg shows her off, we'll be re-introduced, formally this time, and then get to know each other better."

"Something to look forward to," I say.

Viktor licks his lips. "You have no idea."

"About Melford Smith, tell me more about what you want me to do."

"You'll look him in the eye and tell him we are committed to Island Bank, one hundred percent. He'll look you in the eye and confirm that Island Bank is important to the economy of Antigua and as far as he is concerned, its operations there are legitimate, one hundred percent."

"Sounds simple enough."

"It is. Tell him that we appreciate his support. Then let him know an account number in Bank of South Florida, in Miami, where we've made a deposit for him. Read the account number to him. He'll write it down. Don't hand over any paper."

"I'm delivering a bribe."

"You have a problem with that?"

"Not at all. I'll do it."

Forty One

Stairs are wheeled to our plane for passengers to descend to the tarmac at Antigua's V.C. Bird International Airport for the short walk to the terminal. Stepping outside is like entering a sauna going at full blast. I feel sweat running down my sides and back, gluing my shirt to my body like I'd just worn it into a hot shower, and I'm squinting against the sun. Welcome to the tropics: Jacket off, sunglasses on.

The smooth divided road out of the airport soon gives way to potholed two-lane rural roads that my taxi shares with children and chickens and goats. We pass by wooden houses that appear well-tended and others that sag, dilapidated and unpainted; poor people's homes.

Then we turn down a manicured driveway into another world.

The Inn at English Harbour is a refuge of serenity under stately palm trees, cooled by soft breezes. Its fine dining restaurant is perched elegantly on a terrace that overlooks the blue Caribbean and the anchorage of elephantine yachts of the super-rich. My room has a gleaming mahogany floor and a giant bed and a private shaded veranda.

The perks of white collar crime!

Shortly before noon the next day, I take the boat-taxi across the harbor to Nelson's Dockyard, at one time the Caribbean base of Admiral Horatio Nelson.

A woman at the restaurant where I've arranged to meet Melford Smith for lunch tells me that Mr. Smith has already arrived and is seated at a table outside on the patio.

"Can you point him out to me, please?"

She does so. He's slender, has a light coffee complexion, and is sitting alone at a four-seater that's partially shaded by a sun umbrella.

"Mr. Smith," I say. "I'm Jacob Morais. I'm very glad to meet you."

We shake hands and he gestures for me to join him at his table. "Welcome to beautiful Antigua." His accent is British, flavored with a lilt of Caribbean.

"Wonderful to be here. Back in Massachusetts, no one's eating outdoors under palm trees."

I pick up a menu. "What do you recommend?"

"The grilled Mahi Mahi is good," he says. He glances towards a waiter who bustles over. We both order the Mahi Mahi.

We chat for a while about the historic Dockyard, about my fine accommodations at the Inn, and about several of the gigantic yachts in the harbor that have to be seen to be believed.

Now for business. I follow a script that I prepared on my way down to Antiqua.

"We're very pleased, Melford, that you've become chairman of the banking commission. Island Bank has done well in Antigua and we look forward to working with your commission as we have in the past."

"That is my wish as well," he says.

I wonder whether Melford is new to this like I am as we work our way through small talk garlanded with politesse. Perhaps, like me, he's also following a prepared script, unsure how exactly we'll get to our intended transaction. Or maybe he's done this many times and knows what to expect, and I'm the only newbie here.

I say, "I've come down here to assure you personally about our commitment to Antigua. Our CEO, Viktor Rost, wanted me to share this with you directly. He was sorry that he could not come himself due to an urgent business matter in New York."

"Well I'm glad you came, Jacob. I agree that it's important to meet in person."

"Are there any issues that we should know about?"

"Just the normal concerns about procedures to protect against abuse of the bank's charter, which I'm sure we can resolve."

"As you may know, Melford, we enjoyed an excellent relationship with your commission's former chairman. He kept us well informed about rumors that surface every now and again about our bank, as they do about other banks as well, so that we could deal with them directly."

"So I've heard," he says.

"I hope we can continue in the same way with you."

"That is also my hope," says Melford. "Our former chairman told me how much he valued his relationship with you."

The moment of truth. Is *valued his relationship* my cue to offer a token of our esteem?

I take the plunge. "We were glad to show our appreciation to the former chairman. We'd very much like to do so for you as well."

He doesn't reply. Is he wired? Will police materialize suddenly from behind pillars and bushes?

Now or never.

"Do you have paper and pen handy?" I ask.

"Of course," says Melford. He pulls a small notepad and a gold plated ballpoint pen from his shirt pocket.

I show him the sheet of paper on which I wrote his account number.

"Please write this down. It's an account number in a bank in Miami, the Bank of South Florida."

He doesn't say anything but his pen is poised over his notepad.

In case I'm being unclear, I add, "In your name, Melford."

He copies the number and inserts the notepad and pen back in his pocket.

I say, "We hope that when you have a moment to sign into that account, that you'll find everything to your liking."

Melford pushes back his chair, smiling apologetically. "Sorry, I must run," he says. "It was a pleasure to meet you, Jacob. Possibly I'll see you here in Antigua again."

He walks quickly out of the restaurant, just before our waiter comes by with our lunch, both Melford's and mine, and the bill.

Later, as I play back our interaction in my mind, it occurs to me that Melford Smith never said anything self-incriminating.

In fact, once we got down to business I was doing all the talking. Perhaps he suspected that we were being recorded. Perhaps he was doing the recording.

I try to relax.

I stretch out on a padded lounge chair on the private beach below the Inn, shaded by a large sun umbrella, nursing an iced drink that's continually refreshed by an attentive waiter, feeling the rustling breeze off the water, listening to waves lapping gently on the white sand. In the evening I indulge in an exquisitely presented dinner at the Inn's terrace restaurant. After nightfall I lie on my giant bed in my luxurious room with its view of the harbor and of the lights sparkling on the yachts.

Tropical paradise, all expenses paid, but I can't enjoy it. I'm on edge the whole time, expecting a call from the front desk that I have visitors who turn out to be Antiguan officials seeking to interrogate me about my interaction with Melford Smith, especially the part about the bank in Miami when I was the only one talking.

In the end, no one asks for me at the Inn, or approaches me at the airport, officials or otherwise.

I board my flight out of Antigua without anyone trying to stop me from leaving.

I arrive at Newark airport a few minutes early which gives me plenty of time for my connection to Boston.

The US customs officer places my passport on a reader and checks his monitor. His eyes linger there for an extra moment and he asks, "How long were you out of the country?"

"Two days, a quick weekend trip to Antigua."

"Purpose of your trip?"

"Business meeting."

"In Antigua?"

"Yes."

"Nice place to do business."

"Sure is."

He leans forward to see my suitcase.

"Is that all your luggage?"

"Yes."

"Wait here for a moment please sir."

"Is anything wrong?"

"Please wait here."

Two other customs officers arrive, one black, one white, both large and armed and wearing protective vests. The officer behind the window hands one of them my passport. The black customs officer says, "You Jacob Morais?"

"Yes."

"Please come with us."

"What's going on? I have a connecting flight."

"Won't take long."

They lead me to a small room with a table and chairs, grey-green walls that are bare except for an official photograph of the White House's resident moron, and a metal bookcase filled with official looking binders. They tell me to wait there, and then they leave, shutting the room's frosted glass door which is, I assume, locked from the outside.

Ten minutes later, the door re-opens, admitting FBI agents Reilly and Rivera.

"We missed you," says Reilly, as he and Rivera occupy two of the chairs on the other side of the table.

I look for sly hints, winks, or nudges that suggest they know about my connection with Steve Whalen, and find none. Evidently Steve has been true to his word and hasn't told them. As far as they're concerned, I'm the same Jacob Morais they were harassing before I went missing.

"I needed to get away to collect my thoughts."

"Well, that's in the past," says Reilly.

"My answer hasn't changed. I can't help you."

"Yeah, but soon as you returned from wherever the fuck for three months, you went straight back to Viktor Rost like you still don't care what he and Krulik are up to. What's that about?"

"I work at Dazzle for a living. Viktor is my boss."

"So let's talk about your latest trip. Tell us about Antigua."

"What do you want to know?"

"Were you down there on business?"

"Yes."

"You met with an official who regulates banks in Antigua?"

"Yes. How did you know?"

Ignoring my question, agent Rivera asks, "Did you give him a bribe?"

"Are you charging me? Or is that just a friendly question?"

"How about you answer it?"

"No, I didn't, and if you keep asking questions like that one, I'll need to get a lawyer."

"Lawyer up if you want. But your life will be a lot less complicated when we're on the same side. Otherwise..." He spreads his arms to encompass the four corners of our small grey-green room. "...this."

"Harassment."

"You're making this harder than it needs to be.

"Let's get to the point," I say. "You still want me to wear a wire?"

"That's the plan," Reilly replies. "They're miniaturized. So you'll be fine."

"Not going to happen."

"Yeah, it will, hopefully for your sake before your sell-by date. It will be easier for everyone when you stop jerking us around."

"I'm not the one doing the jerking."

"Fuck it," Reilly says. He pushes a business card towards me across the table. "For when you stop playing the fool."

I make a big show of picking up Reilly's card with my fingertips, scanning it carefully as if it might impart interesting new information, and then very slowly placing it back on the table, face down.

"You gave one of these to me earlier," I say. "You came down to Newark for no reason."

"Don't wait too long before you decide to call me," replies Reilly.

Rivera mouths the words, "Perp walk."

They close the door behind them.

Now I'm stuck in the room with nothing to do but wait. I test the door which is locked, as I suspected. My cell is useless; no signal. I finish the last eighty pages of a book that I brought with me. I lean back in the chair with my feet on the table to take a nap. I've missed my connection to Boston.

The door opens to admit the two customs officers.

"I've been here for two hours," I say. "Did you forget about me?"

"No," says the white officer, declining to comment further. There are thoughts and feelings that I want very strongly to share with him, but I manage to keep them to myself.

"We need to examine your suitcase and briefcase," the black officer says. He places a plastic tray on the table. "Empty your pockets into this, and take off your jacket and shoes."

Every item is lifted and turned and squeezed. The suitcase and briefcase are swabbed, flipped upside down, and shaken.

The white officer tells me to raise my arms. Then he wands me and makes doubly sure by vigorously patting me down.

"You have a laptop?"

"I didn't bring it. Short trip."

"You mind if we take a look at your phone?"

"Help yourself," I say, and pass my phone to him after unlocking it with my password.

Whatever they're looking for, they won't find. Fortunately I've cleaned out all implicating text threads and email messages.

They leave with my phone.

After twenty minutes or so, the white officer re-enters the room and returns my phone to me.

"You're free to go, Mr. Morais. Sorry for the inconvenience."

Forty Two

I knock on Viktor's open door. "Thought I'd update you on my meeting with Melford Smith."

"Yeah, tell me," he says.

I describe our meeting in the restaurant and Melford's acceptance of his new bank account in Miami.

He's slumped in his chair, glancing at his monitor. "Okay, good. Anything else?"

"On my return, I was stopped by US Customs in Newark, and then held for questioning by FBI agents Reilly and Rivera."

He winces. "What did you tell them?"

"They already knew about my meeting in Antigua. They asked whether I delivered a bribe and I told them no. Then they left the room and two customs officers arrived to search me and my bags."

"Did they find anything?"

"Nothing to find, Viktor. I'm not stupid."

"Right."

"But the thing is, how did the FBI know that I was going to Antigua and meeting Melford Smith, and the itinerary of my return flight that connected through Newark?"

"You're on their watch list, like me and Oleg. They learn you're heading to Antigua and they get their people down there to track who you meet. They've got nothing on us."

"What about when Melford accesses his new bank account?"

"So what? Lots of people in the Caribbean have bank accounts in Miami."

"But you opened the account for him."

"The account was opened by a name they won't recognize, and money was wired into the account from a shell company based elsewhere that has owners they can't identify. Not a problem."

Viktor's gloomy expression belies his reassuring words.

"You seem pre-occupied," I say. "What's going on?"

"I don't want to talk about it."

"Okay." I start to get up from my chair.

"Just a minute."

After a pause, he says, "New York was bad. Caterina made a big scene about how she was saving herself for her husband, that she was 'good girl,' she kept saying, over and over. That she came to America to be a nanny. That she wanted to go home."

"Are you sending her back to Ukraine?"

"Fuck that. She's mine. I'll have her."

"Right."

"Fucking Nika. She's been getting Caterina all upset. We should never let them stay together in New York. She's a pain, and she's ugly, and with her bad attitude, no one wants her anyway."

"So, you'll send Nika back."

"Too risky. Oleg is shipping her to Miami where they'll teach her manners. If she gives them trouble, they'll sell her organs. We won't take a financial hit, at least."

My face must be revealing less than enthusiastic approval because Viktor senses that I need reassurance.

"It's just business, Jake."

"Sure."

He says, "And as for Irina..."

"Staying with you for now?"

"For now, but not much longer. She figured out she's being replaced. You'll have her soon enough, assuming that you'll take her."

He looks so vexed about Caterina that I just know that he wants me raise another quibble about his generous offer so he'll have an excuse to lash out.

"Of course I'll take Irina."

"Otherwise I'll ship her ass to Miami, along with Nika."

"I'll take her, Viktor, thank you."

Forty Three

My text to Steve Whalen: "One hour, meet Nanook at Hometown Book House."

'Okay," replies Steve. Being a Grand Master in multi-dimensional Scrabble, he'll have no trouble decrypting my code.

I take the Red Line to Alewife, the end of the line where the western edge of Cambridge touches the leafy suburbs. I have my subway car almost to myself, except for a middle aged woman at the other end who is concentrating on her phone. From Alewife, I take a taxi to Winchester's town center.

Seeing no one who appears out of place on the street, I walk up to the town pond. There are benches on the grass facing the pond. I stop at one of them to look around again, casually, like a spy in the movies.

Again, I see no one who makes me uneasy.

I walk up to the Winchester Library Inside, a reference librarian asks, "Can I help you?"

"I'm meeting a friend named Steve."

"What is your name, please?"

"Nanook."

"Love the name," she says, not unkindly, peering at me over her glasses. Given that she's about my age and working in Winchester; we could have been at WHS at the same time. Should I recognize her? Should I ask? Anyway, I don't. This isn't the time or place.

"He's waiting for you in a study room on the second floor, at the top of the stairs."

"What have you learned?" asks Steve.

"Reilly and Rivera knew about my trip to Antigua and were waiting for me in Newark airport when I came through on my return flight. They had me locked in a small room for hours, tried to browbeat me. And when I got back and told Viktor about it he didn't seem nearly as amazed as I thought he'd be, like maybe he has his own sources. Although to be fair, he did have other things on his mind."

Steve says, "The agents believe you'll cooperate once they push you hard enough. They're just doing their job. If they knew you were working with me, they'd leave you alone except to help where they can. Say the word, I'll let them know."

"Don't."

"Okay, up to you."

"Given that the FBI knew what I was doing in Antigua, maybe others in Antigua knew as well, including enemies of the official I met. I could have ended up in jail down there."

"That would be a definite bummer," says Steve, sounding not nearly disturbed enough by this scenario.

"Would you have gotten me out?"

He ponders for a moment. "It depends."

"On what?"

"We'd let Viktor try first. If he failed, or washed his hands of you, then we'd do what we could."

"You'd leave me locked up in an Antiguan jail."

"Hypothetically, but in the real world, the main thing is that we're making progress."

"Hell with that, we're done."

"What do you mean, done?"

"I'm out, finished. I've got a target on my back and you don't give a shit."

"You can't quit now," Steve says. "Not when we're getting close."

I hand him a scrap of paper.

"Here is Melford Smith's account number at the Bank of South Florida. Arrest him when he accesses the account, and use him to get at the bank and at Krulik."

"That's not enough. We're not after Melford Smith. We wouldn't be able to trace the bribe back to Krulik. You're the one who gave him the account number, don't forget."

"Where are my John Dobby IDs?"

"They're coming."

"I want them now, in case I need to run."

"Give us a few more days," says Steve.

I go along with it. I really want those authentic government-issued John Dobby documents. I can wait a few more days, if I have to.

"So I'm back with Viktor," I say. "Now what?"

"Now we'll turn him against Oleg Krulik."

"How?"

"We need to find the right buttons to push," Steve says. "Which is where you come in."

"Why me? I don't have a clue where to start."

"You know both of them. You'll figure it out."

Forty Four

Dazzle's workspace feels empty after the layoffs. Only a couple of employees lounge at work tables that are sized to accommodate eight or more. There's not much for anyone to do. Neither Viktor nor the board will invest in our e-commerce platform. Why bother, while high volume buyers from Russia continue to shovel money into the company?

Our ping pong table is in constant use. The eatery is hopping all day. The beer keg needs frequent refilling. Employees wander around, exchanging jokes and gossip.

Viktor doesn't schedule meetings with his exec team. He has nothing to tell us and we have nothing to report.

The only reason that we have any staff at all is that Dazzle needs to keep up appearances as an ongoing business.

I play my part in the charade. Each day I arrive at work around mid-morning and pretend to do my job. I scan competitors' websites for ideas, catch up on news involving e-commerce businesses, and then, to recover from my exertions, repair to the eatery for snacks and chit-chat with others who are engaged similarly in hanging about.

Most days Viktor doesn't arrive until after lunch and then he holes up in his office with his door shut.

About a week after my return from Antigua, and feeling restless, I drop by Viktor's office when I see that he's gotten off the phone.

"What's on your mind?" he asks.

"Nothing much. I'm just curious about how things are going with Caterina."

"Better. Oleg told me that she's more open to getting schooled now that Nika is gone."

"Okay, glad to hear it."

"You want to come with me to New York? You'll see where the girls ended up, except of course for Nika, and you'll have a good time."

"Great, thanks!"

"Yeah, so when the next shipment of girls arrives, you'll have a better idea how you fit in."

44 Amity Street is a brown brick townhouse on a tree lined street in Brooklyn. Its entrance is twelve white stone steps up from the sidewalk. On either side of the steps, there are black iron handrails over black balusters shaped like urns. The double front door at the entrance is dark mahogany, recessed under a white stone portico, between ornate fluted white pilasters. Curtains are drawn in all of the windows facing the street so that no light escapes from inside.

From the outside, 44 Amity Street looks like a bastion of respectability.

Inside the front vestibule, I hear muffled voices, occasional shouts, laughter, and a track of classical piano favorites, and I see red lights shining through a cigar smoke haze.

Krulik's two heavies, Pavel and the other one whose name I don't know, are checking a visitor ahead of me. The man takes off his suit jacket and places it in a wicker basket being held by the no-name heavy, and then unclips his cellphone from his belt holder and drops it in the basket as well. He's allowed to proceed on through after Pavel passes a wand over his arms, torso, groin and legs, and finds nothing objectionable.

I'm next.

Pavel nods hello, and I nod back. A large bandage circles his head, over his right ear.

"What happened to your ear?" I ask.

"Accident."

"You okay?"

"Yeah." He examines my invitation. "You have photo ID?"

Rather than observing that obviously he knows who I am, I hand him my Massachusetts driver's license. There are rules he has to follow.

He reads and returns it without comment.

"You need to take off your jacket and give us your cellphone."

I place them in a small wicker basket held out by no-name.

"You'll get them back when you leave," says Pavel. "Any other cameras or electronics?"

"No."

No-name passes the wand over my torso and limbs. No beeps or buzzes.

"You may enter," says Pavel.

"Are the girls here?"

A grimace passes across his face like he's been jabbed. "Except for Nika."

The front room has a fireplace and probably once served as a living room. Towards the back it flows into another room, probably formerly a dining room. Each room is lined with sofas and loveseats and has pillows on the floors.

Girls carrying trays of snacks and flutes of champagne circulate amongst the guests. All are naked except for thin panties that are essentially transparent.

In addition there are girls with guests on the sofas and reclining on pillows, while others huddle together, silently, like tethered goats.

The male guests, all of them older, fatter, and hairier than the girls, ogle and grope the servers when they come within reach, pat their rears, cup their bare breasts. On one of the sofas, a man whom I recognize from his bloated artificially-tanned face and his yellow-tinted comb-over as a New York real estate developer who's been in the tabloids, has pulled one of the girls towards him. She stands compliantly before him as he grabs her buttocks. Then he yanks her panties down and draws her in. She undulates her hips into his face, automatically, her eyes blank. A second girl, this one sitting on the sofa beside the man, leans over to take in her mouth his small semi-flaccid penis that's almost hidden by the flab of his overhanging belly.

A few feet away a girl braces herself against a side table as a guest penetrates her from behind.

Viktor touches my arm.

"Quite a scene," he says.

"Yeah."

"If you want to take one upstairs, you only have to ask," he says. "She'll go with you. Lots of rooms up there where you can do whatever you want."

"Looks like they're already doing what they want down here."

"They're just getting warmed up. You want one?" He grabs the arm of a girl who's passing by. "Make my friend happy," he tells her.

She doesn't say anything, just presses her bare breasts against my arm and reaches for my crotch.

I pull away. "Not now," I say. She moves on, unbothered by my rejection, like she's in a daze.

"Not in the mood?" asks Viktor.

"Of course I am. Just trying to decide what I want to do first."

"Yeah. Lots of choices."

"Have you seen Caterina?"

"She's around," he replies, vaguely. Then he adds, "Back near the kitchen. Oleg is educating her."

"Does that bother you?"

Viktor shrugs. "I'll have her to myself after he loosens her up. She'll get into it. They all do. It was the same with Irina."

"What about Gisele?"

"She's very popular. Already upstairs with her second guest tonight."

Viktor looks over my shoulder and mutters about refilling his drink. As he turns away, I remember to ask, "What happened to Pavel?"

"You mean the bandage? His ear got cut off."

"How?"

"With a razor. Oleg told him to put Nika into a van to go to Miami. Nika didn't want to go and Pavel objected to making her. Oleg doesn't like it when his people object."

"So they cut off his ear?"

"Not 'they.' Oleg did it himself as a lesson, with Nika watching, so it was a lesson also for her."

"Pavel is a big man. Why did he submit?"

"Gun at his head. Also family back in Kiev where Oleg can get them. Anyway, that's all done now. Nika is gone. Pavel won't object anymore."

As Viktor says, Caterina is sitting with Krulik on a loveseat near the door to the kitchen. Like the others, she wears only panties. Her knees are pressed primly together and she's staring straight ahead at nothing in particular, a pink porcelain doll with blank powder blue eyes.

Krulik is leaning his large sweaty face close to her ear. Perhaps he's whispering endearments. He's thrusted one of his hands down between her legs.

She looks towards me.

"Fuck off," snarls Krulik.

I do fuck off, back to the front living area.

To be brutally honest, there's a nasty part of me that's turned on by all the naked girls. One knows one shouldn't look, but one does. At the same time, there's another part of me that yearns to grab a fireplace poker and smash the abusers' grotesque piggish faces, starting with Krulik's. However, I'm well aware that I lack a trained fighter's particular set of skills. No question, my noble gesture would end badly. I resist the urge.

Also I'm nauseated by the cigar smoke.

At the front door, I ask Pavel for my jacket and cellphone.

.

I text the Amity Street address to Steve Whalen with a brief description of what I saw there. "Caterina, Gisele, and other girls abused by Krulik and guests."

Steve texts back: "Did you witness violence?"

"No. Abuse. Girls look drugged."

"Consensual?"

"Not really. Coerced."

"But no violence?"

"Not that I saw."

"Already aware of 44 Amity. But thanks for heads-up."

"That's it?"

"For now."

"Viktor says if Nika causes them trouble down in Miami, they'll sell her organs.

"After we get Krulik, we'll rescue Nika and the other girls."

"If she's hurt, it's on you."

"I realize that," replies Steve.

Forty Five

There's a handwritten note that was dropped through my front door mail slot: "Call me. AK."

Annie picks up on the first ring.

"Jake!"

"I got your note."

"I'm so glad you called!"

"Of course I called, Annie. What's going on?"

"Caleb told me everything."

"What do you mean?"

"I'm sorry I misjudged you."

"What did he tell you?"

"You're with us, not with those bastards."

I'm too stunned to reply. Aren't justices on the U.S. Supreme Court supposed to be discreet?

"Don't blame Caleb," Annie says. "He defended you when I complained about what a traitor you were, and I wormed it out of him."

"Whatever he told you about me is wishful thinking. Don't believe it."

"He said you came to his house when you returned from California, and Sophie's brother Steve was there, and that you're working with Steve."

"Well, he's mistaken."

"He told me you'd deny it."

"Look, whether you believe me or not, at least promise that you won't breathe a word to anyone about this. It would put yourself, and me, at grave risk."

"I want to help."

"There's nothing you can do."

"Sophie was my friend. So I'm in, no matter what you say."

"Well... I'll think about it."

"Thank you."

After a pause, when neither of us ends the call, I say, "It's good to hear your voice."

"Yours too, Jake."

Viktor phones me from New York to report his stunning success with Caterina.

"She was all over me!" he exults. "I was coming like a fucking fountain."

"So are you bringing her back with you?"

"Yeah, and Irina can't be in my condo when we arrive. It would spoil the mood with Caterina."

"You want me to take Irina now?"

"Yeah, get her out of there by early afternoon at the latest."

"I will, Viktor."

"She will give you a lot of pleasure."

"I'm sure."

The penetrating October breeze when I go to pick up Irina at Viktor's condo is a bracing harbinger of the oncoming winter.

My welcome from Irina isn't any warmer.

I press the button for 'V. Rost' at the entrance to his condo building.

No response.

I press it again.

This time I hear her voice through the tinny speaker below the condo buttons.

"Who is it?"

"Jake Morais."

"Go away!"

"Didn't Viktor tell you I was coming?"

"I know nothing about that."

"I think you do," I say. "Viktor won't be happy if he hears you won't let me in."

A pause, then her voice on the speaker, "Okay," and the entrance door buzzes.

She's left ajar the door into Viktor's condo so I knock twice and enter.

Irina is sitting by the French doors out to the deck. Her long model's body is dressed in high style, ballet slippers, designer jeans, satiny tank top. Her violet eyes are ringed and tragic.

"Why is Viktor doing this to me?" she demands. "What have I done wrong?"

"Nothing, Irina," I say. "You've done nothing wrong. Viktor just wants to move on."

"He has another girl."

"Yes."

"I am feeling sick," Irina says. She stands up and pulls on a wool jacket. "I need to go outside to the deck for fresh air."

I follow her out.

I stand next to her looking out towards the harbor and Irina whispers hoarsely, "Keep your voice low. Don't turn around. Viktor put cameras in the condo."

"Where?"

"In every room. He likes to watch."

"Kinky!"

"I hate him. I want to kill him."

"Because he has a new girl?"

"Don't be stupid."

"I'm confused."

"You understand nothing."

"I'm trying, Irina. I'll do what I can for you, like I promised."

"Where is my passport?"

"I don't have it. I'm sorry."

"I want to go home to Ukraine."

"What if Krulik sends his men after you?"

"I have a big family. They will protect me."

"When Viktor gives me your passport, I'll hand it over to you."

"What if he doesn't give it to you?"

For that I don't have a good answer. But then it occurs to me that if Steve Whalen's Homeland Security can create official IDs for John Dobby, it can do the same for Irina.

"Then we'll have a new passport made for you."

"I am not going with you!"

"We have to go. Viktor is on his way back here."

"You want to take me to your house to fuck me."

"I won't touch you. You'll be safe in my house."

"Like Nika, and Gisele, and little Caterina were safe? Until you put them in a van to New York to be raped by Krulik and his pigs? Like they raped me before? Don't look surprised. Viktor told me. He was boasting."

"There was nothing I could do."

"And they will come for me also if I am in your house. They'll come to ship me back to Krulik and again you'll do nothing."

"We'll figure out how to keep you safe."

Irina says nothing for a moment, possibly considering her options, then: "I will go with you. For a short time. And no fucking."

"Deal!"

Our Yellow Cab is cutting through downtown Boston on our way to Cambridge when I tell our driver to pull over on Milk Street and wait for us.

"How long?" he asks. "There's no parking here. I could get a ticket."

"Couple of minutes, max."

He sighs operatically but does as I ask.

"I'm expecting a major tip."

"Which you'll receive."

"Better believe it."

I lead Irina into the nearby CVS.

"We need passport photos for my friend," I tell the young man behind the counter.

There's a basket of thumb drives on the counter. I take one of them and hand it to the young man. "Plug this in and copy the photo onto it. We'll pay extra for the digital copy, in cash."

Five minutes later we're out of the CVS.

The cab is still in the same spot. The driver has reclined his seat and is reading a *Boston Herald.*

"All done?" he asks, as we slide into the back seat.

"Yeah, thanks. On to Cambridge."

While Irina is unpacking in my guest bedroom, I text Steve that we need to talk.

When he calls my cell, I tell him that Irina is in my house and needs protection.

"She expects Krulik will ship her down to New York. She's probably right and I can't let that happen. To go home to Ukraine, she needs her passport which Viktor probably won't give me, so she'll need a replacement from you, and also meanwhile a safe house where she can stay."

"Okay, send me her info and a photo for the passport."

"What about a place for her to stay?"

"Don't get your hopes up on that."

"Don't you have safe houses?"

"You've been watching too much TV."

"Then what do you suggest? Krulik could send his thugs at any time."

"Normally I'd tell you to take Irina to the police but that would blow up everything we've been working on."

"So you're telling me tough noogies and good luck."

"I'll look into it, but no promises."

I call Annie.

"You said you wanted to help. I've reconsidered. Maybe there *is* something you can do. But what I'm asking will be dangerous for you."

"Just tell me."

"Come to my house tonight and I'll explain."

"I'll be there."

"Come via the back alley. Stay in the shadows. Text me when you get close and I'll let you in."

"Okay."

"And wear a hood if you have one."

"Are you trying to scare me?"

"Just trying to be careful, Annie."

I snap my Glock into my shoulder holster. From now on I'll have it on me while I'm at home. Next time, I'll be ready for Viktor's mullet-wearing bottom-dwellers. Nor will I stand aside to allow Krulik's heavies to bundle Irina into the back of a van. Fortunately the weather is cooler now so it doesn't look odd for me to wear a jacket that conceals the holster.

I'll need a more accessible hiding place for the Glock while I'm asleep.

Maybe a shoebox under my bed.

Forty Six

Around eleven o'clock that night, Annie arrives in the alley behind my house wearing dark jeans and a dark jacket with a hood that renders her almost invisible in the darkness. Before opening the door, I switch off my kitchen lights to make it harder for anyone watching to see her coming in.

It's the first time I've seen her since the barbeque at Sophie's and Caleb's house, a lifetime ago. She gives me a wicked co-conspiratorial grin, ready for adventure. I'd love to get started on hugging but we have business to attend to.

Speaking softly so that Irina won't overhear, I summarize for Annie the situation at Dazzle and Island Bank, and with the three Ukrainian girls.

"You helped them traffick those poor girls?"

"I had no choice. I'm weaseling my way back into Viktor's circle of trust. Steve Whalen promises the girls will be rescued once we've dealt with Viktor and Krulik."

Annie's eyebrows rise, appalled, or impressed, I can't tell which, maybe both. "You're actually a spy, for real!"

"So it would seem."

"How can I help?"

"My guest upstairs is Viktor's former girlfriend, or possession, since she had no say in the matter. Her name is Irina. Viktor passed her along to me after replacing her with Caterina, one of the three girls who were staying here, who's much younger."

"Of course."

"Irina wants to return to her home in Ukraine. She can't leave right away because she has no documents. She's terrified that Krulik will send his hoodlums to take her back to New York where they'll force drugs on her and prostitute her to their clients."

Annie understands where I'm heading with this. "She can stay with me. She'll camp in the room that I use as a studio."

"Are you sure? If they find out where she is, they'll come after you."

"I'm sure. Now I'd like to meet her."

Annie waits in the living room while I head upstairs to get Irina.

I knock gently on the guest bedroom door.

"Irina, are you awake? I want you to meet my friend Annie."

"You're lying. Go away."

Rather than stand out in the hallway trying to convince her that I'm not planning to rape her, I call down to Annie.

"Can you come up to talk to Irina?"

With Annie beside me, I knock again.

Annie says, "Hi Irina, my name is Annie. I am a friend of Jake's. I'd like very much to meet you."

Shuffling sounds inside the room. The lock is turned. The door is cracked open. Irina looks out at me and at Annie, and then past us checking whether anyone else is on the landing.

Seeing no one else, she pulls the door all the way open and steps out. Tall and thin in a clingy white silk nightgown, her dramatic appearance is accentuated by her woeful violet eyes and downturned lips.

"No one can help me."

"Let's talk about it downstairs," says Annie.

I brew tea while Annie and Irina get acquainted in the living room. I hear Irina laugh, a sound that I haven't heard before.

Both of them go silent as I carry in a tray with a pot of tea and three mugs.

"What were you talking about?" I ask.

"Irina told me what happened at Viktor's party when you were sent to her bedroom."

"When you didn't fuck me," Irina says, clarifying.

"It didn't seem right. Even though I was very tempted."

Annie nods. "Such a gentleman!"

I bow my head, modestly accepting her praise, and then ask, "Have you talked about where Irina will stay?"

"We were just getting to that." Annie turns to Irina. "You're welcome to stay in my condo in Boston until you get the documents you need to return to Ukraine. Please say yes, Irina. You'll be very welcome."

Tears well in Irina's eyes and she starts sobbing. "Why are you so kind to me?"

Annie passes Irina a napkin to dab her eyes. "Because we're on the same side against evil men who murdered a good friend of mine and Jake's."

"Did Viktor murder?"

"Viktor, or Krulik, or both, we don't know for sure," I say.

"They are both pigs."

"You can help us, Irina."

"How?"

"To start, do you know the combinations to open the door into Viktor's condo building and the door into his condo?"

"Yes."

"Please write them down." I hand her a small notebook and a ballpoint pen. After she scrawls the combos, I say, "And also your information for a new passport, your full name, place and date of birth, height, eye color, and your signature."

When she finishes with that, I say, "Now, also, can you write down what happened to you from the time you were recruited to come to the US from your town in Ukraine, until Viktor brought you to his condo, including names of everyone involved? This will help to build a case."

"Now? In this little notebook?"

"You can use a laptop computer in my condo," says Annie.

"Do you know how to use a laptop?" I ask Irina.

"I'm not a child," she replies in a haughty tone, handing me back the notebook and ballpoint pen.

"Of course not," I say. "And, one last thing…"

Annie cuts in, "Give the girl a break, Jake. She's had a hard day."

Irina puts her hand on Annie's knee. "It's okay."

"Final question, did you learn the combination to Viktor's safe?"

Irina smiles. "He was high on cocaine and I was giving him pleasure, so he didn't push me away when he went into the safe for more drugs. I watched him."

I open the notebook to a blank page and hold my pen ready. "Tell us."

She closes her eyes to think.

"He spun the dial. First left four times and stopped at 51, then right to 12, then two or maybe three times to the left and stopped at 37."

I jot all that down in the notebook.

"You're fantastic!" I tell her.

Irina smiles again and Annie takes her hand in sisterly approval.

I ask, "Were you able to get into the safe when Viktor was away?"

"I couldn't," she says. "Because of the cameras."

"We'll have to deal with that."

"What are you thinking?" Annie asks. "That you're going to break into Viktor's condo?"

"I want to see what's in that safe."

Irina yawns. "Do I go with Annie now?"

"No, tonight you'll stay here. I'll report to Viktor that you're here, safe and sound, and that we're having a great time together."

"Fucking."

"We get it," Annie says. "Enough with the fucking!"

Irina laughs, again, a throaty chuckle that's surprising coming from someone so tall and languid.

"Tomorrow night," I tell her, "you'll go to Annie's."

Forty Seven

"Did Irina give you problems when you went to pick her up?" asks Viktor.

"At first she was upset," I say. "So we talked for a while out on the deck, to calm her down, and after that she was okay. She collected her bags, and we left."

"Talked about what?"

"About you, mostly. She was sad that she wouldn't see you anymore. But she realizes there's nothing she can do about it. I think we'll get along fine."

"What did she say about me?"

"That she admires you even though she feels you weren't always nice to her. She thinks you are a very strong person, very manly."

Viktor smiles. "Women prefer strong men. Certainly with me, she knew who was boss."

"So, Viktor, you know Irina. What should I do? Do you have any suggestions?"

"Tell her what you want. You want it, she says yes. She thinks she's special and she is, but you're more special, and she has to know that."

"Good point."

"You'll enjoy her."

"Maybe I'll go home early today so that we can practice how it's going to be."

"What about last night?" asks Viktor. "Did she please you?"

"She did, although we only did it once, just to break the ice. She was crying the whole time which actually was kind of a turn on."

"Yeah," says Viktor, thoughtfully, "the crying .. I like that too."

"How are things with you and Caterina?"

"When I make my wishes clear, she is very accommodating. *Very.*"

"Well, good, and thanks again for Irina."

"My pleasure."

"One thing I was wondering, now that I have Irina, whether I should also have her passport."

"Why do you want it?"

"Holding her passport will make it official, that she belongs to me."

Viktor scowls. "It's official enough."

"Okay, not a big deal."

"Besides," Viktor continues, "it's not like Irina will stay with you forever. There are many other beautiful girls. You'll need space for them when they arrive. We'll have to get Irina out of the way."

"I can make room for them as well as for Irina."

"We can't have Irina talking with the new girls. It would confuse them."

"I thought you gave Irina to me."

"I did, for a time. She's yours to enjoy while you have her. Nothing is permanent, Jake."

"When are more girls coming?"

"Soon."

I get up to leave and am almost out of Viktor's office when he says, "Obviously we cannot allow Irina to leave your house. My guys will make sure she doesn't."

I whirl back, "My house is being watched?"

"You have a problem with that?" asks Viktor, seemingly surprised by my reaction.

"Yeah, I do!"

"Believe me, Jake, we're all better off if Irina doesn't go missing because of how Oleg would react. My guys won't bother you. They're only there for insurance on Irina."

"Are they the same two dirtbags you sent after me earlier?"

"That's not nice."

"Just tell them to stay away from me."

"Don't worry. I'll tell them."

Steve Whalen says, when I call him, "I've got your John Dobby documents. And we're working on a new passport for Irina."

"Good, because I will not allow Krulik to take Irina. I'm moving her to safety tonight."

"How will you explain that to Viktor?"

"I'll say she ran away and that I have no idea where she is."

"He'll be suspicious."

"I'll try to be convincing."

"Have you learned anything useful from her?"

"A lot. She gave me the combinations to the door locks at Viktor's condo building, and the combo to Viktor's safe."

"Good work!"

"I'm expecting to find great stuff in that safe."

"*You're* expecting? I don't think so. This is a job for professionals. We'll send agents who know what they're doing."

"They'll be noticed. I've been in and out of there with Viktor and Irina so anyone who sees me will think nothing of it."

"You're sure?"

"Mostly sure. But if you keep asking, I'll entertain second thoughts."

"Never mind, you're on! You're perfect for the job. Go for it."

"I'll need your help to get Viktor out of town."

"That's doable."

"Also, Viktor has set up cameras in his condo that need to be disabled while I'm in there."

"I'll give you a signal disrupter," Steve says. "You can carry it in your pocket. As long as it's turned on, the cameras won't transmit."

Forty Eight

Irina watches silently as I open my kitchen door. It's dark in the alley, and quiet. The alley looks empty.

"You go first," I tell her in a low voice.

"Okay."

"Go left up the alley, turn left when you get to the street and walk up to Mass Ave, then turn right on Mass Ave. I'll follow behind you and catch up with you on Mass Ave."

She pulls her jacket hood over her head and slips out of the door. She sets off at a fast clip up the alley, making quick headway on her long legs. When she's gone about one hundred feet or so, I also step out, quietly shut the door behind me, and follow her.

I can see her approach the street at the end of the alley which is lit by streetlights. She's walking past a dumpster when a man emerges from the shadows, and she stops.

I approach them as quietly as I can, sticking to the side of the alley where it's darkest.

The man has his back towards the alley.

I'm able to get close enough to them to hear the man say, "You're the Russian whore."

"No," Irina replies. "You are mistaken. Don't bother me."

"I'll bother you all I want," the man says.

Irina must have seen me coming but she gives no sign, and the man doesn't turn around.

Gripping my Glock by the barrel, I smash the steel handgun butt against the back of the man's head producing a satisfying *thunk*. I would have preferred to use a rock but there's never one around when you need one.

The man drops to the ground hard, like a sack of sand. Now that I see his face, the pockmarked skin and scraggly goatee, I recognize him as the lowlife who pressed a gun into my stomach in front of my house, the same one whose image was caught on the security cam on the street where Sophie was attacked. His eyes have rolled back and blood dribbles from his nostrils and out of one of his ears. I can't tell whether he's still breathing. If he's not, so be it, no big loss to the world. I use the man's shirt to wipe his blood and hair off the butt of my Glock, taking care not to get any on my clothes.

I put my finger to my lips to caution Irina not to say anything, in case he's still alive and can hear.

There's no one around on the street and no cars passing by for the moment.

I tug his body back into the darkness of the alley, then motion Irina to grab his legs while I slide my arms under his from the back, trying not to gag from his rancid smell.

We lift him to the lip of the dumpster and heave him in. His body sinks between black plastic bags of trash.

"Is he dead?" whispers Irina.

"Don't know, don't care," I whisper back. "Let's go."

The man's partner must be stationed at the other end of the alley because we don't see him on our way to Mass Ave.

"Change of plan," I say. "You'll go to Annie's on your own. She is expecting you. I have to get back to my house before Viktor's guys realize what's happened."

Irina doesn't object. If she's shaken by our encounter with the man in the dumpster, she doesn't show it. She just looks determined.

"Will I see you again?"

"Yes, we still have to deal with Viktor. But meanwhile Annie will take care of you."

I find a scrap of paper in my pocket and write on it Annie's address and cell number as well as my own cell number. I pass the paper to Irina along with five twenties.

"For your taxi and a bit extra, just in case," I say.

I flag down a cab. As Irina climbs into the back seat, I tell the driver Annie's Pinckney Street address on Beacon Hill.

She gives me a little goodbye wave as they drive off.

I text Annie: "Irina in taxi on her way. She's alone. I need to tend to an issue at home."

Her text reply comes within seconds: "I'll look out for her."

Walking back into the alley, I hear movement in the dumpster, a rustling sound. Perhaps the man is still alive, or perhaps there are rats in the dumpster to keep him company. For the briefest of moments, I contemplate shooting him with my Glock just to make sure. But then I think better of it. A shot would be heard and reported, and a bullet might be traceable back to my handgun.

I avoid the dim patches of illumination in the alley as I make my way back to my house.

Fifteen minutes later, another text from Annie, "She's here. Told me what happened. Be careful."

At five a.m., I call Viktor's cell.

It rings a couple of times before he picks up. "What?"

He sounds groggy.

No time for apologies for waking him up. "Viktor!" I shout frantically into the phone, "We have a big problem!"

"What?" he repeats.

I'm having trouble breathing, too agitated almost to tell him the awful news: "Irina is gone!"

"What do you mean, *gone*?"

"She's not in the house. Her room is empty. I thought she liked what we were doing. She really seemed into it. Everything was fine when I left her room around midnight. I noticed when I got up this morning that her bedroom door was open, and she wasn't there. I've checked everywhere in the house. She must've slipped out while I was asleep. I don't know when she left. She could be anywhere. I don't know what to do."

What Viktor mutters in Russian is probably not complimentary.

"That's not all," I continue. "My wallet is empty. She took all my cash, three hundred plus dollars."

"Fuck the money. Oleg will go ballistic."

"Didn't you say my house was being watched? Why didn't your guys catch her?"

"That's what I intend to find out," says Viktor.

The line goes dead. I don't call him back.

Forty Nine

At around nine that morning while I'm on my way to work, my cell buzzes with a text from Viktor: "My office immediately you get in."

He receives me with a thunderous scowl, veins popping on his forehead like purple ant trails. "Took your fucking time."

"I was racking my brain about how I could have stopped Irina from leaving, what I could have done. She seemed okay to me. She gave no clue that she was going to run."

"She did more than just run. One of my men was found this morning in the alley behind your house, in a dumpster, unconscious, head smashed."

"Did anyone see how he got there?"

"Police aren't saying."

"Do you think Irina was involved?"

"Who the fuck knows?" He gives me a squinty look. "If she was, she had help. She couldn't have lifted him into the dumpster by herself. We'll find out more when he wakes up."

"Certainly hope so."

"I had to tell Oleg. Like I expected, he went raving crazy. He wants to kill someone. Totally crazy. Warned me, one more mistake, and…"

Viktor slices his hand across his throat.

"He told me I should've sent Irina back to him directly or dumped her in the Boston fucking harbor. He asked me why the fuck I gave her to the shitfuck Jake Morais, his exact words. And now I'm asking myself the same question."

"That is a fair question."

"You think?"

"Obviously I couldn't hold onto her. Maybe she liked me, like you said, but it wasn't enough to keep her in my house."

"You're too weak."

"You're right, Viktor. I'm too weak. I messed up. I'm sorry."

"You're not fucking forgiven."

Viktor is breathing hard, thinking about the situation, so I hang my head for a bit until he regains control, then I ask, meekly, "When Irina was with you, how did you make sure she didn't run off? And now Caterina, how are you doing it?"

"Fear," replies Viktor. "Irina feared me. Now Caterina does too. When I tell them stay, they stay. Also they have no ID, no money. Where would they go? They know they'll be found, and then they'll be very sorry."

"What about when you travel, like down to New York? How can you be sure that Caterina will still be in your condo when you get back?"

"You don't need the details. Let's just say, she wouldn't get far."

"Well, about Irina, she's gone," I say. "I'm sorry, but it happened. What do we do now?"

"No longer your concern. We'll find her and ship her down to New York. Oleg wants proof of death. He'll accept a body part so long as it's one she can't live without. He doesn't care about the rest."

"I liked her," I say.

"I did you a favor letting you have her, and you lost her, and now Oleg doubts me. So no more fucking favors."

"Okay."

"If this happens to me," again he slices his hand across his throat, "you'll get it too, count on it."

"I understand."

"Get out of my office."

Late that afternoon, I take the Red Line to Kendall Square, one stop before my usual stop in Central Square.

On the short walk to the nearby Marriott, I pause to re-tie my shoelaces and see no obvious evil doers on my tail.

Inside the Marriott, I take an elevator to the tenth floor, walk down a flight of stairs, than take another elevator from the ninth down to the fifth floor. I knock softly, twice, on the door to Room 512, where Steve Whalen said he'd be waiting for me.

Steve's room has the basic Marriott layout with a large king size bed, work desk, chest of drawers and minibar, sofa, and coffee table.

I take a spot on the sofa while Steve pulls the chair from the work desk over to the coffee table.

"So," he says. "What's the latest?"

I tell him that Irina is safe for now. He doesn't ask where she is. Maybe he already knows, being from Homeland Security. I leave out the part about clubbing the lowlife with my Glock and depositing his body in the dumpster.

I report that I'm now banished from Viktor's circle of trust. Also that Krulik says I'm a shitfuck.

"Some people are just fickle."

"Yeah. And Viktor believes Krulik will have him killed if he makes another mistake."

"Good to know."

Steve lays an envelope on the table. Inside I find a US passport for John Steven Dobby, born in 1974 in Rushmore County, New York State, as shown on the birth certificate that I provided to Steve for reference. Also a New York State driver's license, issued to John Dobby at his address in Sprightly Falls, New York. And a card in John Dobby's name from the Social Security Administration with his official nine digit SSN.

"Are these linked to entries in government databases?" I ask.

"Sure are! John Dobby is real!"

"What about Irina's passport?"

"Here."

The passport he holds in front of me is blue with a silver shield in the center. Over the shield is wording that I assume to be Ukrainian, and under the shield, in English, 'Passport Ukraine.'

Steve opens to the identity page, which shows Irina's photo from the CVS and the particulars for Irina Melnitsky that she provided to me.

"She'll be glad to get this," I say, and reach to take it.

He pulls it back.

"No, sorry, we can't let her leave the US just yet. We'll need her testimony against Viktor and Krulik."

"Irina is writing all that up."

"That's fine. Can't wait to see what she writes. But we also need her to testify in person at trial. We'll charge Krulik with sex trafficking and related crimes so that we can hold onto him while we unravel his money laundering network. Irina's testimony will help to make those charges stick."

"So she'll still be a prisoner."

"A witness, not a prisoner. We'll protect her. She'll be well treated. After the trial, we'll send her home, even pay for her ticket."

"Not good enough!"

"If she prefers, assuming she cooperates, we can offer permanent residency in the US."

"She'll want that in writing."

"Not a problem," says Steve. "Now, let me show you the signal disrupter."

He holds up a compact black device about the size and shape of a deck of cards, with an antenna tucked to the side.

"It's got two hours of battery life so turn it on only when you need it. Just lift the antenna from the side and press the ON button. It has a range of about three hundred feet, like typical WiFi signals and within its range, it will block all wireless transmissions from cameras or other sensors."

"We need Viktor to take a little trip outside Boston to give me time in his condo."

"We'll arrange that."

"And pull FBI surveillance off his condo. I don't to be seen there. Word would get back to Reilly and Rivera."

"Will do, Mr. Dobby. Agents will stay on Viktor's tail rather than watching his condo."

"Okay."

"Be ready to move tomorrow."

Fifty

Now that I have authentic John S. Dobby IDs for Plan B, Version Two, I deal with another issue, BLT Properties' questionable ongoing value as a shell company.

That evening, I use the same online incorporator as before to create a second shell company, which I call Guardian, LLC.

Like BLT Properties, it is based in Nevis.

Also as with BLT Properties, Guardian's beneficial owner, John S. Dobby of Sprightly Falls, NY, is not publicly identified in any of its founding documents, consistent with Nevis' privacy laws.

Unlike BLT Properties, Guardian won't be compromised by owning the building in Montreal where I'm living, and where Steve Whalen was able to track me down.

I don't know yet how I'll use Guardian, LLC, but it's comforting to have it available, just in case.

Fifty One

Next morning Viktor tells me that they still haven't found Irina. "That's not the worst of it. The bitch is talking to the FBI."

My look of alarm isn't entirely faked. Irina was supposed to stay out of sight in Annie's condo, not involve the FBI. *Especially* not the FBI!

I ask, "Does this mean I'm in trouble?"

"This isn't about you. FBI agents called on Oleg down in Brooklyn. They knocked on his front door with no warning. They told him that a person had contacted them and named names including his, and they wanted to ask him questions. Naturally he told them to fuck off, but…"

"Did they say it was Irina?"

"Who else would it be?"

"Maybe Pavel. Mr. Krulik did slice off his ear. That can make a person resentful."

Viktor pauses for a moment before rejecting my suggestion. "No, it was Irina. She's out there. She's fucking trouble."

"If you say so."

"Anyway, that's not the point. When Oleg called me last night to tell me about the FBI, we both heard clicks on the line, like we were being tapped."

"Holy shit! Are you sure?"

"It's not the first time, so we know what we heard. Now he wants me down in New York to talk in person where they won't be listening."

"Do you want me to come with you?"

"Not good for your health for Oleg to see you, not that I give a fuck about that. He could lose control and have me killed too, if we're together."

Viktor tears off to catch the ten fifteen Acela to New York City.

According to the Amtrak website, his train departs on time from South Station. I have to assume that he's on it.

I tell Brittany I'm going out for a walk to get fresh air, and that I can be reached on my cell if anyone calls.

I think I hear her say, "When the cat's away..." but she seems innocently busy at her desk when I glance back.

I meet Annie and Irina on the roof of the parking garage across from the New England Aquarium. Annie has found a space where she can see who else is around. At the moment, we have the garage roof to ourselves.

Our plan: I will accompany Irina to the entrance of Viktor's condo building but hug the side of the building so that I won't be seen by its surveillance camera. Annie will wait at the Starbucks one block up on Atlantic Avenue.

At Viktor's building, I activate the wireless signal disabler and after a second or two to let it do its thing, Irina presses the buzzer for Viktor's condo.

A woman's voice comes through the small speaker, "Yes?"

"Caterina?" asks Irina.

"Yes."

Then follows an exchange in Russian, or maybe Ukrainian, I can't tell the difference.

A buzzer sounds and Irina pulls the door open and enters. I slide in just behind her.

Irina takes the elevator to Viktor's third floor. I take the stairs so that we're not seen together by anyone who might be in the third floor hallway when the elevator door opens.

Irina knocks on Viktor's door. From my hiding spot down the hallway in the stairwell of the emergency stairs, I hear talking between her and Caterina. Whatever Irina says must be convincing since the two of them leave together, riding the elevator down to the ground floor. According to our plan, Irina will treat Caterina to lunch in the Rowes Wharf Sea Grill in the Boston Harbor Hotel, adjacent to Viktor's condo building.

As soon as their elevator begins its descent, I go to Viktor's door and enter its lock code. There's a click, unlocking the door.

No time to waste.

In the bedroom, I hold my breath while entering the combo to Viktor's safe, as recalled by Irina.

Spinning the dial left four times, stopping at 51, then right to 12, then two spins to the left, stopping at 37.

Doesn't work.

Not to panic. Irina may have made an error of a digit or two in her recollection of one of the numbers.

I test the first stop at 49, 50, 52, and 53. No luck.

Then return the first stop to 51, and test the second at 10, 11, 13, and 14. No.

Then the third stop at 36, and at 38. No.

Okay, maybe panic just a little.

I try other small changes to Irina's numbers, now in various combinations. The first number higher by one, the second number up by two, the third unchanged. The first number down one, the second still up by two, the third still unchanged. The first unchanged, the second down one, the third unchanged. And so on.

None of these changes works. I could be more systematic, but I haven't anticipated a problem with Irina's numbers, and I'm no longer thinking calmly.

Finally, about to give up, I re-read my notes of what Irina said as she recalled the combination.

Everything she said matches what I've been trying. Except that she wasn't sure about last spin of the dial. She recalled that for the third number, Viktor had spun the dial to the left twice, but maybe not, maybe it was three times.

For the final spin of the dial, I try three spins to the left, rather than two.

And hear a blissfully reassuring click.

Inside the safe there's a well-stuffed manila envelope, a handgun, a box of bullets, a large white envelope, and a leather change purse.

I take out the handgun, a Luger, and place it to one side along with its supply of bullets.

Inside the white envelope there are two thick packs of crisp hundred dollar bills, one hundred bills per pack, twenty thousand dollars total in cash.

Inside the change purse are plastic packets of white powder.

The manila envelope is jammed with papers, a notebook, a thumb drive, and three passports, two of them Ukrainian, Irina's and Caterina's, and one Russian, Viktor's.

I pile these items on the floor in the same order as they were packed in the envelope.

Then, using my cell, I take photos.

I'm photographing pages in the notebook when my phone vibrates, a call from Viktor.

"Hi Viktor," I say.

"Where the fuck are you?"

"Out taking a walk. Why?"

"I got an alert from my surveillance system. The cameras in my condo aren't transmitting."

"That's not good."

"If Caterina runs, I'm a dead man. And you are too."

"You should contact the management of your condo building. Or one of your neighbors. They can check..."

I hold my breath for Viktor's response.

"I don't want anyone talking with Caterina. Could get awkward."

I breathe again.

"You go make sure that she's there," says Viktor.

"I can't get into your building."

"Just buzz my condo from the entrance, find out if Caterina answers."

"She doesn't speak English."

"Doesn't matter. You don't need to have a conversation. Just confirm she's in there."

"Okay. I'm at the far end of the Seaport District. I'll need to find a cab."

"Make it fast. Let me know."

"Will do."

I speed up my already frantic photographing.

On one of the pages in the notebook, under the heading IB, there are handwritten entries, a word in Cyrillic followed by a colon, then another word in Cyrillic, then a line of phrases and numbers. Although I don't have time to study the notations, in my mind I'm doing a happy dance. Most likely these are logins and passwords for accounts at Island Bank.

Also there are pages listing names, mostly Russian, followed by amounts of US dollars, sorted in columns under Incoming, Outgoing, Current Balance, and Notes. The notes are written in Cyrillic. After each name, in brackets, there's a twelve digit number that looks like a bank account number.

I photograph each of these pages.

I debate pocketing the thumb drive. The files stored on it might answer a lot of questions. But I have to decide, would Viktor notice that it's missing?

What would I do if I were Viktor, having just returned to my condo after my surveillance system fails mysteriously? I'd interrogate Caterina. And I'd check my safe. And assuming there are sensitive files on the thumb drive, I'm pretty sure that I *would* notice that it's no longer there.

Too risky for me to take it with me.

I repack Viktor's safe with his thumb drive inside.

Annie saunters past Irina and Caterina's table at the Rowes Wharf Sea Grill, our signal to Irina that time is up.

Although Irina and Caterina haven't yet finished their seafood salads, Irina, glancing at her watch, says they have to hurry. At any moment Viktor might check on Caterina's whereabouts.

In the background, Annie takes care of their bill so that Irina and Caterina can push back from their table without waiting.

As we've rehearsed, Irina tells Caterina that if Viktor interrogates her about what happened while he was away, that she can describe their lunch together, and tell him that Irina just wanted to meet the young woman who replaced her, in order to give her advice about ways to make Viktor happy."

From my vantage point behind a pillar, I watch Irina escort Caterina back into the condo building. A minute later, I see her leave the building and stride towards the Starbucks a block away.

I turn off the wireless signal disrupter.

Then I jog to the condo building entrance, this time in full view of the building's camera, and press the buzzer for Viktor's condo.

"Yes?"

"Caterina?"

"Yes."

"It's Jacob Morais. Viktor asked me to check. Are you okay?"

"Yes. Okay."

I call Viktor.

"She's in the condo."

"Are you sure you talked with Caterina?"

"I think so."

He says, "Just a minute," and puts me on hold.

When he comes back to me, he says, "She's there. The cameras are working again."

I join Annie and Irina at the Starbucks.

"Success?" asks Annie.

I give her a thumbs-up. "I took a lot of photos. There's a lot to review."

I copy my photos of Viktor's documents from my phone to my PC.

From my PC, I upload a copy of the file to the Hightail large file transfer service, and text Steve to check for an email from Hightail that it's ready for him to download.

I store an encrypted copy of the file onto a thumb drive and deposit the thumb drive in my toiletries bag. Then I delete the file from my PC to sanitize it in case it falls into the wrong hands.

And I clean my phone, deleting all the photos and the text threads with Steve and Annie, and my recent phone call history, just in case Viktor asks to take a look.

There's so little trust nowadays, even among friends.

Fifty Two

According to Viktor, while he was in New York and his video cams weren't working, Irina came to his condo, introduced herself to Caterina, and invited Caterina out to lunch.

"Wow!" I exclaim. "Did Caterina go with her?"

"They went to the Rowes Wharf restaurant next door. Irina fed her a line about making me happy."

"I don't get it. Doesn't make sense. Why would Irina...?"

"Shut the fuck up!" he snaps, and locks on me his goggle-eyed stare.

"What?"

"Just tell me, were you involved?"

I am irate.

"I had nothing to do with it, I swear! How would I? I don't even know where Irina is. I haven't seen her since she took off from my house."

"Are you lying to me, Jake?"

"No."

"You said you liked her."

"Yeah, I did like her, and so did you! Jesus, Viktor, after all the grief she's caused us with Mr. Krulik, do you really think I'd have anything to do with her?"

"You told me Caterina was in the condo when you rang the buzzer."

"She was. Didn't you confirm that for yourself?"

"Yeah, but they were only half finished their lunch when Irina told her they had to leave. It was very sudden, Caterina said. And then somehow, like magic, just after she got back, she heard the buzzer and your voice asking if she was okay."

"And now you're accusing me! I did as you asked. Grabbed a cab, dashed to your condo building as fast as I could, and checked that Caterina was there. Also, let's remember that when you needed to check on Caterina, you sent me. You're down on me because of Irina, I understand that. I'm sorry for what happened. But I'm the only one here you can count on. You know that."

Finally, Viktor relents and averts his eyes.

"Oleg told me to ask, are you still getting contacts from FBI agents?"

"Not since my return from Antigua, at Newark."

"You sure?"

"I made myself very clear. I have nothing to tell them. Since then, I haven't heard from them."

He takes another moment to consider what I've told him, then says, "So Oleg and I agreed, we have a proposition for you: We're making you Dazzle CEO."

"What do you mean, CEO? Why?"

"Oleg is going away, maybe to Venezuela. I have other options. Maybe Venezuela, maybe somewhere else."

"You're leaving too?"

"Yeah, but we'll still control the business. You'll report to me remotely, and I'll report to Oleg. We'll work it out."

"I don't know…"

"Don't waste my time. You'll do it."

"But if you and Mr. Krulik are leaving, maybe I should go as well."

"No need. Irina's got the FBI investigating our business with the girls which is not your concern."

"Three of the girls stayed in my house."

"You were just doing me a favor. You thought they were here as nannies. Anyway, we're getting out of that business. We'll sell the ones we have, even make money on the deal."

"Including Caterina?"

"She'll fetch a good price," says Viktor. "Because of Irina, we're done with this business for now. But we can't give up on our clients who use Island Bank. They have big money at stake and long arms, and we must keep them happy. So you'll stay here for that."

"When are you and Mr. Krulik leaving?"

"Soon."

Fifty Three

Once I'm outside, I call Steve Whalen.

"Viktor and Krulik are spooked. They think the FBI is closing in on their sex trafficking. They're going to sell their girls and run. Viktor told me that I'll be appointed the new CEO at Dazzle to keep the Island Bank transactions going."

"Congrats on your promotion."

"Thank you."

"When are they planning to leave?"

"Viktor says soon, so you'd better act fast."

"We're already acting fast," says Steve. "I've got a team working on the documents from Viktor's safe. Turns out you found the motherlode. Names of Krulik's clients, how much money they sent to Island Bank, and when, and where it went afterwards, mostly to shell companies in the Caymans, Panama, and Antigua. Now that we've identified these companies we can trace the money further to investments in the US and elsewhere. It's amazing what we've got here. A detailed map of dirty money trails."

"Enough to put Krulik away?"

"We can't use these documents at trial. They weren't obtained legally, as you know."

"So get a warrant to search Viktor's condo. You'll find the originals in his safe. Plus even more, potentially. There was a thumb drive that I had to leave there."

"Too late now," Steve says. "If Viktor and Krulik are spooked, the docs are probably already gone. We need Viktor to testify. He's the key."

"He'll only testify if he believes Krulik is a threat to him."

"We're already part way there," says Steve. "Didn't Krulik warn Viktor that he'll tolerate no more mistakes?"

"So Viktor told me."

"Then, what additional transgression by Viktor would turn Krulik into his mortal enemy? What's the one thing that Krulik values above all else?"

"Money."

Silence on the line while we ponder.

Then, Steve says, "Viktor gave you an advance on your annual payout from your equity share in Island Bank."

"My one quarter of one percent."

"Right, and when you asked him about it, he told you he has discretion to allocate money from the Island Bank partners' general fund."

"And he also said that Krulik checks on what he does."

"What if Viktor were to take more than his share for himself?"

"He *could* do that. But Krulik would find out."

"Right," says Steve, "Thing is, would Krulik find it credible that Viktor would take the money?"

Warming to this scenario, I reply, "They're both preparing for life on the run. If Krulik discovers that Viktor took more than his share, he might conclude that Viktor figures that he can escape to his hideaway in time."

"You know Viktor. Would he actually steal from Krulik?"

"Never, ever, not in a million years," I say. "Viktor is terrified of Krulik."

"So, how do we make it happen?" asks Steve.

More pondering, and then the lightbulb goes off.

"We'll do the stealing for him," I say. "We'll pad Viktor's account. Krulik will be tipped to take a look. Viktor will discover too late that he's got all that money that doesn't belong to him and that Krulik won't believe his protests that he's innocent. They're thieves, after all. It's in their nature to steal. Then you step in to offer protection."

"Great idea. Start padding."

"Me?"

Steve intones, "The United States Department of Homeland Security would never…"

"So it's up to Nanook to do the funky stuff."

"With our totally deniable approval."

"You'll owe me."

"I'm adding to the tab as we speak."

"I'll need Viktor's Island Bank logins and passwords. The ones I saw in his notebook are written in Cyrillic and knowing Viktor, they're probably also in code, which I assume you've broken by now."

"Actually, we haven't," Steve replies, "His passwords are combos of Russian words and numbers. We tried them as written and they don't work, so you're right, he's using a code. We tested related words, synonyms, opposites, English translations, nothing working so far."

"Are you saying that Homeland Security is stumped?"

"Correct."

"Despite all your world class experts that are the best that billions in tax money can buy?"

"Yeah, despite all that."

"I can't pad Viktor's account without passwords that work."

"So why don't you take a crack at breaking his code? Get Irina to help. She knows Viktor. She's a native Russian speaker. Maybe fresh eyes can see what the experts are missing."

"Fine, send me what you've got."

Fifty Four

A Cambridge police car, a black and white Ford Crown Vic, pulls beside me as I'm walking back to my house from the Red Line station in Central Square. I assume that this has nothing to do with me specifically so I keep walking.

Then its siren emits a loud *blurt* and its blue lights start flashing, so I stop.

The passenger side window slides down to reveal the driver, Sergeant James Murphy.

"Got a minute?" he asks.

"Sure."

He hauls himself out and comes around the car to stand in front of me, blocking my way. He notches his thumbs into his duty belt with his right hand close to his holstered gun, a gesture that I notice as I'm sure he intends.

"Couple of nights ago, there was an incident in the alley behind your house. Do you know anything about that?"

"No," I reply. "What happened?"

"A man was attacked and left in a dumpster with a severe head wound."

"Sorry, this is the first I've heard of it."

"Strange."

"Why so?"

"In the hospital, he told officers that he was talking with a woman, a Russian whore, when he was struck from behind, and he seemed to think you were involved."

"That's nuts. I don't know anything about it."

"So you don't know a Russian whore who was in your alley?"

"No."

"The man said, 'Had to be the asshole Morais.' Why would he think that?"

"I have no idea."

"Is there more than one asshole Morais in your neighborhood?"

"I don't know, but the man must be mistaken, whoever he is."

Sergeant Murphy looks at me like I'm vomit he almost stepped in, and I ask, "By the way, who is he?"

"He goes by Sean Kelleher."

"Nope. Doesn't ring a bell."

"Our Sean is well known to police. It's not a surprise that he'd end up in a dumpster."

"So you don't put any weight on what he tells you."

"Certainly not when his story conflicts with yours," replies Sergeant Murphy. "We both know you'd never lie."

"Well, I'm not lying about this."

"Good to hear, because the man's buddies don't take it well when one of their own dies at the hands of the likes of you."

"He died?"

"Docs couldn't stop the bleeding in his brain."

"Well, that's…"

"Yeah, a great loss."

Out of respect for the deceased I don't comment further for a couple of beats.

Then, "Was he conscious long enough to talk to his buddies?"

"No, but word gets around."

"Should I be worried?"

"I would be," replies the Sergeant.

Fifty Five

I apply my usual tricks to leave my house undetected: Lights off, dark alley, Mass Ave bus to Boston, and taxi for the final leg to Annie's Beacon Hill apartment on Pinckney Street near Louisburg Square.

This is my first visit to Annie's new place, a fourth floor walk-up overlooking an alley. She shows me around. Her bedroom has a high ceiling with a ceiling fan in the center, a fireplace which Annie says is no longer functional, and a four poster bed, queen size, which I remember fondly. Her kitchen has granite countertops and a moveable island. Her living area, which doubles as her studio, has a second ornamental fireplace, a small round dining table, an easel and painting supplies near the windows, a flat screen TV, and two sofas, one of which is folded out for Irina.

"More windows than in my last place," Annie says. "Much more light."

I take her word for it, given that it's dark outside.

On the fold-out sofa, Irina is lying on her side watching a reality TV show about the emotional torments of California models. Fortunately, the sound is muted.

"How are you both managing?" I ask.

"We're doing okay," replies Annie.

Irina looks at me sleepily, dazed by the TV, before pulling herself up to sit at the edge of her bed.

"Annie is very kind," she says.

"That she is."

Annie asks me, "Have there been any developments?"

"We're having a problem cracking Viktor's passwords and I'm hoping that Irina can help."

"Let me see," Irina says. After she and I take chairs at the dining room table, I show her the copy of the page from Viktor's notebook that's headed IB, for Island Bank. Steve's team has written English translations just above the Cyrillic words.

As translated, the first entry is titled 'master' followed by *Vrost* and the second entry is 'personal,' also followed by *Vrost*.

"*Vrost* looks like his standard login that he uses for both accounts," I say.

Irina is studying the lines of letters and numbers after each of the logins, *npaBga3eHut66* after the first, and *Bop3aKoH99* after the second

"His passwords," I say. "Written in Cyrillic."

Irina nods agreement as she continues to study them.

"Obviously they are Russian words," she says. "Plus numbers."

"Tell us what you see."

"The first password starts with the Russian word for truth, followed by Zenit, which is the name of the soccer team in St. Petersburg, then the number 66. The second password has the Russian word for thief, then the Russian word for law, and the number 99."

"Homeland Security analysts see the same Russian words. But these words don't work as written. Viktor is using a code. They tested variations like opposites, and synonyms, and English translations. None of these worked."

"What's the opposite of the St. Petersburg soccer team?" asks Annie.

"They tried Spartak, a Moscow soccer team."

"Very interesting," says Irina, as she studies the sheet.

"What?"

"Maybe his code has nothing to do with the meanings of these words, one soccer team instead of another. Maybe the words are just to help him remember."

"So what are we looking at?"

"Viktor boasted all the time about his English. He said he could switch back and forth from Russian better than anyone, Russian to English, English to Russian, like he's a great genius." Staring at the sheet, she says, "The way they sound, most of the Cyrillic letters in his passwords correspond to different letters in English. Can I write on this page to show you, down where it is blank?"

"Yes, please," I say, handing her a ballpoint pen.

Irina jots down two columns of letters:

Cyrillic >In English Sounds Like

n	>	*p*
p	>	*r*
a	>	*a*
B	>	*v*
g	>	*d*
3	>	*z*
e	>	*e*

299

$H >$ n
$u >$ i
$t >$ t
$o >$ o
$K >$ k

"So, you're saying we should substitute the English letters that correspond to the sounds of the Cyrillic letters."

"Yes!" declares Irina, as she re-writes the passwords using the English letters. "Like I'm doing here, *p-r-a-v-d-a-z-e-n-i-t-6-6* and *v-o-r-z-a-k-o-n-9-9*."

"Worth a try," says Annie.

"I have a good feeling about this," I say.

"Let us hope," Irina says. "Make the rat fucker pay."

Fifty Six

Back at my house, I use the Tor browser on my thumb drive to navigate anonymously to the Island Bank website, and cross my fingers that this will be sufficient to mask my identity and location.

There's a sign-in box requesting a login ID and password.

I take a deep breath.

For the login, I type *VRost*.

Then, trying Viktor's personal account first, I type our version of his password by inserting English letters to represent the sounds of the Cyrillic letters, as Irina has written them, *v-o-r-z-a-k-o-n-9-9*. And, it... *works*. Viktor's account balances and transactions are displayed on my PC screen.

His current balance is four hundred and fifty three thousand US dollars. During the previous six months, his account has received deposits each day of three to four thousand dollars, give or take, and then each day transfers out approximately the same amounts, to an account at Panama Bank and Trust that's held in the name of a company called VR Enterprises.

So far, so good.

Then, I access the 'Master' account logging in with *VRost* and typing in our version of Viktor's password for that account, *p-r-a-v-d-a-z-e-n-i-t-6-6*.

What appears on my screen isn't a bank account but rather a front end program, set up like a dashboard, to manage transfers of money into and out of multiple accounts.

Open Sesame!

I have to work quickly. If Viktor signs on while I'm also signed on, he might be blocked by a bank security system, or a note might pop up on his screen advising that he's not the only one accessing the account.

First, I boost the fee charged by the Island Bank partners to Krulik's clients for their phony jewelry transactions. 'Boost' is an understatement. The twenty percent that they are currently paying amounts to around forty thousand dollars per day. After my upward adjustment, the clients will pay one hundred percent, or roughly two hundred thousand dollars per day; in other words, every last one of their unwashed dollars.

Then I allocate the entire increase into Viktor's account rather than depositing into the partners' general fund, thereby enhancing Viktor's take by one hundred sixty thousand dollars per day, plus or minus.

The other Island Bank partners will continue to receive the same income as they did before because Viktor is now capturing only the *increase* in the partners' fees. The partners won't notice anything amiss, a clever ploy for which I take a silent bow on Viktor's behalf.

On the other hand, some of Krulik's *clients* whose ill-gotten dollars are being laundered, and who happen to be monitoring their transactions, will soon discover that they are left with nothing after paying confiscatory fees to the Island Bank partners.

They will be understandably upset.

Krulik will hear about it. He'll check the numbers, and discover what Viktor has done.

Fifty Seven

At around three o'clock the next afternoon, I hear Brittany's raised voice and, looking towards the reception area, I see Pavel looming over her desk.

In the past Pavel has taken up a position on the street outside our building but this is the first time he's come inside. I amble over to find out what's going on.

"Do you know this man?" asks Brittany. Her face is flushed and she doesn't wait for my answer. "He says he's here to pick up Viktor but he won't let me call Viktor to tell him."

From the entrance, I can see Viktor at his desk in his glassed-in office on the far side of our open work space. His door is shut so he must not have heard the commotion.

"Is there a problem?" I ask Pavel.

"Mr. Krulik sent me to get Viktor."

"He said he'd hurt me if I tried to call Viktor," says Brittany. "He threatened me. I'm calling the police."

She moves her hand towards the phone on her desk. Pavel gets there first, and snaps the wires from the back of the phone.

"No calls," he says.

When Brittany eyes her cell which is on her desk beside her purse, Pavel puts his giant hand around it and slides it into his jacket pocket.

"No calls," he repeats.

"Give me back my phone," Brittany says, again raising her voice. "Or I'll start screaming."

"When we leave," Pavel says. "Viktor and me."

This is not the plan. We need Viktor alive.

"Let's all calm down," I say. "First, Brittany, you should know that Pavel would never hurt you. He's big and ugly and has a bloody bandage on his head but he doesn't hurt women. Do you, Pavel?"

Pavel scowls. I'm not helping his intimidation thing. On the other hand, he doesn't deny what I said.

Brittany says, "Then tell him to give me back my cell."

"Will you let me try to work this out before you call the police? I don't think we need them at the moment."

She looks up at Pavel, and then at me, and nods her head, closing the deal with an indignant sniff.

"Pavel?"

He shifts his huge shoulders in what looks like a shrug.

"Here," he says, handing Brittany's cell back to her.

"You okay?" I ask Brittany.

"Yeah," she says. "Pavel's your problem now. I'm going out for a coffee."

I ask Pavel, "Is Mr. Krulik angry with Viktor?"

"He just told me to bring him back to New York."

"Then I'll let him know you're here and to get ready to go with you."

"Okay." He arranges his huge body in one of our reception area chairs. "Don't take too long."

Viktor waves me in when I rap twice, politely, on his closed glass door.

"What?"

"Pavel is out front. He says Mr. Krulik sent him here to pick you up and bring you back to New York."

Viktor stands at his desk to get a clear view of the entrance. As I told him, Pavel is there, sitting massively by the front door.

"I know nothing about this," he mutters.

"Maybe you should call Mr. Krulik to find out," I offer, helpfully.

"Yeah, leave now. Wait outside."

I watch Viktor make the call. He speaks normally at first, which comes through the glass as just a mumble, probably asking why Pavel is at Dazzle and why Krulik wants him to accompany Pavel back to New York. Then Viktor yelps, *nyet, nyet,* and starts yelling.

Suddenly the call ends. Perhaps Krulik has disconnected. Viktor glares at his handset. Then he slams it onto its cradle on his desktop phone.

He swivels towards his monitor, taps furiously on his keyboard, and stares disbelievingly at what it reveals.

"Fuck!" he screams. "Fuck! Fuck! Fuck!"

I give up all pretense of not overhearing and return to his office.

"What's wrong?" I ask.

"My account is fucked up. Oleg thinks I'm stealing."

Without a mirror to check, I'm not sure how I look but my expression *feels* sympathetic. "Viktor, I'm sure you can explain to Mr. Krulik that there's a misunderstanding. He knows you would never steal."

"He wants me dead," Viktor means. "He believes what he sees, and what he sees is too much money going into my account."

"So just give the money back."

"Too late. Oleg would say I'm only doing that because he found out. I'm as good as dead."

"What are you going to do?"

"What can I do? Pavel is here to take me to New York. I'm fucking dead."

"I'm so sorry. Is there any way I can help?"

"How the fuck could you help?"

"I do have an idea about that," I say.

"What?"

"Only if you're absolutely sure that you can't persuade Mr. Krulik to give you another chance."

At the entrance, Pavel stands up like a grizzly on its hind legs and catches my eye through Viktor's glass wall. He taps his watch. I acknowledge with a wave. He sits back down.

Viktor sees Pavel's gesture. He stares at me, clutching at straws.

"Tell me."

"This is a long shot," I say. "But only if you're sure..."

"Just tell me!"

I hand to him Reilly's business card

"You could call agent Reilly, offer to talk to him about Mr. Krulik. He'll come here to pick you up. Pavel won't be able to take you."

"The FBI? Then I'll be truly fucked!"

"You don't have a lot of time to decide. Pavel is getting restless."

"Can I trust Reilly?"

"I have no idea," I say. "Like I told you, I refused to talk to him."

He studies the card, turns it over, trying to decide.

"You'll also have to tell Reilly about Sophie," I say.

"What about her?

"They think you had a hand in her murder."

"Who gives a shit about that?"

"Her husband, for one. He's a big deal lawyer and politically connected. He's making a lot of noise. They won't protect you unless you tell them everything."

"It was Oleg's idea," Viktor says. "I just set it up."

"So tell them."

He rubs his face, glances again at Pavel waiting by Brittany's desk, and says, "Fuck it!" and makes the call.

"This is Viktor Rost. I'm calling agent Patrick Reilly."

Pause.

"Agent Reilly?"

Pause.

"Viktor Rost, from Dazzle.com."

Pause.

"I got your number from Jacob Morais. I'm in trouble. I want to turn myself in, for protection.

Pause.

Right now. Please. There's no time."
Pause.
"Yes, I'll tell you what you need to know."

Fifty Eight

Brittany has returned to her desk and is ignoring Pavel who is ignoring her in return, when agents Reilly and Rivera arrive five minutes later. I watch from Viktor's office as they talk to her, and she points them towards us.

"Will you protect me?" asks Viktor, when the agents enter his office.

"You cooperate and you'll be taken care of," says Reilly.

"I will cooperate."

"We'll take this," agent Rivera says, as she closes Viktor's laptop and drops it into a shoulder bag. "Also your cellphone."

Viktor holds it out to her.

"We'll get the rest of your stuff later," Rivera says.

Reilly turns to me.

"Don't touch anything here. Don't remove anything. You understand?"

"I do."

"Also don't even think about traveling anywhere."

"Okay."

"Jake," says Viktor, as he's being led out of his office, "you are my one true friend. Thank you."

"My pleasure," I reply, and this time I mean what I say, one hundred percent.

Dazzle staff watch Viktor's exit. He's done nothing for them, scarcely paid them any attention. But even a stranger's misfortune attracts rubberneckers.

One of our engineers calls out to me, "What's going on?"

"Viktor has legal problems," I say. "I don't know what this means for the company so you'll have to make your own decisions."

They know: This gig is done, the well-stocked eatery, the creativity-rebooting recliner, the ping pong table, the nap room, the having nothing much to do. Dazzle is history. Time to move on.

To Pavel, I say, "Let's talk in Viktor's office."

"You tricked me."

"No, Viktor made his own decision. Come on, let's talk."

Pavel follows me into Viktor's office and I shut the door behind us.

"Now you have a choice," I say. "If you return to Mr. Krulik without Viktor, he will be unhappy with you."

Pavel watches as I touch my right ear which unlike his is still whole and bandage free. He gets the message.

"Or you can stay in Boston for a while. Caterina is in Viktor's condo. Now that Viktor's gone, she'll need company."

"Okay," Pavel says.

"Authorities will come to pick her up so that she can go home to Ukraine, which is what she wants. Are you okay with that?"

"Yes," Pavel says. "She should go home."

I call Steve Whalen.

"Viktor's in custody," I say.

"I know. Agent Reilly contacted me."

"Krulik will find out soon. You better grab him while you can."

"Happening now," Steve says.

"Once you have Krulik, I'll arrange for you to take charge of Irina. Also you can rescue Caterina, who's in Viktor's condo. Krulik's man, Pavel, will be there, but he's protecting her, not working for Krulik anymore, so be gentle with him."

"We will."

"Since Viktor is suddenly cooperative, maybe he'll give you permission to open his safe, so you won't need a warrant."

"Right."

Is Steve miffed that I'm firing off instructions like he works for me? Too bad.

Viktor in custody, Krulik about to be arrested, their trafficked women rescued, their money laundering enterprise exposed, Viktor's confession and his implication of Krulik for Sophie's murder : *mission accomplished.*

Text from Steve Whalen: "Krulik escaped."

"What the fuck?" I say, when he answers his phone.

"He was under surveillance at his home in Brooklyn. When agents went in, he was gone. He slipped away before you called me, apparently. They're still trying to figure out how."

"So he was alerted about Viktor."

"Looks like it. Although it could be a coincidence. He may just have decided it was time to go."

"And not wait for Pavel to deliver Viktor to him in New York? He wouldn't leave before dealing with Viktor. How would he explain that to their clients?"

"Good point."

"Viktor told me that Krulik was planning to run to Venezuela. I assume you've alerted airports and airlines to watch for him."

"Yeah, but if I were Oleg Krulik, I wouldn't rely on commercial airlines. He'll lease a private plane and take off from an airfield where there's no TSA."

"It wasn't Pavel who tipped Krulik off. He didn't know what was happening until FBI agents arrived at our office. I had him in sight the whole time. And obviously Viktor didn't tip him off either. Who else knew that Viktor offered to cooperate?"

Silence on the line.

I answer my own question, "The FBI agents."

"Uh-huh."

"I never trusted them."

"So you told me."

"What are you going to do about it?"

Steve goes silent for a moment, and then says, "I'll get back to you," and disconnects.

He doesn't call back. After twenty minutes of staring at my cellphone, I call him, and reach his voicemail. I'm not a big fan of voicemail so I end the call without leaving a message. Instead I send a text: "What?"

"Problem with Viktor," he texts in reply. "I'm on my way to Boston."

"What problem?"

"He's dead."

"Dead, while in FBI custody?"

"Yes."

"How?"

"That's why I'm on my way to Boston. Looks like suicide. Used his belt to hang himself."

"You believe that?"

"TBD when I get to Boston."

"Viktor wasn't suicidal. He called the FBI to save his life, not end it."

"We'll see."

I wait twenty minutes in Louisburg Square before I see Annie walking up Willow Street alongside the Square towards her place on Pinckney.

I step out of the shadows to stand under one of the old-fashioned Beacon Hill streetlights so that I won't startle her.

"Hi Annie."

"Jake! What are you doing here?"

"A lot happened today that you need to know about."

"Do you want to come in?"

"No, we should talk here."

"Because of Irina?"

"Yeah, and also it's personal, between us."

I tell Annie about Viktor, how he died in FBI custody, and about Krulik's escape.

"What does this mean for Irina?"

"I'm going to arrange with Steve Whalen to have her picked up at the Starbucks on Charles Street. I'll text you the time.

Steve doesn't know that she's staying with you and he's not going to. I'll keep you out of it."

"What about you, Jake? Are you in danger?"

"Apart from Viktor, the bad guys are still out there and I'm not their favorite person."

"So you're here to say goodbye, again."

"I'm radioactive right now, Annie. It's unsafe for you to be seen with me."

Annie uses a knuckle on her right hand to brush wet off her cheek.

"Annie…"

"Yes?"

"I love you. Always will. I want you to know that."

"You're freaking me out."

"I should have told you that more, when we were together. I should have told you everything."

"There's still time to make amends."

"I hope so. But for now, whatever happens on my end, please remember that I care for you."

We hug hard under the streetlight and I kiss her cheeks, tasting the salt. She breaks free and walks on towards her place on Pinkney.

Fifty Nine

Sophie's sacrifice and everything that I've done since the day I joined Dazzle, are all for nothing.

Viktor has been silenced.

Krulik has escaped and once he reaches Venezuela, he'll issue a fatwa on the shitfuck.

The last time I was in Montreal, I ran low on cash. That's not going to happen again.

I sign onto Viktor's account at Island Bank. It's still open, and his passwords still work.

My first tweak is to sever the link from his Island Bank account to his shell company, VR Enterprises LLC.

Then I transfer his entire account balance, now six hundred and twenty thousand dollars, into *my* new shell company, Guardian LLC, and also redirect to Guardian the daily flow of money from his enhanced share of the Island Bank money laundering transactions, a hundred and sixty thousand dollars per day, plus or minus.

Am I stealing? Yes, sort of. On the other hand, being dead, Viktor has no further need for dollars. Also his money is already stolen several times over. It doesn't even belong to him, may he rest in peace, since it was siphoned from his and Krulik's clients, admittedly by me on Viktor's behalf, but they're crooks too, so it wasn't really their money either.

Will I get away with it? That's my plan. I've done what I can to cover my tracks. I'm already on Krulik's kill list, so what's there to lose?

Sure, I could channel Viktor's loot to worthy charities. A better person might make that choice. But then the charities' accountants would have to report the mysterious donations and set the money aside until questions are answered, which they wouldn't be, so in the end the charities would receive no benefit. Let's not sugarcoat the truth: Right now, worthy charities are not top of mind.

Dazzle's website runs on automatic pilot. It could well continue to support transactions for weeks or longer before it shuts down. The Island Partners' dashboard shows that fake jewelry purchases are still being processed. Apparently Krulik neglected to alert his less observant clients that their scheme is compromised, probably to give himself time to get safely to Venezuela.

Meanwhile, the coffers of John Dobby's Guardian, LLC, will fill quite nicely, thank you very much.

I leave a handwritten note on my desk:

To whom it may concern:

Today Viktor Rost, Dazzle's CEO, was escorted from our premises by the FBI. Soon after, he was found dead in FBI custody. The Chairman of Dazzle's board, Oleg Krulik, has fled. Krulik has indicated that he blames me for his troubles so I may be targeted by his associates. In addition, I have reason to believe that I may also be targeted by FBI agents

Patrick Reilly and Charlene Rivera. I suspect that Reilly, and possibly also Rivera, are working for Krulik. If I disappear, police should focus on Krulik and his associates and on agents Reilly and Rivera. Attached to this note is a signed and notarized Transfer of Deed for my residence in Cambridge, MA, to my parents. Jean Michel and Marilyn Morais. Also attached is a copy of my last Will & Testament. Yours truly, Jacob Morais.

Then I call Steve Whalen.

"Have you got Krulik?"

"No."

"So he got away."

"Seems so."

"When will you be ready to pick up Irina?"

"As soon as you let us know where she is."

"I want the FBI kept out of it."

"We'll send U.S. marshals for Irina. She'll be safe with them in their witness protection program."

"And Caterina?"

"Boston police have her now."

"What about Nika, in Miami?"

"No luck there, Jake. She's disappeared."

"Damn!"

"Miami-Dade police found a man in an apartment where Nika was last seen. He was dead, stabbed multiple times."

"Do they think Nika did it?"

"That's the current theory."

"So she may still be alive."

"Yeah. We'll keep looking."

"Let me know when you find her."

"I will."

"I'll text you a time and place to get Irina."

Annie calls me after Steve and a female U.S. marshal have picked up Irina at the Starbucks on the corner of Charles and Beacon Streets, across from Boston Common.

"I watched them from a bench on the Common," she says. "They went in, introduced themselves, and left together in a black SUV with tinted windows."

"Did they see you?"

"I don't think so. They weren't looking in my direction. Irina is fine. She's delighted that Viktor is dead. Looking forward to testifying against Krulik when they catch him. She's keen to move to California to become a reality TV star."

"Thank you for taking care of her," I say.

"Glad to do it, for Sophie, and for you."

"Well, still... I hope that you..."

I pause. Hope what? That Annie will have a happy life? That she won't forget me?

"I know, Jake," Annie replies. "Same for you."

Sixty

Montreal.

Paola accepts me back. I returned like I promised and that's enough for her.

Her daughter Elise is less forgiving. She barely tolerates my presence. When I try to talk to her at breakfast, she rolls her eyes and studies her phone, or her plate, as if I'm not there.

When I reactivate Jewels by Paola on Etsy, Elise protests that I'm profiteering from selling her mother's creations, that I'm just a useless middleman.

"Elise is right," I tell Paola. "You should take this over."

"Internet commerce is not my thing."

"Then let Elise do it for you."

So I transition Jewels by Paola to Elise. She's almost cordial while I'm showing her how to post items and manage transactions. But before long, her suspicions of me resurface.

One Saturday afternoon, while Paola is out back in the garden, Elise drifts into the living room where I'm reading.

"Why are you here?" she asks.

"Thought I'd just relax for a while with a book."

"You know what I mean, in our house, with my mom all the time."

"Because your mother and I enjoy each other's company."

"I don't trust you."

"Sorry to hear that."

"You hurt Mom again, like before when you took off and never called, I'll hunt you down, I swear."

"I'm glad you're here to protect your mom," I tell her.

Paola appears in the doorway.

"You two having a nice chat?" she asks.

"Not really," Elise replies. A moment later, the slam of her bedroom door makes the house shake.

I say to Paola, "She doesn't believe that I'm good for you."

Paola shakes her head. "Don't pay…"

"She may be right, Paola."

Paola's large dark eyes lock on mine. "That's for me to decide."

I touch my forehead to hers. Just a touch.

"Thank you," I say.

Between Christmas and New Year's, when Paola's shop is closed, and Elise is spending the holiday week with cousins at a cottage up north, Paola and I visit Quebec City, three hours from Montreal by train.

Our room at the renowned Château Frontenac faces out over the long wooden boardwalk of Dufferin Terrace. Below the boardwalk are the stone buildings of historic Old Quebec, and in the distance the St. Laurence River, which is frozen and covered by snow except in the middle where there's open water.

I arrange to take a nap while Paola leaves to explore the shops in the Château's lobby.

"Back soon," she says.

It's already getting dark out at around four thirty when I wake up. Paola hasn't returned, or if she has, she's left again. Her goose-down winter coat is still hanging in our room closet.

I text her: "Where U?"

No response.

My call to her cell goes to voicemail.

By six o'clock, I'm getting worried. I leave a note for Paola on our bed, "please call my cell," and head down to the lobby to try to find her.

No luck in the hotel's vast wood paneled lobby, nor in its café, nor in the stores on the lower level that sell Inuit artifacts, jewelry, books, and paintings by Quebecois artists.

Back in the lobby, about fifty feet from me, I see two men at the hotel concierge's kiosk. Their heads are shaved and they're wearing black leather jackets. One is compact and the other much larger. I can't be sure, since I only see them in profile, but the larger one resembles the Krulik heavy whose name I can never remember.

My cell buzzes. Finally, a text from Paola: "In room."

I text back: "Please wait for me there."

I hustle down the stairs to the lower lobby where I buy a pair of sunglasses and a peaked cap souvenir of Quebec with 'La Belle Province' printed above the bill.

On my way to the elevator past the two men in black leather jackets, my cap is pulled low, sunglasses are on, and I keep my head down.

Paola is nestled in a chair.

"Where'd you go?" I ask.

She smiles deliciously and stretches. "I treated myself to a soak and a massage in the spa."

"You do look relaxed."

"I saw that you called. Sorry. My cell was turned off, by orders of the spa."

She notices my new cap and sunglasses.

"Are we going to a beach?"

"Someday, I hope so," I say.

"Let's pretend we don't have to wait. Let's pretend that we've strayed onto a clothing optional beach."

She sidles over to the bed and pats the space beside her.

"Don't be shy," she says. "On this beach we can do whatever we want."

In the morning, I wear my sunglasses when we go out although the day is overcast and cold, with more snow pending.

Paola looks at me curiously but doesn't say anything, and I don't volunteer a reason.

Also, once again, I stop shaving. From now on, John Dobby will have a beard and long hair, and will always wear glasses in public.

I don't see the two men again in the Château Frontenac lobby, nor during our walkabouts through the charming cobblestone streets of the old city.

Perhaps I was mistaken. Perhaps they were just attending the convention of insurance brokers that was at the hotel.

Sixty One

The late February snow storm hits Montreal shortly after midnight. By mid-morning, ten inches have fallen and it's still coming down hard, blowing sideways and swirling in the biting wind. Cars and buses slowly follow deep ruts left by vehicles ahead of them. Signs jammed in the snow along Sherbrooke Street warn that any parked vehicles will be towed.

It's brutally cold. People slogging forward on the snowy sidewalks have their heads down and scarves wrapped up to their eyes like bandits. Some walk backwards to protect their last remaining exposed skin from the freezing wind. Probably like me they've got their fingers curled into fists inside their mitts to stop them aching from frostbite.

I take shelter in the Second Cup on Sherbrooke across from the McGill campus where I met earlier with Steve Whalen, and watch through the café's window as the first tow trucks arrive. One after the other they haul off parked cars. Next comes a massive snow plow pushing snow towards the curb, followed immediately by a second plow shoving it still farther and higher to the right, and then by a snow blower, diesel engine roaring and blades spinning, that devours the piled snow and fires it back out through its overhead chute into a dump truck that's keeping pace alongside. As each dump truck is filled, it trundles off and is replaced by another. Within only a minute or so, the convoy of tow trucks, plows, snow blower, and dump trucks has cleared the portion of Sherbrooke Street in front of where I'm watching and has moved on.

A man in a trapper hat with ear muffs enters the café. He has a large scarf around his neck and a heavy wool coat. He stomps his boots and slaps his gloves together to shake off snow, and looks around the café. He catches my eye, and comes towards my table.

"Hey, Nanook," he says. "How do people survive in this insane climate?"

"Hey Steve," I say.

He shakes his hat and gloves again to remove the last remnants of snow, and places them on the window shelf beside my table, and takes a seat, laying his coat on the back of an empty chair beside him.

I don't waste time with pleasantries. "Whatever you need to finish the job with Krulik, that's on you. I'm gone."

"But not forgotten."

"Forget me."

"Don't get your panties in a twist," Steve says. "I won't blow your cover."

"So why are you here?"

"I'm bringing news."

"Good or bad?"

"Well, they got to Krulik. A team from Russia caught up with him on his island in Venezuela. They executed his bodyguards who tried to defend him and let the others go. Then they went to work on Krulik, once they had him."

"So he's dead."

"Very dead. But they made sure he didn't die quickly. They were very thorough."

"Ahh!"

I'm picturing Krulik's face in an agonized yowl, eyes gouged, Teddy Roosevelt choppers blood stained and broken. I've no idea why this image comes to mind. But from now on, I won't be able to forget it.

"He was a murderous thug who deserved everything he got," Steve says. "But, still."

"Yeah."

"The men that killed him are professionals, probably ex-KGB hired by Krulik's former clients."

"Putin's cronies."

"Yeah. Making sure he'd never cooperate with us. Also delivering payback for costing them money. About that, on the plus side, the clients' accounts at Island Bank are frozen. We've identified US investments from their shell companies that we can confiscate. We've got enough on several of them to bring charges that we're working on now."

"Good."

Steve pauses, and I ask, "Anything else?"

"Irina's in LA where she's auditioning to get into reality TV."

"Seems an odd way to keep a low profile."

"You wouldn't recognize her with her changed hair and eye color. She answers to Brianna Meznick, born and raised in Orange County. She'll blend right in."

"What about Viktor's death while in FBI custody?"

"Agent Patrick Reilly is on leave and under investigation."

"How long before he's charged?"

"Hard to say. If he was paid off, he's done a good job of hiding the money. And there are no witnesses. Agent Rivera insists she knows nothing and is shocked about Reilly."

"Nika?"

"We still haven't located her. We'll step in if she's arrested by Miami-Dade PD. Make sure she's treated properly."

"Okay."

"Annie called me. Said the last time you and she talked, it sounded like you were saying goodbye. She wanted reassurance that you're among the living. I told her that you're like a cockroach, hard to kill."

"Just how I'd like to be remembered. Thanks."

"No problem. Also she's been in touch with your parents. They don't know what to think given what happened last time. But they're worried. When they tried to get the Cambridge PD to look for you, they were advised to wait a few more months. Apparently the cops feel burned."

I feel guilty about how I've treated my parents, disappearing on them a second time. On balance, given my entanglements, they're better off with me gone. At least that's what I tell myself.

"They're safer if they have no idea where I am," I say.

"I'm sure you're right."

"For what it's worth, I signed over my house to them."

"I'm not judging."

"The hell you aren't. What do you suggest?"

"I can ask Annie to let them know you're alright and not to worry."

"Okay. Please do that."

"And now we come to the part about Viktor's money."

"What about it?"

"You did a great job funneling the money into Viktor's account. He was well framed."

"As we planned."

"But then I tracked his filthy lucre a bit farther. Know what I found?"

"Tell me."

"His money did a hop, skip and jump to an account in Nevis that we traced to John S. Dobby."

I keep my face blank.

"Not a surprise?" asks Steve.

"No."

"Did you think I wouldn't find out?"

"It wasn't Viktor's money. Why shouldn't John Dobby take it?"

"You're right," says Steve. "Keep the money. I don't care."

"Okay."

"It's not me you should worry about. It's the Russians."

Now, Steve has my full attention.

"After Sophie died, I came for you and you stepped up. So, because of my sister and as my good deed for the day, I'm here to warn you that the Russians suspect that it wasn't Viktor who stole from them."

"How do you know that?"

My voice is surprisingly calm as if these Russians have nothing to do with me. But what am I supposed to do, tear off my clothes and run screaming out into the blizzard?

Steve says, "We know by listening in, obviously. The team that caught up with Krulik in Venezuela reported back that he was eager to share his suspicions, although in the end that didn't help him much. In any event since their visit with him there's been chatter about someone else, not Viktor."

"Chatter about the shitfuck?"

"The very same. They'll work it out. It's only a matter of time."

"Yeah."

"I know, it sucks."

"Do you know what they look like, this team?"

"Sorry, no. If we had photos, I'd pass them along."

"Well, anyway, thanks for the heads-up."

"You're welcome," Steve says. "You okay?"

"Yeah, sure."

"You look pale."

"Haven't seen the sun for a while. I'm okay."

"Then I'm out of here."

He pushes back from the table and layers on his coat, scarf, hat, and gloves. "Stay warm, Nanook."

Flexing his arms and inhaling sharply like he's about to dive into a cold swimming pool, he pushes the café's door open, stamps his feet, and charges outside.

I open my laptop and load the Tor browser from my thumb drive. Normally I would go to the Atwater Library for more complete Internet anonymity but there's no time to lose and I'd have to walk to get to the library in the midst of the storm, and most likely it's closed anyway.

I access Viktor's account in Island Bank. A note on the account states that due to reported irregularities, transfers of funds into or out of the account will not be permitted until further notice.

However, I *am* able to delete the link between his account and Guardian, LLC. Probably too late, but right now anything is better than just sitting in the café thinking woe is me.

Then, in the month that follows...

Guardian purchases a building in Montreal that's being converted into luxury condos, paying two million four hundred ninety five thousand dollars s. The four story building is located on Avenue de L'Hotel de Ville, a few blocks from my place on Duluth and St. Dominique.

Guardian holds title to the building for only a day, before flipping its ownership to NextVentures LLC, a newly formed holding company based in Panama, in payment for "consulting services."

The day after *that* deal closes, NextVentures places the building back on the market.

Attractively priced for a quick sale slightly under the original price paid by Guardian, it's snapped up by Cromwell Properties, a big property owner based in Toronto.

As NextVentures' representative in Montreal, I close the deal, and hands are shaken all around, in a Cromwell Properties meeting room in an office tower on René Lévesque Boulevard.

Cromwell Properties' check is deposited into NextVentures' bank account in Panama.

Meanwhile, also in payment for consulting services, BLT Properties transfers to NextVentures its ownership of the building which was bequeathed to me by Grandpa Alain, and where I still live, on Duluth and St. Dominique.

NextVentures then flips *this* building to a Montreal-based developer, Edifices Bedard, for one million one hundred thousand dollars, which also is deposited in the NextVentures account in Panama.

Then I transfer the entire balance from NextVentures' Panama bank account to an account in John Dobby's name in TD Canada Trust in Montreal.

Then, I shut down Guardian, BLT Properties, and NextVentures, and their associated bank accounts in Nevis and in Panama.

Despite these maneuvers, I have to face facts.

Krulik's former clients are Putin cronies. They have access to advanced technical resources that will enable them eventually to track my money trail to Montreal.

And when their assassins arrive, most likely they'll follow me to discover my relationships, and before they put me out of my misery they may well go after Paola and Elise, and maybe even Sara and the Maqbools, as a lesson to others.

I'm lying on my back in bed with Paola whose lovely body rests against mine with her head on my chest.

"I have to tell you something," I say.

"Can it wait?" Paola asks, sleepily.

"Sorry. It can't."

"Do I need to get up to hear this?"

"No, please don't get up. Stay close to me so that we can feel each other."

Paola nestles in tighter against me. "Okay," she murmurs. "Tell me."

"I need to go away, soon, and this time I may not return."

Paola lies still, saying nothing, just listening.

"Down in the US, my name is not John Dobby and I don't own a house in Sprightly Falls, New York. In fact, I've never been there..."

I tell Paola how I was hired by an old friend to work at an e-commerce company in Boston where she was CEO, how our company was used by Russian criminals for money laundering, how they murdered my CEO friend, how I was working with Homeland Security to bring them to justice, how one of them was taken into custody by the FBI where he died under questionable circumstances, and the other, his boss, escaped to Venezuela, but has since been killed. I tell her that before I left the US, I accessed a bank account in the Caribbean in order to take the money launderers' money, and they are on my trail.

"You stole money from Russian gangsters?"

"Yes."

"So now they're after you."

"Yes, so I need to leave before they track me to Montreal which could happen any time now. I can't take the chance that I'll lead them to you. I don't want you and Elise to be harmed because of what I've done. I need to disappear."

"We do have police in Canada," Paola says, softly. "They could protect you, and us."

"I'd prefer not to get them involved," I say. "I'm not entirely innocent."

"Alright."

"I wish I could stay. This is not what I planned."

Paola shifts to lie on her side, tucking her arm under. She looks down at me, hair rumpled, and scary beautiful.

"I was upset when you left the last time," she says. "I came to terms with it. I resolved that if you came back I would enjoy our time together without worrying too much about the future. I'm sad you're leaving again. I'll miss you. But I understand."

"Elise threatened to hunt me down if I hurt you."

"I'll talk to her."

"Thank you."

"If you do return to Montreal, you will call me?"

"My very first call."

"Promise."

"I promise."

I sense that Paola has more to say, but is hesitating.

"What?"

"You're such a smart man," she says. "Why did you take their money?"

Sixty Two

In Tudorsville, Vermont, my name is Wally (Skip) Stone.

My house sits on a small rise leading down to Lake Parker. There are a couple of other houses on the lake but I haven't met the people who live in them. Our properties are separated by woods and we each have our own private access road.

The entry to my access road off of scenic Route 100A is unmarked except for a 'Private - No Trespassing' sign. It's a dirt road, about a half mile long, and hard going over frost heaves and ruts and gullies. Any vehicle that attempts it will make slow progress, bouncing and swaying and straining its engine. I'll hear it coming.

Any mail that I get, which isn't much, is held for me at the post office in Woodstock, the next town over.

I'm not a recluse. I see other Tudorsville residents on shopping trips into town. I attend concerts at a community center that the town took over from a cult a few years back.

My hair is long and my beard is full. I wear glasses and work boots. My attire is loose-fitting Vermont agri-casual. I never leave my home without a Glock in my shoulder holster.

I drive a used Toyota Tacoma pickup that I bought for cash across the state line in Lake George, New York. It's registered to John Dobby of Sprightly Falls, New York. No one has bothered me yet for driving a pickup with New York plates. I guess the cops here have better things to do.

People in Tudorsville know me as Skip. They don't ask for my surname and I don't volunteer it. Clearly I've come from somewhere else after removing myself from a situation that I don't choose to talk about, and that's fine with them. They believe in minding one's own business. They protect my privacy. Anyone asking about me will receive a blank stare and I'll hear about it later, in due course.

I don't use credit cards and I don't write checks. For whatever I need, I pay cash, which I withdraw from my TD Canada Trust account using ATMs in the city of Rutland, a few towns over. Utility bills and property taxes are paid online by the owner of record of my house, WSSTrust, LLC (Delaware).

TD Canada Trust has as my home address a small condo in Rutland that I visit only after dark and on an irregular basis, and only on foot after parking my truck in a downtown garage, doubling back often to check for followers, and always wearing a peaked cap pulled down low on my forehead.

The balance in my TD Canada Trust account is ample for my needs. Still, to keep myself busy, I run a small business peddling authentic Vermont antiques on eBay and on Etsy. Getting product to sell isn't a problem. Every weekend there are barn and rummage sales nearby where rustic treasures are laid out to be perused and bargained for.

My friend Marlee Austin manages the Aubuchon Hardware in Tudorsville. Blond, divorced, no kids, we get along well. Her great eye for collectibles is a big help in identifying what will appeal to my online customers.

Like at a recent church rummage sale in Tudorsville, when she picked out a small mirror in a silver frame.

"Take a look at this," she says.

The chatty lady at the table, Suzie Prestowicz according to the tag on her sweater, chimes in, "Isn't it charming?"

"Yeah, I suppose."

Marlee says to me, with a hint of sharpness, "Well, if you don't like it, let's move on."

"Do *you* like it?" I ask, my tone mollifying.

"It has possibilities. Make an offer."

I toss out a low ball number.

Suzie shakes her head. "No can do."

"Oh well," says Marlee to Suzie, sympathetically. "He's hard to impress."

"I know the type," replies Suzie.

"Thanks," I say, and we start to wander off. Suzie calls out, "Come back! You have a deal!"

Sometimes I stay over at Marlee's place down near Ludlow, a nice cottage with a view of the Okemo ski resort. She isn't looking for a commitment. Nor am I.

She's never been to my house. Never asked to see it.

My house looks modest from a distance, just another single story Vermont country house.

Appearances can be deceiving.

It has bullet-proof windows, steel doors, and fire-retardant siding and metal roof, all installed by a contractor from Rutland. I paid him extra to employ illegals who don't know anyone in our area with whom they might gossip about the bearded guy's fortress.

At the Vermont Gun Mart in Rutland, I'm buying three Glocks and associated magazines and rounds of ammo, when the sales guy says, "Before you go, you've got to take a look at this." He lifts an AR-15 semiautomatic rifle off the rack. "Feel this baby."

Its skeletal metallic protuberances give it the look of a lethal alien insect. It radiates fear. I find holding it strangely pleasurable.

"You want this firearm, I can tell," says the sales guy.

"Good guess. I'll take it."

Plus a box of grenades that he assures me will work, "They're authentic military from Croatia, left over from their war over there."

I pay cash, no questions asked.

I practice shooting my AR-15 until I can hit targets that I've attached to trees about a hundred feet distant. If anyone comments about the gunfire, I'll say that deer have been munching vegetables in my garden. This is Vermont. They'll understand.

My access road is monitored by tree-mounted wirelessly-connected surveillance cameras that are invisible from the ground. When signaled by sensors, floodlights illuminate my property as brightly as daylight behind my house down to the lake and for several hundred feet on the sides and in front.

Buried plastic explosives that ring the perimeter around my house are rigged to blow with a signal from my cellphone. When they do, they'll spray shrapnel and create a moat of fire, which should give attackers pause.

The food, water, and meds stored in the bunker in my basement will keep me going for a couple of months.

Whatever bad stuff happens, I'm ready.

Using my Tor browser, I track incoming emails mirrored to my fourth tier AOL email address.

Annie is getting married. I'm happy for her.

My parents took possession of my house in Cambridge and sold it. They still live in Winchester. They report that Annie talked to them and they aren't worried about me anymore, and they hope I've found someone.

Paola is coming to Vermont. She has no idea whether her email to me will be read or where I'm living now, but she wants me to know that if I turn up at the Burlington Sheraton where she'll be staying, she'll love to see me. She has news she wants to tell me in person. Also she passes along that Elise says hi.

I miss Paola. I think about her a lot. I'd like to see her. I'm curious what she means by her 'news' and Burlington isn't far from Tudorsville, only a two hour drive. But why would Elise say hi? She never warmed to my presence. Is Paola using a code to warn me? Are the Russians looking over her shoulder? It could be a trap.

Still, I'm tempted.

I'll get to Burlington early, park blocks away from the Sheraton, watch who comes and goes, and verify that Paola arrives alone. I won't reveal myself unless I'm totally sure.

I'll be careful.

Acknowledgements

Heartfelt thanks to Elizabeth Shapiro and Bernadette Nelson Shapiro for their multiple readings and brutally candid reviews of early drafts, and to Alison Backman for her comments on versions of the cover, and to editor Amaryah Orenstein and literary agent Janet Reid for their valuable guidance on how to improve the story, and to Yulia Musayelyan for her tips on matters Russian, and to international artist Adam Shapiro for the use of his haunting painting "Self Portrait" for the cover.

About The Author

Originally from Montreal, Canada, Peter David Shapiro
now lives in the Boston area.
His website is www.peterdshapiro.com.

Also by Peter David Shapiro

"A captivating spiritualist mystery with three dimensional characters in a vividly real environment." (Amazon, 5 stars).

In 1896, renowned psychic Ignatius Jones commissions his portrait to be painted and promises his followers that he will communicate with them through the portrait after he passes to spirit. On the day that he is murdered in 1903, his portrait is stolen. It turns up 100 years later at a church rummage sale in Tudorsville, Vermont. Current-day psychic mediums are invited to see the long-lost portrait at the newly-established Ignatius Jones Center for Spiritualist Discovery. When Boston psychic Dr. Frances Gourmelon (from *Ghosts on the Red Line*) arrives at the Center, she discovers that things there are very odd. Charles Philip Tucker, former con man and the Center's founder, says that he's channeling Ignatius Jones when he selects an eighteen-year-old girl to bear his children on Ignatius Jones' behalf. Frances decides to get involved.

"Marvelously twisty thriller." (Amazon, 5 stars) "Truly entertaining, very well-crafted tale that will keep you away from bedtime turning pages." (Amazon, 5 stars)

Consultant Harry West is hired by the government in Hong Kong to evaluate a business deal. But after Harry arrives in Hong Kong, he discovers the assignment is not what he expects. His client wants him to find evidence of money laundering and corruption, evidence that will kill the deal. Harry is all too aware that the people he would expose will stop at nothing to protect themselves. However, he needs the work. He takes the assignment, which soon requires him to draw on resources that he never knew he had. Along the way, Harry's journey is shaped by two women in Hong Kong, an American journalist who is investigating the same deal and a long-lost love who comes back into his life. A suspenseful story about intrigue, revenge, and the bonds of love and memory, *The Trail of Money* keeps the reader guessing until the end.

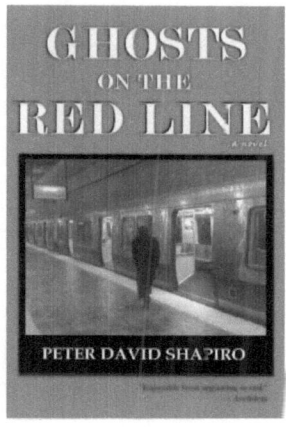

"Wonderful unlike anything I've read before." (Amazon, 5 stars). "One colorful scene, character or plot turn succeeds another without losing a hint of coherence." (Amazon, 5 stars).

Boston subway riders see their Departed on the Red Line trains and consultant Harry West is hired to investigate by the Massachusetts Bay Transportation Authority. His project turns personal when his ex-wife Alexandra Ben-Tov meets their beloved daughter on the Red Line, who looks like the teenager she might have become if she had lived. Are the visitors on the Red Line ghosts or hallucinations? Either way, when Harry's team discovers the source of the visitations, the MBTA declares it will bring them to an end. Alexandra has a brilliant idea: Build Visitation Rooms that replicate the features of Red Line train cars so that people can continue to meet their loved ones. But not everyone approves. The Archbishop of Boston seeks to get Visitation Rooms banned in Massachusetts. And a gangster who frets that his victims might return from the dead warns Harry and Alexandra: Cancel Opening Day for the Visitation Room, *or else!*